W9-BTZ-289

DISCARD

Until July

Aurora Rose Reynolds

Copyright © 2015 Crystal Aurora Rose Reynolds
Print Edition

Cover and Cover design by Sara Eirew
Designs: Formatted by BB eBooks

All rights reserved. No part of this book may be reproduced or transmitted in any form or by any means, electronic or mechanical, including photocopying, recording, or by any information storage and retrieval system, without permission in writing.

This is a work of fiction. Names, characters, places and incidents are the product of the author's imagination or are used factiously, and any resemblance to any actual persons or living or dead, events or locals are entirely coincidental.

The author acknowledges the trademark status and trademark owners of various products referenced in this work of fiction, which have been used without permission. The publication/ Use of these trademarks is not authorized, associated with, or sponsored by the trademark owner.

All rights reserved.

Dedication

To Corina, may you never settle until you find the man who gives you butterflies and takes your breath away

Table of Contents

Prologue

I TURN ONTO the highway and pull back on the throttle, watching as the speedometer reaches sixty. I tuck the upper part of my body behind the windshield where there is less wind resistance and yell out, "Wahooo!" when the feeling of flying hits my stomach. This is what I love. *Freedom.*

I sit up when I see a few bikes in the distance. I don't recognize their patches, but that doesn't surprise me. Tennessee has a huge MC community, and there are always new clubs popping up all over the state. I slow down as I close the distance between us.

The closer I get, the more details I can make out. The group of about five bikes in front of me are all Harleys, all ranging in colors from almost purple to black. None of the men are wearing helmets, which is the complete opposite of me, who is covered from head to toe in black leather. Even my helmet is all black, with leather piping.

I take the men in, noticing they are all well-built, their leather cuts displaying a large eagle, with its wings spread wide like it's midflight. The talons of the bird are carrying a long stem rose, with petals falling off it onto their club name, The Broken Eagles. I begin to speed up and pass them one by one, thankful for the security of my helmet, the black visor making it impossible to see me.

I keep my head straight until the last guy, the one who is at the front of the group, catches my attention. From the back, his hair is the first thing I notice. It's slightly long on top and buzzed on the sides. My eyes move to the expanse of his back, the wide set of his shoulders, and the tan skin covering his lean muscles. His bike is low to the ground, and the bars are in front of him in a way that he has to stretch his arms straight out, causing every muscle to flex and move, making it look like the tattoos are alive and dancing.

My eyes skim farther down over his chest, which is covered in a white tank top tucked into a pair of light jeans, and around his waist is a black belt with a large silver buckle. I continue to pass him, my eyes shifting from the road to him and back again. This time when I look over, his head is turned towards me, and if I didn't know any better, I would have swear he is looking directly into my soul.

"Holy shit," I whisper, taking in his hair, the set of his jaw that is covered in days of stubble, and a pair of light eyes I can't quite make out through the tint of my helmet. He is seriously hot, but equally scary-looking. I look from him back to the road. It must not have been even a second, but when my eyes go to the asphalt in front of me, I see a bird that is trying to make its way across the road, its wing hanging in an awkward position. I swerve to the right just in time to miss the poor animal.

"What the fuck?" I hear roared, and I look over my shoulder at the man who is now coming up quick on my right side. I yell an apology over the sound of my engine and his pipes. Do a quick wave and take off, lowering my body and pulling back the throttle, wanting to get away from them. Dude looks seriously pissed off, and even though I hate leaving the bird behind without helping it, I would like to live to see my next birthday.

I think I'm in the clear, but then the sound of pipes fills my ears, and I don't even know how it happens, but they all catch up with me, surrounding my bike. I can't make out what they're saying, but my stomach starts to roll at the sound of their voices. I feel my side to make sure I have the Taser my dad insisted I carry.

I see a clearing and pull my bike off to the side of the road. I know this is probably one of the stupidest things I have ever done, but if they keep chasing me like they have been, we could all end up seriously hurt. I pull over and don't even shut down my bike. I just lower my kickstand as my heart, which was already beating hard, begins to bang violently against my ribcage as they surround me.

"What the fuck is wrong with you?" the guy who was at the head of the group asks, stepping in front of my bike.

I shake my head as my words get lodged in my throat.

He pulls me off my bike, and the men who are with him begin yelling obscenities as well.

"Sorry," I croak out, and I don't even know if he hears me as his hand goes to the collar of my leather jacket, where he shakes me hard. My hand accidently presses down on the button that ignites the Taser. The loud crack fills the air, and his eyes go wide then he falls to the ground, and I fall on my ass and crabwalk backwards. I look up when I hit something, only to meet the eyes of another man, who looks pissed.

"Get up," he growls, picking me up. My feet flail under me as I'm lifted off the ground with my hands restrained behind my back.

"Hold him still," the guy who I had tasered growls in front of me as I try to get away from the anger I feel coming off him. His hands go to my head and he rips my helmet off, causing my hair to float down around me.

Complete silence descends. I swear no one even takes a breath.

"Um." I bite my lip and the guy in front of me blinks a couple of times before his hands at my shoulders release then tighten.

"What the fuck were you thinking?" he barks, dipping his face closer to mine, and the scent of him fills my lungs. He smells like leather, musk, and man.

"I..." I start to explain to him what happened, when he cuts me off.

"Fucking bitches always trying to be fucking hard."

Oh, hell no, he did not just call me a bitch. "You did not just call me a bitch," I lean forward and hiss in his face.

"Yes, bitch, I asked you what the fuck you were thinking?"

"You cannot be serious right now!" I scream. Have I mentioned that I may have a little bit of a temper? I come by it honestly.

"You gonna explain yourself?" He crosses his arms over his muscular chest and then lifts his chin to the guy behind me, who immediately lets me go, causing my feet to hit the ground hard without warning, making me stumble.

Once I right myself, I turn around quickly to face the guy that just dropped me and get up on my tiptoes, even though that is not even close to reaching his face, and growl, "That was rude."

Then I swing my body to face the scary, hot biker dude. "First of all, I didn't want to kill a poor, innocent bird, so I swerved to miss it. I apologized for almost hitting you, but then you proceeded to chase me down like this is an episode of *Sons of Anarchy*, which it is not, I might add," I yell, flinging my arms around. I hear someone chuckle, but I'm too caught up in my own tirade to pay any attention to how crazy I might appear.

"You flipped me off," he says.

I look at him and my eyebrows pull together as I reply, "I totally did not flip you off." I'm pretty sure that I didn't flip him off. *Did I flip him off?* I ask myself then shake my head. "I did not flip you off," I confirm out loud.

"This bitch is crazy." I turn my head and come face-to-face with a guy who is at least a foot and a half taller than me. He's slim, and kind of cute in that 'I just got out of prison. Wanna take a walk on the wild side?' kind of way.

I swing around in a circle, stating, "The next one of you assholes who calls me a bitch is going to get tasered." I stop on skinny cute guy and hold the Taser out in his direction, causing him to suck in his already thin stomach.

"Watch it," he complains, but I swear I see his lip twitch.

"Stop fucking around," Hot Biker Dude says, grabbing the Taser from my hand.

"Hey," I protest, and turn to face him, holding out my hand while putting my other hand on my hip. "Give it back." I wiggle my fingers and he looks me over, making every inch of me tingle. "I'm not kidding; give it back. It was a gift from my dad."

He looks me over again then looks over my head, and says, "Lets roll."

"What?" I look at him then all the guys walking away and getting on their bikes. I don't know why I'm not happier about them leaving, but I swear I want to run up to that guy, jump on his back, and wrap myself around him. I shake my head at my stupidity and yell, "Good riddance!"

That comment must have come too soon, 'cause Hot Biker Dude slips off his bike and comes back to me. I think he's going to be a jerk, but instead, he hands me my Taser and mutters, "Be safe, babe."

I watch him walk away; his ass in jeans is like nothing I have seen before. He lifts his leg and straddles his bike, and I stay in place, watching his arm muscles flex from behind. "Holy shit," I whisper as they all pull off. I get on my bike quickly and head back towards the area I saw the bird. I finally find the poor guy off the side of the road near the edge of a field. Once I have him in my hand, I get back on my bike, and that's when I hear the sound of pipes once again. A shiver slides down my spine, but I ignore it and focus on what I need to do.

I unzip my leather jacket and unfold the bird's wing so that I can tuck it closer to his body. Once I have his wing adjusted, I place him near my belly with one hand.

"What are you doing?" a dark, rich voice asks, and I startle almost dropping the poor bird, so I lift my head and glare.

"He broke his wing."

"It's a bird," Hot Biker Dude says, looking at the tiny animal in my hand.

"I know that." I roll my eyes and zip up the lower part of my jacket so the little bird is secure against me, with his miniature head sticking out the top of the zipper.

"What are you doing with him?"

"Taking him to my office, where I can hopefully get him fixed up."

"You a doctor?"

I lift my head and our gazes connect. This time, without the visor, I can see his eyes are green, a green so light that they remind me of mint chocolate chip ice cream.

"You gonna answer, or just stare at me?"

What the hell is wrong with me? "I'm a vet." I feel my face pinking from being called out. "Sorry about earlier," I murmur, picking up my helmet from behind me and slipping it on, feeling instant relief when he's blocked out. I lean forward and start up my bike, being careful of the bird that is now sitting close to me. I look at Hot Biker Dude one more time and lift my chin. He smiles, crosses his arms over his chest, and leans back in his seat. I know right then that if I ever see him again, I'm screwed.

Chapter 1

"HEY, DAD." I smile, walking into my parents' house. My dad lifts his head from the papers in front of him on the island and smiles as I slide onto the seat next to him, leaning my head on his shoulder.

"Hey," he says, tenderly pressing a kiss to the top of my head then wrapping his large arm around my shoulders. I set my bag down on the counter and lean forward, picking up the coffee cup in front of him and taking a sip. "What's going on?"

I let out a shaky breath, set the cup down, and lean back so I can look at him.

"There was another dog left on the hospital's doorstep this morning," I tell him, and anger instantly fills his features. "I hate it, Dad," I whisper. "I hate knowing someone is fighting dogs and getting away with it. I hate that when they get to me, they are so badly broken I don't have any choice but to help them pass peacefully." I feel tears sting my nose, but I fight them back. You can't cry in front of my dad. He doesn't deal well when his girls cry.

"What did Uncle Nico say?"

"He's putting up cameras out front to see if he can catch anyone, but there isn't much he can do right now," I mutter, picking his cup of coffee back up and taking another sip.

"I'll call your cousins and see if they can have some of their boys do a round in the area."

"Dad, seriously, they're busy." I shake my head. I know my cousins would do rounds if I asked them to, but I hate the idea of them worrying about me. They may be my younger cousins, but you would never know it by how they treat any of us girls. They make my uncles and dad look tame.

"If things don't pan out with the cameras, I'm asking them."

I roll my eyes, knowing there is no point in arguing. There are times you may as well be talking to a brick wall when speaking to my father.

"Hey, honey." My mom smiles, walking into the kitchen, wearing a robe that isn't exactly appropriate, but still looks good on her. My mom is beautiful, and judging by the look on my dad's face, he seems to think so too. *Which is my cue to leave.*

"Hey, Mom," I mumble as her arms wrap around me and she kisses my cheek.

"I didn't know you were coming by." She looks at my dad over my head, but I still catch the look she gives him. *Gross.*

"I just wanted to come steal some food before I went home," I tell her, and then want to take it back, 'cause I need to get out of here.

"Do you want me to make you something?" she offers, going to the fridge.

I shake my head. "No, I'll stop at the store," I assure her.

I swear my parents are complete freaks, and I do not want to witness anything that will have me bleaching out my eyeballs later. Been there, done that, never going back.

"Are you sure?" She frowns, looking me over.

"Babe, she's leaving," my dad growls at her, making me smile.

"Asher Mayson." She puts her hands on her hips and I almost laugh.

"I'm sure, Mom." I pick up my bag and kiss my dad on the cheek before giving my mom another hug. I yell, "Love you, guys," over my shoulder as I rush out of their house.

I drive twenty minutes to my house across town. I live in a yellow, three-bedroom, ranch-style home with a huge front porch that sits two rocking chairs. Even though my house is in town, the houses in my neighborhood are all spread out, each of us on my block having around one-acre lots.

I shut down my car in my driveway, not bothering to park in the garage since I would have to crawl out my trunk, and grab my bag before making my way up to my front porch. I grab my mail from the mailbox next to my door before making my way inside, quickly closing the door behind me so that Juice doesn't have a chance to escape.

"Hey, big guy." I drop my mail and bag on the entryway table and pick up Juice when he jumps up, making the contents of the table rattle. "What have you been doing?" I rub my face into the soft fur of his neck and smile when he begins to purr. "I think it's going to be an early night," I tell him as I walk back to my bedroom and toe off my shoes in my closet before dumping Juice onto the bed.

He walks around in circles for a moment before curling himself up into a ball and closing his eyes. I shake my head, wishing I could fall asleep as easily as he does. I always find it hard to sleep after work. My body is normally exhausted, but my mind is in a constant state of worry. I'm always wondering if I missed something, or if I should have done something differently with one of the animals in my care. I slip off my clothes, pull on a pair of cut-off sweats that are now shorts, find a tank top, and put that on before making my way into the kitchen.

"Hey, Taser," I say as I go to the cage that is now on a stand near the double doors that lead to my back deck. His little bird head turns towards me, and I check to make sure he has enough water and food before placing a sheet over the top of his cage. Since the day I brought him home, Taser has been improving, but judging by the way his small wing still hangs awkwardly, I don't think he will ever be free again.

I fix myself a peanut butter and banana sandwich and a glass of milk then carry both back to my bedroom, turn on the TV, and get into bed.

I make myself comfortable while flipping through channels until I find one of my favorite shows, *Ancient Aliens.* I lean back and pick up my sandwich, taking a large bite before moaning at its perfection, and then wash it down with a gulp of milk. After I'm done eating, I take my dishes back to the kitchen then go handle my nightly routine before getting back into bed. I make sure I hold back the covers for Juice, who, like always, curves himself against my stomach as I watch the supposable hidden secrets of an ancient alien race until I fall asleep.

I LOOK AT my receptionist, Kayan, and feel my eyebrows pull together when she taps franticly on the glass and waves her hand at me. "I'll be right back," I tell my patient's family, and follow Kayan out of the exam room and down the hall towards the waiting area. "What happened?" I ask her, and she pauses just around the corner and points. I look around to where she's pointing, instantly regretting it when I see the profile of the man I wished I would never see again standing near the reception desk. "What did he want?" I whisper, taking Hot Biker Dude in, in all his jeans-and-leather glory.

"He said he wants to adopt a dog. I sat there staring at him for five minutes, not able to even speak, and I could tell he was becoming pissed off, so I figured you could help him."

"Do you remember when I told you about the bikers who chased me down a couple weeks ago?"

"Yeah," she mutters dreamily.

"He's the one I tasered," I tell her, watching as her eyes get big and her mouth form an O.

"No," she whispers, looking around the corner at him.

"Yes." I nod then pat her shoulder. "Good luck."

"No…please." She shakes her head franticly, grabbing onto my hand.

“He’s not that scary.” I frown.

“No, he’s scary hot.” She shakes her head again. “I could deal with him if he was just hot, but no, he’s scary *and* hot. That is a no-go for me. You know this.”

“Fine.” I stand at my full height, which is only five-four, and adjust my shirt, pressing my boobs up a little higher, which makes no sense, because I’m wearing scrubs. “Can you go make sure the Thompsons have the supplies they need for Tutu?”

“Of course.” She breathes a sigh of relief, and I inhale a huge breath before stepping around the corner.

“Hi, Kayan told me you were interested in adopting?” I say, pretending like I have no idea who he is. His head turns toward me, his gaze locking with mine, and my heart stutters in my chest. Everything I remembered about him was wrong. He is way hotter than I recalled, the scruff darker, his lips fuller, and his eyes greener.

“You,” he mutters as his eyes travel over the length of my hair, the tops of my breasts, down to my waist, and then slowly slide back up, making every inch of me feel exposed. “July,” he says when his eyes meet mine again.

“How do you know my name?” I ask, feeling completely baffled.

His head dips towards my chest and I look down, seeing my nametag attached to my top. “Oh,” I say, feeling like an idiot, my hand going to my chest to cover the piece of plastic.

“Wes.” He smirks.

“Pardon?” I blink, wishing I had forced Kayan to do her damn job.

“Name’s Wes.”

“Cool name,” I mutter, and then wish I had grown up with a filter that worked properly when I see his smirk turn into a smile. “So you want to adopt?” I ask him, knowing that if he says yes, his hotness points are going to increase tenfold.

"Thinking about it." He shrugs, shoving his hands into the front pockets of his jeans, forcing the well-worn black shirt he has on to stretch across his chest and abs. I swallow and mentally kick my ass around in my head until I pull myself together enough to speak again.

"Well..." I clear my throat, and then narrow my eyes when I see he's smiling at how uncomfortable I am. "Follow me," I snap, and stomp down the hall in front of him then push through the double doors at the end of the hall that leads to the kennels out back. I hear him chuckle, but I ignore him. "Those are dogs. Those are cats." I wave my hand back and forth. "Come back up front when you're done." I start to storm past him, but his hand shoots out, wrapping around my bicep stopping me in my tracks and sending a zip of electricity up my arm.

"Slow down, babe," he says, and my heart stops, and a shiver slides down my spine from the tone of his voice.

I shake off his hand and turn to face him, trying to be casual, even though my heart is beating so hard I swear it's going to pound right out of my chest. "Did you need something else?"

"Can you tell me a little about some of the dogs you have here?"

No! I mentally scream, but my stupid head nods up and down. "What would you like to know?" I ask, and am proud my voice sounds normal and not breathy like I expected it to.

"Are any of these guys here known to be good guard dogs?"

"Yeah, Capone," I tell him, walking toward the kennel at the end of the hall. Capone needs a home. He's been with us for over six months, but no one wants the poor guy. He's ugly, but very sweet. If my heart weren't still broken from losing Beast years ago, I would have adopted Capone myself.

"This guy here is really vicious; he would kill someone if they looked at him the wrong way." He looks at me doubtfully. "Don't be fooled. He would rip your face off if he was given the chance," I tell

Wes, crossing my arms over my chest while stopping in front of Capone's kennel. Capone sits up, his large bulgy dog eyes looking between Wes and me, the hair on top of his head sticking up in every direction and his long tongue hanging out the side of his mouth where a few teeth are missing.

I look from Capone to Wes and see his eyes are on me, and there is something in his eyes that causes my lungs to freeze.

"Three," he says in a tone that is so deep that the space between my legs tingles and the breath I was holding whooshes out.

"Three what?"

"Three times you've fucked with me."

"Capone is a badass," I insist, and his hand runs over his mouth and his eyes travel leisurely over me from head to toe.

"Three times you've made me want to fuck you or fill that smart mouth of yours." He steps towards me, his body pressing me into the wall behind me, and his large hand takes hold of my waist. I get lost in his eyes and words for a moment, but then I remember where we are and who he is. His head dips towards mine, and I do the only thing I can think of—I cover my mouth with my hand.

His head pulls back and his eyes search my face as his brows pull together. "That's a first," he mumbles, but doesn't exactly sound disappointed. "You don't want to kiss me?" he questions, running his nose over the back of my hand that's still protecting my mouth. My mind screams, "Yes!" but my head shakes no.

"So sweet." He skims his nose along my hand until he brushes my ear. "Bet once I'm in there, I won't want to leave," he murmurs, and I swallow hard, fighting the instinct to remove my hand, turn my head, and kiss him like my body is begging me to. "Bet you'd go wild for me the minute my hands were on you." The fingers of his hand at my side press in. "Bet you want it as badly as I do."

He inhales at my neck and his tongue touches the skin behind my ear, making my knees actually shake. I have been in love; I've been in lust too, but this is something new, something that makes me feel like every cell in my body is fighting to pull me closer to him, and that scares the shit out of me. I duck down and slide under his arm then walk backwards until there's at least twelve feet between us. Only then do I remove my hand from my mouth.

"So what do you say? Do you want to adopt Capone?" I ask, ignoring whatever the hell it was that just happened.

His brow that was furrowed after I stepped out of his embrace smooths out and he smiles. "I'll take him," he says, looking at Capone then me.

"Really?" I whisper as my heart flutters in my chest.

"I still need a guard dog, but I'll take him too."

"Why do you need a guard dog?"

"I have a shop, and around back, there's a lot with cars. The last couple weeks, someone's jumped the fence and broken into cars, stealing stereos or other parts out of them."

"You can't leave a dog outside." I frown at him.

"Didn't say I was going to. You can even come check it out for yourself."

"That won't be necessary," I mutter as he smirks.

"So do you have another dog? One that is actually dangerous?" he asks, and I frown.

"Dogs are not dangerous. Stupid dog owners are dangerous."

"Okay…do you have a dog that's protective?" He shakes his head, and I let out a breath then lead him to the back of the shelter, where Max is kept. Max was the only dog from the fighting ring that I was able to save. He is blind out of one eye and mean, but I love him and just couldn't bring myself to put him to sleep.

"This is Max." I crouch down in front of Max's cage and press my hand through the bars, rubbing his dark head.

"What happened to him?" Wes asks, crouching down next to me. I expect Max to growl, but he just looks at Wes then me. Wes slowly presses a finger through the cage, and Max starts licking him, making my heart feel lighter. I hate that Max is here and stuck in a kennel all the time.

"He was here one morning when I got into work. He was almost dead, his eye was missing, and he couldn't walk. I realized then that he had been fought and obviously lost."

"Normally when dogs are fought, they kill them for losing," he tells me, something that causes tears to pool in my eyes.

"I know," I whisper, petting Max's head. "He was the first to be brought to me, but every few days, I get to work and there's another. Max is the only one I have been able to save.

"What the fuck?"

"I don't know." I stand up, walk over to one of the visiting rooms, and open the door. "Wait in here. I'll bring Max in so we can make sure you guys get along," I tell him. I wait until he's in the room then shut the door and get Max, taking him into the room with me.

"Hey, bud," Wes mutters, petting Max's head when he comes to sit in front of him.

I watch them for a few minutes, and then ask, "Do you want to see how he and Capone get along, or were you just saying you wanted them both in order to earn brownie points?"

His head tilts back to look at me. "Go get Capone, babe. I need to make sure my boys are cool," he mutters.

"Be right back," I mumble and head out of the room.

In front of Capone's kennel, I jump up and down, shaking out my hands. He watches silently, while the rest of the dogs go crazy. I make sure Capone is on his leash as I lead him into the room, where he meets Wes and Max. Max sits nicely, while Capone sniffs around before jumping up to sit on Wes' lap.

"You guys look good together." I smile at the image, reach into my back pocket, and grab my phone. I slide up the camera, taking a picture before I can think better of it. My head bends and I look at the photo, not quiet sure what the feeling in my stomach means.

"You wanna have dinner with me?"

My head flies up and my gaze collides with his. I have read a lot, and I do mean *a lot* of biker books, and not once has a biker taken a girl out to dinner. "Um…" I whisper.

"I know a great Mexican spot."

"Mexican?" I repeat.

"Or if you want something else…" He shrugs.

"I like Mexican." I clear my throat and look at Max and Capone.

"Tonight?"

I look at him again, and he has one hand on Capone and the other on Max, two guys I believed would be forced to live out the rest of their lives in cages. He's saving them, so that tells me a lot more than knowing him for weeks could.

"Okay," I agree, then move away from the bench when he stands. "Let's get you guys out of here."

It doesn't take long to fill out the necessary paperwork, and when it's done, I help him get both boys into his Escalade.

"I'll see you tonight."

"See you tonight," I confirm, watching him.

He swings up into his truck and shuts the door, pulling on a pair of sunglasses. His head dips towards me and I wave. The truck fits him as much as his bike does. He looked hot getting behind the wheel.

I feel for my phone in my pocket, making sure it's still where he put it after he programed his number into it. I go inside and come to a complete stop when Kayan looks at me and smiles.

"What?" I ask, and she presses her lips together—to keep from laughing, I'm sure.

"Shut up," I say, walking back into my office and shutting the door.

I have a date. I have a date with a hot biker who just adopted two dogs. Yeah, I was right in my last assessment of him. I'm screwed.

Chapter 2

I LOOK AT myself in the mirror and turn from side to side, checking myself out. I have on a kimono jacket, and I've paired it with a red tank and dark denim capris. I walk to my closet and pull out my beige wedges that wrap around my ankle and have a peep toe. I slip them on, tie them up and around my ankle, and then walk back to the bathroom. I apply some bronzer, a little blush, and a whole lot of mascara. I tease the top of my head and bend over, using some spray before flipping my head back over, pulling the bottom pieces down over the tops of my breasts.

I do not look like a biker's girl, but I do look cute.

I head out to my Jeep and toss my bag across the seat. It takes ten minutes to get to the restaurant that Wes asked me to meet him at, and when I arrive, the parking lot is packed with cars and tons of bikes. It's late spring, so the evenings are warm, and the whole outdoor patio is packed with diners wanting to eat outside under the stars. My phone starts to ring, and I answer it without checking who it is.

"Hello?"

"Babe, the lot's full."

"I know; there's no parking."

"I'll follow you home and you can ride back with me," he says, but I don't know if that's smart. I'm not sure I will be able to be pressed close to him with my thighs around his, my hands on his body.

"Babe."

"Huh?"

"I'll follow you." I turn around and see him straddling his bike with his cut over a plaid shirt in blues and blacks with the sleeves rolled up, the top buttons open enough to see the tank he has on under it, and a pair of jeans with his black boots.

"Okay," I whisper, and pull around the parking lot then onto the main road. He follows me the few minutes to my house, and I park in my driveway, getting out quickly and meeting him at the back of my car.

"You wanna get your helmet?" he asks.

I look at my bag in my hand and realize that if I'm riding with him, I need to lighten my load. "Be right back," I mutter, opening the door to my car and bending across the seat to press the button for the garage.

"Babe."

"Hmm?" I turn to look over my shoulder at him.

"You look good, baby."

My stomach starts to turn, not with unease, but with excitement.

"Thanks." I smile with a shake of my head and go into my garage, pulling the stuff I need out of my purse and shoving it into my bra and pockets before carrying my helmet back out to where he's waiting.

"Your car good?" he asks, lifting his leg over the seat of his bike and taking my helmet from me.

"Yes," I whisper as his smell surrounds me. His fingers tuck my hair behind my ears, and then he places the helmet over my head and hooks the button under my chin.

"That okay?" he asks, and I nod as he tosses his leg over the seat once more. I've ridden bikes since I was fifteen and begged my mom to teach me to ride. She and I both like riding sports bikes, but my uncles and cousins who ride like Harleys, so I know what I'm doing. But I have never been on the back of a bike with a man I'm attracted too. I slide on, and the moment my ass touches the seat, his hands go to the back of my calves, where he pulls me tighter against him.

"Hold me tight," he instructs, looking at me over his shoulder. I place my hands on his waist and squeeze him a little tighter as the bike takes off, which is a huge mistake, because I feel hardness like I've never felt before right under my palms. I didn't even know abs were something that actually exist in real life. I try to keep still, even though my hands itch to press into him to see if what I think I'm feeling is really real.

When we pull into the parking lot, I remove my hands quickly and get off the bike. I pull off my helmet and bend over, fluffing my hair before swinging my head back upright.

"You need to watch who's around when you do shit like that," Wes says taking ahold of my hip.

"What?"

"That bending over, hair-flip shit you just did." I look at him and see that his eyes are pointing toward the outdoor eating area, where there is a group of guys all watching us. I ignore his comment and start walking into the restaurant, or try to, but his finger hooks into the back of my jeans and he pulls me into step with him. Then he wraps his hand around my waist, his fingers curling into my side.

"How many?" a cute Spanish girl asks as soon as we enter the restaurant.

"Two," Wes tells her, and she leads us to a booth near the bar and gives us our menus, telling us our waiter will be right with us.

My gaze connects with his, and I bite my lip and lift my menu up. The intimacy of being in the booth with him is causing me to suddenly feel nervous.

"Wes."

I turn and look up at a guy who is wearing something similar to Wes, only he has on a red and blue plaid shirt, with his cut over it.

"How're you?" Wes shakes his hand and they begin to talk about something to do with bikes, or some crap I don't understand. I look at

Wes, and I doubt he even remembers I'm here at this point. I test my theory by saying, "Excuse me," to the guy, and telling Wes I'm going to use the restroom. His eyes don't even come to me when I speak. I slip out of the booth and go to the restroom then back to the table. The guy is still there and has now taken my seat, and they each have a beer in front of them. I stand there waiting for a few minutes, wanting to see if Wes realizes I'm not there, but his eyes don't search the room for me.

"Screw this," I whisper, suddenly feeling sorry for myself. I pull out my phone, call a cab, walk out to Wes' bike, and grab my helmet off the seat. It takes three minutes for the cab to show up, and the moment I slip into the back seat, my phone starts to ring. I click the end button, and do it again when it rings two more times. When we reach my house, I give the cabdriver a ten and tell him to keep the change.

I head up my walkway and into my house, when the roar of a motorcycle fills my ears. I go inside, close the door, take the stuff out of my pockets and bra, and set all of it on my entryway table. "Open the door, July. I know you're in there." Wes yells from outside but I ignore him and walk back to my bedroom, take off the kimono jacket and my heels, and walk back out to the living room, opening the door when he begins to pound so hard the pictures on my walls shake.

"Can I help you?" I raise a brow and his eyes narrow.

"You wanna be a smartass after walking out on dinner?"

"Oh, honey, you're confused." I put on my biggest smile, open my screen door, and step out onto my front porch, shutting the door behind me. "You say I walked out on you, right?" I ask, crossing my arms over my chest.

"You did," he growls.

"Interesting," I mutter, leaning back on the heels of my feet, looking him over. "I sat across from you for fifteen minutes, got up from a table I was sitting at with you, and you didn't notice. I stood across the room from you for five minutes before I said 'Screw it', and left. I don't know what type of women you're used to, but I'm not one of them. Good luck in life, Wes," I tell him, opening my door, stepping inside, and then closing and locking the door behind me.

I plop down on my couch for a minute and put my face in my hands. This was not how I expected my evening to turn out. After a few minutes, I stand and head for the kitchen, scooping up Juice on the way, letting his soft purrs sooth my wounded ego. Then I go to Taser and check on him before placing Juice on the counter, and pull down one of my large mixing bowls from one cupboard and a box of Fruity Pebbles out of another. I fill the bowl half-full and go to the fridge to get milk, and pour some on top of the cereal. I grab a spoon from my cute holder on my counter and take the bowl with me, heading towards my bedroom, when there is another knock on my door.

"What?" I ask, wrapping my arm around the bowl of cereal as I open the door.

"You're not eating that. I ordered pizza," Wes says as soon as he spots my Fruity Pebbles.

"Are you drunk?" I ask him as he pushes past me into my house, taking the bowl out of my hand.

"No, and don't do that shit again, unless you want a red ass," he says, and I ignore his comment and follow behind him. "Sean had some information I needed, so I didn't even think; I just went into work mode." He walks into my kitchen, sets my bowl of cereal in the sink, and turns the water on.

"You did not just do that," I hiss, watching my favorite food in the whole world literally go down the drain.

"I ordered us pizza."

"Did you hear the part where I said 'have a nice life'?"

"I'm ignoring that, 'cause I know you're pissed, but I also know you'll get over it."

"Get over it?" I breathe out, watching as he takes off his cut and places it over the back of one of my kitchen chairs.

"You're right. You're not like any woman I've been with before." He runs a hand over his jaw, and I notice he didn't say 'dated'.

"No shit." I shake my head, crossing my arms over my chest, and his lips twitch.

"I also know that's the reason I'm pursuing you. I can get pussy anytime I want. But a woman I see myself having a future with," he shakes his head, "never had that."

"Uh…I just met you, and I hate to be the one to bust your little bubble, but you're not someone I see myself having a future with. I can't even see us having a second date."

"We'll see," he mutters, walking over to Taser's cage.

"No, we won't see. You need to leave." I pick up his cut and head towards the door, hoping he'll follow but when I open the door, the pizza delivery guy is standing there with his hand in air, ready to knock. *Crap.* I step back as Wes comes to stand in front of me, talking to the delivery guy.

"Babe, take this into the kitchen while I pay for it," he tells me, handing me the pizza box and pulling his wallet out of his back pocket.

I stand there for a moment, looking at him like he's insane, but then stupidly walk the pizza back to my kitchen, setting it down on my counter. Then I put his cut on the back of my chair again and stand there in the kitchen with my arms crossed over my chest as I wait for him.

"You gonna get plates?" he asks, walking around the corner.

"No."

"Are you always this difficult?"

"I would like to remind you that I went out to dinner with you, but you ignored me," I say haughtily.

"Told you it was business."

"And I told you I don't care."

"I know you believe in second chances. Most people, especially a vet, would take one look at Capone and Max and put them to sleep, but you didn't do that."

That was a low blow. I look at him, and my gut is telling me to do it, to give him a second chance, but my brain is screaming at me, telling me that if I do it, then it will be the end of life as I know it.

"We can be friends," I compromise, and he grins.

"Sure, baby. Friends," he mutters then steps closer to me, and I cover my mouth again when I see his eyes drop to my lips. "Don't worry. I won't kiss you until you're begging me to," he says, and I scoff, take a step back, reach up with my free hand, and open the cupboard that holds my plates. I pull two down and shove them at him, and then remove my hand from my mouth when I open the fridge to grab two beers.

He opens the box of pizza, and the smell filters to my nose, causing my stomach to growl. "Ewww, you got Hawaiian and supreme." I scrunch up my nose. His eyes come to me and he blinks as I press my lips together to keep from smiling.

"You're a pain in the ass," he mutters, shaking his head and smiling as he slides a slice of each on a plate and hands it to me, then does the same for himself. I walk back to the living room, and he comes with me, setting his plate and beer on the coffee table and looking around. "Where's your TV?" he asks, confused.

"In my bedroom," I tell him, taking a bite of pizza.

"You only have one TV?" He frowns, and I frown back.

"Yes, why? How many TVs do you have?"

"A couple." He shrugs.

"When I'm home, I usually hang out in my room," I tell him, watching as he takes a bite of pizza. *How can eating be sexy*? I think, and then realize I forgot napkins, and I will definitely need them. I set down my plate, get up, and go to the kitchen, grabbing some paper towels off the roll before coming back and handing one to him.

"Thanks," he mumbles, taking a drink of beer.

"So what do you do?" I ask, sitting back on the couch and pulling my feet up under me.

"Me and a few of my brothers have a parts store and bike shop." He says then wipes his mouth.

"Brothers, like *brothers,* or brothers, like 'This is my brother'?" I ask, doing a fist bump in the air.

"It's all the same." He smiles. "We were all in the military together, and when we got out a couple years ago, we decided to settle down and start a business together."

"That's cool," I murmur, taking a drink of my beer then pulling the crust off my pizza before finishing it off.

"What about you? How long have you been a vet?"

"A couple years."

"How old are you?" he questions, and I feel my skin heat as his eyes roam over me.

"Twenty-six." I shrug then continue when he looks at me doubtfully. "I graduated high school at seventeen then started college right away. I knew I wanted to be a veterinarian since I was a little girl, so I worked extra hard until I got my wish."

"Why?" he asks, and my heart squeezes painfully in my chest.

"We had a dog growing up, and his name was Beast. He was a black and white Great Dane, but to me, he was my best friend. When he got older and became sick, I knew one day I wanted to be able to help other people who loved their animals as much as I loved Beast," I whisper, taking another sip of beer, hoping it will help wash away the pain of talking about my best friend.

"Is that why you don't have a dog now?" he asks, reading me, and I nod.

"I don't want to replace him."

"I get that," he says gently, setting his empty plate and beer on the table.

"How old are you?" I ask, setting my own plate down but keeping my beer in hand.

"Twenty-nine. So how long have you been riding?"

"Since I was fifteen. My mom is actually the one who taught me to ride. My dad hates it, but knows he can't stop me. It was one of my mom's hobbies, and something that only she and I share, so it makes it that much more special."

"You have brothers and sisters?" he asks.

"I have four sisters, all younger, all in college." I smile. "What about you? Any siblings?"

"No, I'm an only child, raised by a single mother."

"How did you end up in Tennessee?"

"My mom lives in Nashville, and when I came out to visit her, I drove through this town and liked the feel of it, so I talked to my boys and we packed up, got on our bikes, and drove out here from California."

"That must have been scary, huh?"

"None of us had anything to lose," he says, and I try to think of something else to say then look around my living room, wondering why the hell I didn't just buy another TV.

"Do you want to go to bed with me?" I ask then cover my mouth and feel my eyes grow large.

"Sure." He smiles, and I cover my face.

"I mean do you want to watch TV with me?" I say peeking out from behind my hands.

"I know what you meant." He chuckles, and I feel his hand on my knee. I remove my hands from my face and look at him, shaking my head.

"Let me just clean this stuff up," I mutter, standing and grabbing my plate.

"I'll help," he says, picking up his plate and taking mine from me, so I pick up his beer bottle and follow him into the kitchen, watching the way his ass moves as he walks. "Are you checking out my ass?"

"Definitely." I smile, walking past him to the garbage can.

"Pain in the ass," he mutters, but I hear the smile in his voice. "You kept the bird," he says, standing in front of Taser's cage.

"Yeah, he probably won't be able to fly again. His wing didn't heal like it was supposed to." I smile when Taser tweets at Wes as he sticks his finger into the cage. "Do you want another beer?"

"Sure." He nods, and I open one for him and another for myself then lead him back into my bedroom. I set my beer on my nightstand before climbing up on my bed. I watch as he walks around to the other side, his presence making my room feel small. My insides start to twist thinking about how my ex-boyfriend was allergic to cats, so we always spent time at his house, and the only guys who have been in my room since I moved here are my cousins.

I try to see what he sees as he takes in my room. I painted the walls a light blue that matches an antique chair I set in the corner of the room. My dressers and night stands are all antiques, as well as being all different in design, the old cream paint chipping and peeling, giving them character. My bedding is ruffled white duvet that covers the large down comforter I have inside it. You can tell it's a girl's room, but it isn't covered in pink flowers.

I watch as he slips off his boots then slides onto the bed, sitting back against the headboard and crossing his ankles. I let out a breath and flipped on the TV, and Juice decides to come out of hiding, jumping up on the bed and climbing into my lap.

"Do you like cats?" I ask Wes while running my fingers through Juice's soft fur.

His eyes come to me, and I see something flash within their green depths before he replies, "I love pussy."

I start to giggle and bury my face in Juice's fur. I hear Wes chuckle, and I shake my head and hand him the remote, not knowing what he likes to watch. "You can pick whatever," I tell him, curling up on my side with Juice curled into my belly.

He flips through the channels for a few minutes then stops on the movie *Back to the Future.* He leans back farther, putting his hand behind his head and resting the one holding the remote on his abs. The urge to scoot closer to him is almost painful, but I keep myself still, making sure to keep my breathing normal.

"So…can we at least cuddle?" he asks, and I tilt my head back to look at him then without thinking I move Juice and scoot over to him, and his eyes get wide. He shakes his head and holds his arm up, and I lay my head on his chest. Both my hands pillow under my cheek while I pull my knees up, tucking them against his side.

"That was easy," he mumbles, wrapping his arm around me.

What can I say? I'm a girl; I like to cuddle. And no one in their right mind would turn him down if he asked them.

"Babe." I hear Wes say but I'm so comfy that I don't want to open my eyes or move.

"Hmm?" I mumble.

"I gotta head out."

"Later," I mutter.

"Babe."

"What?" I whine, and he starts to laugh.

"You gotta come lock up."

"It's fine. I don't need to lock up," I grumble.

"Baby." I open one eye and look at him. "Come on." He pulls me out of bed and sets me on my feet.

"I'm up." I yawn, stumbling out of the room and to the front door. I open it for him while he goes to the kitchen, gets his cut, and slips it on over his shirt then comes toward me and I cover my mouth, making him smile.

"I stole a kiss while you were sleeping."

"Liar." I say as he stops in front of me.

"I told you I won't kiss you until you beg me to." I pull my hand away from my mouth, and bite my lip when my eyes drop to his mouth.

"Thanks for the pizza, Wes," I tell him as my gaze travels back up to his.

"I'll call you, baby."

"Sure." I nod, and he leans in and presses a kiss to my forehead that catches me off-guard.

"Lock the door," he says over his shoulder, and I roll my eyes then open them wide when something I hadn't even thought about clicks into place.

I have grown up around crazy-ass alpha men my whole life, men like my dad and uncles, and as I watch Wes walk to his bike, I know the kind of man he is.

"Babe, lock up," he shouts, swinging onto his bike. I slam the door shut, lock both locks, go to the blinds, and peek out as he pulls away.

"What have I done?" I whisper as he drives out of sight.

Chapter 3

"HEY, WHAT ARE you doing here?" I ask Jax as I open the front door.

"I need to use your shower."

"Why?" I ask, seeing that he's carrying a large bag in his hand.

"Water heater went out and I don't have time to wait for the repair guy to come look at it before I have to be somewhere."

"Oh, well you know where it is." I swing my arm out for him to enter, and then I go to my kitchen and start a pot of coffee, set out food for Juice, and clean Taser's cage. Once my coffee is done, I take my cup out to my back deck along with my Kindle and start to read.

"What the fuck are you doing here?" I hear roared through the glass of my sliding door, and I get up, quickly setting my stuff on the table, slide the door open then make my way to my living room, where Wes is standing in the doorway with Jax, standing in front of him, wearing nothing but a towel around his waist.

"What the fuck are you doing here?" Jax asks Wes instead of answering, and I step into the mix, push my cousin back, and stand in front of Wes.

"You go finish showering," I tell Jax, shoving him away.

"Are you shitting me?" Wes snarls, and I wait glaring at Jax until I see him go back into the bathroom before I face him.

"What are you doing here?" I ask then look down and see that he's juggling two cups of coffee and a bag, and my heart melts, because he brought me breakfast.

"What am I doing here? Are you fucking kidding me?" My head flies up and my eyes meet his. "I left you last night, and you already have Jax Mayson in your house, showering? Now you're asking what I'm doing here?"

His words punch me in the gut as his eyes roam over me in my long shirt that hides the boxers I have on. He shakes his head and mutters, "Bitches," as he walks off.

I stand there for a second as my stomach crawls up my throat, and watch as he opens the door to his truck. My mind is reeling from what he just said.

"You said his name's Jax Mayson, right?" I shout, and he looks at me then shakes his head.

"Well, you fucking asshole, my name is July Mayson. He's my cousin, and you're a fucking scumbag," I yell then slam the door shut and stomp down the hall to my bedroom, getting my scrubs on quickly, and then my shoes. I don't even bother with makeup. I just tie my hair back into a ponytail, walk to the guest bath, and knock on the door, calling to Jax that I'm leaving and to lock up.

I grab my bag, stomp out to my garage, pull on my helmet, and shove my purse under the seat. I put on my helmet and press the remote for the garage. I get on my bike start it up then pull out of the garage, noticing that Wes is still sitting in my driveway. I close my garage, shove the remote in my pocket then flip him off while simultaneously trying to kill him with the lasers I can feel coming out of my eyes.

When I get to work, I look at my phone and see that Wes has called every few minutes since I left my house. I turn off the stupid thing and head to the building. The moment I get to the front door, I see a large black mass in front of the double doors and my heart instantly sinks, because I know exactly what it is. I have already had such a horrible day; this just makes it worse.

"Hey, guy," I whisper, crouching down in front of the dog that is bleeding from his mouth and ears. His head barely lifts then drops to the ground again and his eyes close. I scoot closer and can see that his breaths are few and far between, and the blood coming from his nose tells me he's not going to make it. I head around the back of the building, go through the back door, drop off my bag, and get a small stretcher. Carrying it out front, I carefully get him on it before taking him inside.

"Another one?" Kayan asks as I check him over, seeing if there is anything I can do to save him before I unwillingly put him to sleep.

"Yeah," I whisper as I force myself to accept there is nothing I can do. Tears begin to fill my eyes, but I fight them back and do my job, making sure he's comfortable before I give him the injection that will help him go to sleep and never wake up again.

"Do you want me to call your uncle and have him come out?" Kayan asks as we walk toward reception.

"No, I called. He's checking the cameras he set up. He said he'll stop by at some point today."

"Are you okay?" she asks, looking me over.

I let out a long breath then tell her what happened with Wes last night and this morning. The more I talk, the bigger her mouth opens, and by the time I'm done, her jaw is almost hitting the floor.

"So, no, I'm not really okay," I tell her.

"I bet not," she mumbles then sits back in her seat. "So you really didn't kiss him?"

"No."

I shake my head and laugh when she whispers, "Wow."

"He is a jerk, and I'm glad I found out now, rather than later."

"Yeah." She nods then her eyes get glossy. "So what does Jax look like wearing nothing but a towel?"

"You do know he's my cousin, right?" I frown at her.

"Your cousin is hot."

"You're delusional." I roll my eyes then walk down the hall, yelling that I'll be in the back.

"SO DID YOU see anything on the video?"

"Nothing, kiddo," my uncle Nico says on a sigh.

"I don't know what I should do," I mumble. Watching the video that he had pulled up, the only thing you see is taillights then the image of someone wearing jeans and a black hoodie carrying the dog and setting him down in front of the double doors.

"You're doing nothing."

"Okay," I say, but a plan starts forming in my head.

"We'll get it worked out, kiddo." He gives me a hug and I hug him back then walk him out front and watch him pull away in his truck. Then I go over to where Kayan is still looking out the door.

"He's really hot for an old dude."

"Can you stop lusting over my family members?" I laugh.

"Whatever." She smiles then her face goes serious. "So did he tell you anything?"

"Nada, but I have an idea. How do you feel about having a stakeout with me?"

"A stakeout?" Her eyes flash and a smile spreads across her face, making her already beautiful features striking. "Hell yes, I'm down."

"Okay, we'll start tomorrow."

"Good. Tonight, we can go shopping."

"Shopping for what?" I ask, and she looks at me like I'm crazy.

"We need gear. We need black clothes and a camera, maybe some kind of device that lets us know when someone is coming. I don't know for sure, but I'm thinking the police supply store will have some stuff we can use."

"I just wanted us to sit in my jeep and wait until someone came." I frown, and she lets out a huff of air.

"You have so much to learn."

"And where did you get your stakeout knowledge?"

"TV." She shrugs then looks to the left when the bell over the door goes off. "Uh oh," she whispers as Wes walks in.

"Can I talk to you for a second?" he asks as his eyes come to me.

"Sorry, do you have an appointment?" I ask, tilting my head to the side, studying him.

His eyes go to Kayan and he bends slightly over the desk. He takes the calendar that's in front of her and looks at it then pulls a pen from the jar that sits on the upper ledge and writes his name in one of the boxes.

"Looks like I have an appointment." He sets the calendar down.

"Great, follow me," I mumble, leading him back toward one of the exam rooms. Once we're inside, I go to the opposite side of the counter from him. "What can I do for you, Mr. Silver?" I raise an eyebrow, using his last name I learned yesterday when we filled out paperwork.

"Fuck." He runs a hand over his head then down his jaw, which is covered in stubble that makes me want to rub up against him.

No, you don't want to rub against him, I remind myself.

"I don't have all day," I say, making a point to look at the clock.

"I shouldn't have jumped to conclusions."

"Really?"

"I came over wanting to see you, and Jax answered the door in a fucking towel, then you in only a shirt. I saw red."

"I had shorts on."

"Pardon?"

"I had shorts on under my shirt," I tell him then wonder why, because it seriously does not matter at all.

"I shouldn't have said what I said."

"No, you shouldn't have."

"Can you forgive me?" he asks, and I see he's sincere. I'm sure it looked that way to him, and I'm still pissed, but at the end of the day, it doesn't matter.

"Absolutely, apology accepted." I stick out my hand and he looks down at it, his frown lines growing deeper.

"Fuck," he whispers, and his gaze comes up to lock on mine again.

"Well, if that's all, I really need to get to work." I walk to the door and open it up. "See you around, Wes." I walk out then head to one of the other exam rooms. I hear Kayan talking as I wait behind the closed door until I hear the front door alarm go off, letting me know he's gone. Only then do I head back out of the room.

"So, your biker dude just ruined my whole calendar," Kayan grumbles, and I peek over the counter to see what she's talking about, and everyday at noon, it says 'Lunch with Wes'.

"Not happening," I tell her, and she looks at me doubtfully. "I'm serious."

"Okay," she whispers, looking down at the paper, but I can still see the smirk on her lips.

"I need a drink."

"Yeah, a tall drink of hot biker."

"Shut up," I mumble as disappointment floats through my system. Wes was hot and edgy, and obviously a man with issues, so sadly, we were never going to explore things, but that didn't mean I didn't wish things had turned out differently.

"Your two o'clock is here." Kayan says and I come out of my daze mutter.

"Thanks." Then smile at my patient's family before kneeling down to greet Cloyed a very hyper Yorkie who makes me wish that men were as easy to understand as dogs.

The rest of the day passes quickly between patients and back work that I have to catch up on. I don't leave the building until it's dark outside, leaving Kayan to go shopping alone, which I regret the next evening when she shows me what she picked up.

"I'm not wearing that." I look at the black full bodysuit that Kayan just pulled out of the bag she set on my bed.

"You are." She smiles then walks to the bathroom and comes back a few minutes later wearing a matching black bodysuit that is unzipped, showing cleavage, and a pair of black boots that go to her knee, with three-inch heels. Her black hair is up in a high ponytail, and she has put black smudges under her eyes.

"Come on, go get dressed." She pushes me toward the bathroom, and I go unwillingly then frown when I put on the outfit. I have no idea how I let her talk me into this. I leave my hair down. The bodysuit shows off every single curve and dimple of cellulite that I have. I don't have a choice but to leave the top unzipped, because my breasts are so large the zipper is likely to bust. When I come out, she's in my closet and she comes out with a pair of boots I wore once for Halloween. They are basically stripper boots that are shiny and have five-inch heels.

"I'm not sure about this." I frown.

"We need to blend in," she tells me, and my frown grows deeper.

"Blend in where? At the strip club?" I ask, and she laughs, handing me the boots that I reluctantly put on.

We get in my Jeep and go over to the office, and we park off in the distance where it's completely dark. It's after ten at night, and from the video footage timestamp, I know whoever dropped the last dog off had done it after midnight.

"What's that?" I ask as Kayan pulls a bag from the backseat.

"Supplies," she mumbles distractedly and begins pulling items out. The first is a camera that she sets on the dash. Next is a pair of walkie-talkies that she sets next to the camera, and then a thermos and a box of powdered doughnuts that she holds in her lap.

"I think you're taking this too far."

"The guy at the cop store didn't even let me get everything I wanted."

"What?" I laugh.

"I wanted to get one of those things you roll out to blow out tires, but he told me I needed to be a cop in order to buy them, along with smoke bombs."

"Ugh." I look at her and she smiles.

"This is going to be so much fun," she whispers, and I shake my head and look out the front window. At one o'clock I'm just about ready to give up and go home, when lights flash and a car pulls into the parking lot. I tap Kayan, who had fallen asleep after eating the whole box of doughnuts while drinking the thermos of hot cocoa.

"What?" she mumbles, and I elbow her again.

Her head comes up as I hiss, "They're here."

"Oh shit," she whispers, pulling the camera off the dash.

I pull out my phone and call one of the vets, Mark, who has been working with me over the last few months. I tell him he needs to get to my office and take care of the dog that was just dropped off, and to call the vet tech on call. He agrees, and I watch as the person drops the dog at the door then gets back in the truck.

Everything in me wants to go to the poor dog, but I know there will be someone coming to help him soon so that I can follow the truck. I need to see if I can find out any more information. When the person gets back in the truck and pulls off, I make sure my headlights are off before I start up the Jeep and follow him out of the parking lot.

"I wonder where he's going," I say as we head out of town on one of the back roads.

"Don't know," she mumbles, watching the truck in the distance, which pulls into a large parking lot that is packed with cars. That's when I remember it's a Friday night. I pull in and park a few spaces behind him then wait until the driver gets out before I open the door to my Jeep. I watch him, taking in what he's wearing so that I know what to look for if we lose sight of him inside.

"Just so you know, I'm firing you on Monday," I tell Kayan as I realize the outfit I have on.

"You look smoking hot," she whispers, but I can tell she's nervous as well.

I shake my head, slam the door, and head into the building. The moment we walk though the door, the loud country music hits my ears. I follow the guy toward the bar, feeling every single person in the bar looking at Kayan and me. Hell, if I were them, I would be looking too. It's not everyday you see two chicks dressed like cat-women walk into a country western bar.

"Your dad's in back, bud," the bartender tells the guy we followed here. He looks probably twenty-five. He takes his hat off and runs his hand over his hair then gets up and starts walking toward the back of the bar. I start to follow him, when an arm bands around my waist and breath whispers against my ear.

"Where you going, pretty girl?"

I elbow the guy holding me then back up, grabbing Kayan's hand and pulling her with me toward the restrooms saying. "You're really getting fired." As my gaze connects with Wes', who is standing near a pool table talking to some guy, his eyes sweep over me, and even from across the room, I can see anger enter his handsome features.

"Oh no," Kayan whispers, and I remind myself to start looking for a new receptionist and best friend on Monday after I have a full-face transplant.

"Run," I breathe.

"What?"

"I said run!" I cry, and we both turn and start toward the front of the bar. We get down the hall, almost to freedom when I'm suddenly pulled back into a hard body.

"What the fuck are you wearing?" is growled near my ear, making my whole body shiver.

"What are you doing here?" I ask, trying to get away.

"Z, watch her," Wes tells a tall guy with a bald head and tattoos that run from his neck and down his arms, which you can see from the white tank and leather vest he has on. His arm muscles look even more intimidating as he stands, crossing his arms over his chest while looking down at my very petite best friend.

"That's not necessary; we were just leaving," I say as I'm walked backwards into the men's restroom through a swinging door.

"Out," Wes growls to some guys who are standing near the urinals. They all look between Wes and me, zip up their pants quickly, and then rush out of the room.

"That was rude," I mutter, then my breath comes out in a whoosh as my body is pressed into the wall behind me.

"What are you doing here, July?" he rumbles.

I feel the vibration of his words against my chest as he speaks, and I ignore the butterflies that have erupted in my stomach since seeing him. "I wanted to learn how to line dance?" My answer sounds more like a question.

"Don't lie to me." He presses deeper into me, and I can feel every hard inch of him through the thin material of the bodysuit I have on. I hold my breath and squeeze my eyes closed, trying to get my body back under control. "There are some fucked up guys here right now, babe, and you can't be here."

I open my eyes and search his face. "Are you in trouble?" I ask, and his eyes sweep over me as he mutters, "Yes," making my insides turn liquid.

"Wes, you're too close," I whimper, feeling like his presence is suffocating me.

"Not close enough, baby," he whispers back as his hands framing my waist press in deeper and his erection presses into my belly.

"Oh, God," I moan as his face lowers and his mouth hovers over mine, his breath brushes across my lips, making me crave him in a way I never, ever thought possible.

"Don't," I tell him, closing my eyes, and after a long moment, I open them back up and meet his eyes when I realize that he didn't kiss me like I expected him to.

"I'm gonna walk you out to your car. I want you to go right home, and don't ever come back here again," he tells me, placing his forehead to mine.

"I—"

"No, babe, you need to swear to me that you will never come back here again."

"I won't come back."

"Come on." He pulls me with him and leads me back out of the bathroom. Kayan is leaning against the wall, looking at the floor, while biker guy 'Z' stands blocking her from everyone's sight.

"I remember you," I tell Z when I realize he's the guy who picked me up like I was as light as a feather the day I tasered Wes. He grins then looks at Wes and shakes his head.

"Let's get the girls out of here, and then we'll come back and finish up," Wes states.

"Sure," Z mutters, wrapping a hand around a struggling Kayan's waist and walking in front of us out of the bar. I try prying Wes' fingers off my waist as we walk, but he only holds me tighter. My legs work double-time in the boots I have on to keep up with him, and I let out a relieved sigh once we reach my Jeep.

"You're as shy as a kitten. Don't think I've ever had shy in my bed," I hear Z say as we get into the Jeep. I look over at Kayan, who has her eyes pointed at her lap, but I can see there is dark blush covering her cheeks. "Be good, Kitten," Z rumbles, shutting her door. I start to shut my own door, when a body cages me into my seat.

"Straight home."

"Straight home," I repeat then lick my lips when I realize how close his mouth is.

"We have some shit to work out, but I'll get in there," he tells me. My eyes flutter up to meet his, and my heart starts to pound when I see the promise in his eyes. His head dips to the side and his lips brush my ear, making my core convulse. "Be good."

I nod my head as my voice box closes up. He backs up and slams my door. I start up my Jeep and pull out of the lot then look over at Kayan when I'm at the stop sign. When her eyes meet mine, a smile alights her face.

"That was scary, but oh, my God," she breathes out, making me giggle.

"No more stakeouts," I tell her, and she smiles and whispers, "No more stakeouts."

Chapter 4

I CALL MARK on the way back to town, and he tells me he wasn't able to save the dog that was dropped off. My heart breaks yet again for another dog. I vow then that I will get to the bottom of what's happening, if it's the last thing I do.

"I'll see you Monday," Kayan mumbles solemnly when we pull up in front of my house since I got off the phone with Mark, the energy in the car has changed.

"See you Monday," I tell her, shutting down my car and heading toward the house. I watch her pull away before heading inside and closing the door.

"Hey, Juice." I pick him up off the small table and press my face into his fur while I walk into the back bedroom. I dump him onto my bed then pull off the heels and bodysuit before finding an old t-shirt and getting into bed.

I lay there for a long time looking at the ceiling and just as I'm about to fall asleep, there is a pounding on my front door, and I hear Wes yell, "Open up!" I stumble out of my room and go to the front door to see that he's standing there with Z, who has his arm around Wes' shoulders.

"What's going on?" I ask sleepily.

"He got shot."

My eyes go to Z then get big when I see he's holding a towel to his shoulder and there is blood soaking through. "You need to go to the hospital."

"Can't."

"Wes, I'm a vet, not a doctor."

"Jesus," Z grumbles, and Wes gently presses a hand into my belly and pushes me out of the way as he walks into the house and helps him get seated in one of my white kitchen chairs that creaks like it's going to give out under his weight.

"Baby," Wes comes and stands in front of me, and his palms hold my face gently as he nudges my cheek so that my eyes focus on his and not Z. "I need you to help him. The wound is clean through, so all you need to do is sew it up."

"Wes," I whisper, looking away from him to Z.

"Look at me." I do, and his face lowers toward mine. "I need your help, baby."

I search his face and whisper, "Okay," then clear my throat. "I need to go to the clinic and get supplies. I don't have anything here."

"I'll take you."

"No, you stay with him. I'll go and be back quickly." I go to my room and get on a pair of jeans, a sweatshirt, and a pair of sneakers. I walk past the guys, head out of my garage, and open the door, and that's when I see that I'm blocked in by Wes' SUV.

"I'm driving you," Wes says, stepping out into the garage. He takes my hand, leads me to the passenger side of his truck, and helps me inside before jogging around to his side. It takes less then five minutes to get to the clinic, and by the time we arrive, my body is shaking with nervous energy.

I've never done any kind of stitching on a human patient before, or been around anyone who had ever gotten shot.

"It'll be okay," Wes tells me, placing a hand on my lower back as I open the back door. I go right to the supply room and gather the necessary provisions into a shopping bag before locking the building back up and heading to my house. When we arrive, Z is sitting at the table still, but he now has the bottle of Jack my sister June and I bought when she was home visiting from college.

"You better not neuter me, girl." Z smiles, and his words make some of the anxiety that I was feeling leave and a laugh to bubble out of my mouth.

"You probably need to be neutered," I tell him, and he grins then eyes the stuff I begin to set out on the table.

"Can I ask how this happened?" I question softly, pulling the towel away from his shoulder and looking at the wound.

"No," Wes says, pulling out a chair and taking a seat.

"You don't think I have the right to know, when you show up at my house in the early hours of the morning, asking me to stitch up a guy with a gunshot wound, while refusing to take him to the hospital?" I narrow my eyes on him, and he doesn't even flinch.

"Nothing you need to worry about." He looks at Z, and I see some kind of silent conversation happening between the two of them, which pisses me off.

I dump some alcohol onto a piece of gauze and begin wiping down the wound as I look at Wes. "This is the last time I see you," I tell him, even though the words leave a nasty taste in my mouth.

"You already know that's not happening, July," he says as his jaw clenches tight.

"No." I shake my head, getting a new piece of gauze so I can clean the backside of his shoulder.

"I know twice you've called me a bitch without cause." I shake my head then turn it so my gaze connects with his. "I know you made me feel like crap when you found my cousin in my house."

"I—"

"No," I cut him off before he can say anything. "You didn't even ask; you just jumped to conclusions." I finish cleaning Z's wound then look at Wes again. "Then you show up at my house and ask me to do you a favor, refusing to tell me anything. So, yes, this is the last time we see each other. I think it's obvious we have no reason to stay in contact," I mutter the last part then frown when I see Z is smiling at me.

"You are so fucked, brother," he mumbles, looking at Wes. I ignore them both and start to thread up the needle. It doesn't take long to get the wound closed up, and I'm surprised that Z doesn't even flinch as I work on him. By the time I'm done putting a bandage over the wound, the sun is beginning to rise, casting an orange glow throughout the room, and my eyes are so heavy I can barely keep them open.

"Thanks, girly," Z rumbles, standing up.

I sway on my feet in front of him, and a hand slides around my waist and Wes leads me back toward my bedroom. "Go wash up and go to bed, babe. I'll clean the mess up." I nod, not even caring. At this point, my body is completely exhausted. I'm running on empty, and not even coffee could help me now.

I go into my bathroom and take a quick shower then put on my robe from the back of my bathroom door, not even bothering with clothes, and climb into bed, where I immediately fall asleep.

I wake up to the smell of bacon, and roll to my side, coming face-to-face with Capone, who is looking at me with his tongue hanging out of his mouth.

"What are you doing here?" I sit up and look at the clock, seeing it's after three in the afternoon, and then look around the room, making sure I didn't just dream that I came home last night.

Capone climbs into my lap and licks my cheek then jumps off the bed and leaves out of the small gap in the door.

I stand up, tie my robe tighter around me, open my bedroom door, and head through my living room. Coming around the corner into my kitchen, I stop dead when I see a shirtless Wes standing in front of the stove, wearing only a pair of jeans and necklaces that hangs between his pecs, with a cross and dog tag on it. I blink, trying to clear my head as my body reacts to the way he looks.

"You're awake."

I lift my eyes and take in the extra scruff and the way his eyes are soft, like he just woke up as well. "What are you doing here?"

"One of the brothers came and picked up Z last night, and I stayed so that we would have a chance to talk when you got up."

"Why's Capone here?" I ask as the dog sits down at Wes' feet, looking between the two of us.

"I had him dropped off. I didn't like the idea of him being at my place alone for so long."

"Oh," I mutter, wrapping my arms around myself.

"I'm not good at this kind of thing," he says, and I feel my nose scrunch up. "As you may have noticed, I can be harsh and jump to conclusions. But I can admit when I'm wrong and when I've fucked up. I've done both with you more times than I want to count. I won't apologize for being me, but I will apologize for being an asshole. You didn't deserve that."

Wow. Okay, I didn't know how to recover from that. I never expected him to apologize and to admit that he was an asshole.

"As for last night, not happening. I appreciate you helping Z, but this is not a situation that I would ever let you be involved in."

"Thank you for apologizing." I bite the inside of my cheek, not knowing what I should say or do, and my stomach takes that moment to remind me I haven't eaten in over twenty-four hours, breaking into the moment with a loud growl.

"Sit, I made you breakfast." He points towards my kitchen table and I take a seat, and the second my ass hits the chair, I immediately realize I have no panties on and my robe is not exactly long. He brings the plate over and sets it in front of me before I have a chance to get up and go to my room. Then he comes back a second later, setting down a cup of coffee. He gets a plate for himself and a cup of coffee, sets it on the table next to mine, and then sits next to me, his jean clad leg rubbing against my bare thigh. I squeeze my legs together as tightly as I can and pick up the coffee in front of me, taking a sip.

"Is it okay?"

"Perfect," I mumble then look down at my plate. "You made this?" I look up at him then back down at the perfect omelet that is sitting on my plate next to two pieces of flawlessly cooked bacon.

"I did." He smiles, taking a bite of his, and I follow suit and moan as the taste hits my tongue.

"Holy crap, you can cook," I mumble, taking another bite, then I swing one leg up to cross over the other without thinking. His fork that was halfway to his mouth pauses and his eyes drop to my right thigh. I quickly uncross my legs and pull my robe back down to cover myself up.

"Please tell me you have something on under that thing," he rumbles, and the deepness of his words vibrates between my legs.

"I—"

"Fuck," he clips, making me jump slightly. He stands from the table and walks to the fridge. "Go put something on before I set your little ass up on the table and eat you for breakfast," he growls, clenching his fists at his sides.

HOLY COW My pulse kicks into overdrive, and I feel my core clench at his words and the way he's holding himself. "I..."

I start to...I don't know, apologize, when his eyes flash again and he snarls, "Now," making me jump out of my seat and run to my room.

"Holy shit," I whisper. I go to my dresser and grab a bra and panties, slipping them both on quickly. Then I dig through my closet until I find a pair of sweats, and pull them on with a t-shirt before slowly making my way out of the room and back into the kitchen.

"Is this better?" I ask, not even sitting down until I know I'm safe.

His eyes sweep over me and he nods, so I sit back down, pick my coffee back up, and shakily take a sip.

"Until I get in there, and I mean *really* get in there, you need to wear clothes when I'm around."

"This is my house," I mutter, ignoring the part about him getting into me, because that image caused my whole body to heat up, and I could feel myself turning red from the thought alone.

"Never said it wasn't, baby," he murmurs, taking a seat next to me.

I try to think of something to say, but my mind is so focused on just trying to breath that nothing comes to mind.

"You wanna tell me why you were dressed like Catwoman last night at Mamma's Country?"

"Nope," I reply immediately definitely not wanting to fill the silence with that conversation.

"Why were you there, July?" he questions more firmly.

"So you don't have to tell me why you showed up at my house last night, but you expect me to tell you what happened?" I lower my eyes to my plate, saying, "Not likely," under my breath.

"Is it about the dogs?" he asks gently as his fingers pull up on the underside of my jaw, causing my gaze to meet his. "Talk to me." The gentleness of his voice and softness in his eyes causes the words to come tumbling out.

"The morning Jax was here, there was another dog left outside the clinic."

"Fuck, I'm sorry, baby," he says as his fingers come up to run down the side of my face and I try to ignore the way his touch feels.

"I want to find out who's doing this." I lower my gaze when I feel tears sting my nose from thinking about the helpless animals that have lost their lives just so some asshole could have a few minutes of entertainment. "I will find out who's doing this."

"Do you believe the person who's connected to the dogs was at the bar last night?" he asks gently.

I nod, still looking down at my plate. "Kayan and I followed the guy after he dropped off another dog."

He lets out a loud puff of air and I can feel the energy change. "Don't go there again." My head comes up and our eyes connect. "I know you have no reason to trust me yet." His eyes drop to my mouth and his thumb touches the edge of my bottom lip before they meet mine again. "But I need you to promise me you won't go back there."

"Why?" I ask softly.

"Babe." He shakes his head then frowns when pounding starts on my front door. "Who's that?"

"I don't know." I get up and head toward the door when Wes pulls me behind him and opens it.

"Do you want to live, Silver?" Jax asks, shoving his way into my house.

"Fuck you, Mayson," Wes replies, and Jax looks me over then shakes his head, looking at Wes again.

"You told me you were serious about my cousin, and then you let her walk right into the fucking snake pit where someone could see her?" Jax asks, and my eyes go between him and Wes and I feel my brows pull together.

"Don't go there," Wes growls.

"You," Jax turns on me and shakes his head, "what the fuck were you thinking?"

"What?" I ask, confused.

"Why were you at Mamma's Country last night?"

"Uh…"

"I don't have time to babysit you," Jax growls.

"Hold on one damn minute." I put my hands on my hips and get in his face. "I have never, *ever* asked you to babysit me, so you need to get off that high horse you rode in here on and back off."

"You're family."

"And?" I ask, making my eyes big.

"Does Uncle Asher know you're seeing Silver?" he asks, and my body freezes and my heart speeds up.

"I'm not seeing him." I bite the inside of my cheek. I wasn't technically lying, was I? I peek over at Wes, who's frowning, then swing my head to look at Jax.

He growls, "Two days he's been here in the morning."

"So?"

"So, I haven't told my dad or anyone."

"I haven't told anyone about all the women you have in and out of your house," I tell him.

"I'm a dude. No one would care."

"Your mom would." I smirk. Aunt Lilly would kick his ass if she knew the way he went through women.

"Do you think my mom's dumb?"

Okay, he's right. Aunt Lilly knew he had never been in a committed relationship, but she still didn't like it. "Whatever. We're getting away from the point," I say, crossing my arms over my chest.

"Yeah, the point being that *he*," he points at Wes, "should have made sure your ass was nowhere near Momma's Country last night, or *any* night for that matter."

"I would like to remind you that I'm a grown woman."

"You're also a woman who has no idea the kind of fucked up people there are in this world."

"I don't?" I ask, narrowing my eyes on him.

"You don't," he confirms, crossing his arms over his chest.

"Every week, I have animals that have been abused or left for dead come into the hospital. Helpless animals that cannot defend themselves. So, yes, I do know the kind of horrible people who live in this world. I do not have rose-colored glasses on, Jax." I choke on the last words as tears fill my eyes.

Wes steps toward me and pulls me into him, tucking my head under his chin.

"I was talking to her about going there when you showed up. I told you I had her, and I do." I hear and feel Wes rumble as he speaks.

"Why was she there?" Jax asks.

"Someone's been leaving dogs outside the hospital that have been fought. She followed a guy from there to the bar last night."

"You think Snake is in on it?" Jax asks, and I turn my head against Wes' chest to look at Jax.

"Not sure, but I wouldn't doubt it," Wes tells him.

"You're not seeing him?" Jax asks doubtfully as his eyes sweep over us, and I realize my arms have wound themselves around Wes, my cheek is pressed to his chest, and one of his arms is wrapped around me, with the other hand cradling the back of my head.

"What's going on between July and me has nothing to do with you."

"Whatever you say, Silver. You have no idea the kind of men my dad and uncles are."

"I've dated before." I frown, stepping away from Wes while defending myself. *Not that it matters,* I reminded myself. I'm not dating Wes, but still. Yes, my dad is overprotective, but he accepts I'm not a little girl—or I should say my mom talks him down every time he forgets I'm not a child anymore.

"You have," he agrees then looked at Wes, "just not a guy like him."

Okay, so he had a point, but I was done. "Don't you have somewhere to be?"

"I do, but before I can go do my job, I needed to come over here and rein you in."

"Well, now you can leave," I tell him, opening the door and sweeping my hand for him to walk out.

"If she gets into any trouble, I'm holding you accountable," Jax tells Wes as he walks through the door.

"Bye." I roll my eyes and shut the door, coming face-to-face with Wes, who is smiling.

"You want to finish breakfast and go for a ride with me?"

"A ride?" I ask suspiciously, and his lips tilt up farther.

"Just a ride."

I study him for a moment, and just like every time he's near, my gut is pulling me toward him, telling me that if I miss out on the promise of him, I will regret it. "Sure," I agree, ignoring my brain, which is roaring at me that I have just changed the course of life as I know it.

Chapter 5

I HOLD ONTO Wes' waist and memories from today wash over me. After we finished breakfast, I went and got dressed in a pair of jeans, my high-top Chucks, and a black tank top. When I walked into the living room, Wes was sitting on my couch with Juice and Capone, who had somehow became best friends. Seeing them all sitting there together made everything stop.

As a little girl, I told myself that my Prince Charming would love to ride motorcycles, have a soft spot for animals, and be strong like my father. When I got older, I realized I would have a better chance of finding the Holy Grail than the man I envisioned spending the rest of my life with.

I didn't know much about Wes yet, but I did know he was gorgeous, when his arms wrapped around me when I was crying, I felt sheltered, he loved riding, and he had a soft spot for animals. So far, he had more going for him than men I thought would be my perfect match.

Wes' hand coming to rest on top of mine lying against his stomach brings me out of my thoughts, and I feel that strange feeling in my chest again, the one that somehow makes me feel like I'm connected to him in a way that goes beyond this lifetime. When the bike starts to slow, I pull my face away from his back and look around, realizing we arrived at his clubhouse.

Earlier today, we dropped off Capone and his truck at his place, which was about ten minutes from my house. He lived in one of the newer apartment buildings in town. My friend Ken lives in the same building, so I know the kitchens are open, with granite and stainless steel, and the rooms are all large enough that you don't feel like you are in an apartment. When we arrived at his place, I declined going inside and waited near his bike. He took Capone inside and came back out a few minutes later with his helmet.

He told me he didn't have anything in mind for the day, just that he wanted to ride, and I was completely okay with that. The sun was out, and there was a nice breeze in the air. Plus, I liked the idea of being wrapped around him.

After an hour of riding around on the back country roads, he pulled over to a small white shack that was set up along the highway, the sign out front offering homemade frozen custard. We got off the bike, and he didn't get anything for himself, but ordered me a cone and stole occasional bites as we sat under an umbrella, eating and laughing. I had the best time with him; more fun than I've ever had with a guy I was interested in.

I've had three boyfriends. One was my high school boyfriend, the guy I gave my virginity to. He was sweet, but when I went to college, we lost contact. He still lives in town, but we don't speak. My second boyfriend was in college. He was a pre-med student who I realized was more interested in the image of having a girlfriend than actually having a girlfriend. We never even kissed, and truthfully, I think he may have been hiding his sexuality from his parents. Then there was my last boyfriend, Harvey. He was nice enough, but he was also boring…so boring that I could actually tell you what he would say before he'd say anything, and I never even bothered asking him what he wanted to do, because it was always the same.

Wes…he's nothing like the men I've dated. None of them would ride a motorcycle, get a tattoo, or live a life where they picked up and move to another state because they liked the feel of a town they drove through. None of my exes made me feel as comfortable as Wes did. None of them made me feel the way Wes made me feel. Just one look from him had my skin feeling too hot and my belly dipping.

After we ate custard, he asked me if I wanted to go to a club party with him. I have been to parties, sure, but partying with bikers was not something I had ever done. But I hated the idea of missing out on time with him, so I agreed, and he dropped me off at home so I could get dressed. He came back an hour later to pick me up.

When I opened the door to my house, I found him on the other side wearing his normal black boots, a pair of jeans that look like they were washed one too many times, the cuffs and pockets fraying, and a black shirt that fits him like a second skin, with his cut over it. His hair looked like it always does, messy, and his green eyes grew darker as they made their way back up my body.

That one look shot a thrill through me. I did my hair big, like I did on our first date, but this time, instead of simple makeup, I went with smoky eyes and a light lip that made me feel like a vixen. I chose my blue jeans that were so dark they almost looked black. I cuffed the bottom and paired them with peep-toed booties and a simple tank and one of my big chunky necklaces that made the outfit look dressier than it actually was.

"You okay?" he asks, pulling me out of my thoughts as his hand runs over the top of my fingers, which are still wrapped around his waist.

"I'm good." I remove myself from him and get off the bike, looking around. I haven't been to this part of town in years, and I'm not really surprised that this is where they would have their biker headquarters. When I was in high school, this whole area was an industrial park. But over the years, the factories have shut down one-by-one, and the empty buildings have been put up for sale.

The outside of the building looks normal, with a large sign that offers 'Car, Motorcycle Repair and Parts'. Next to that is a short alley and another building. Without even looking, I know where we are going. There's a metal gate that has to be at least fifteen feet tall. It looks like something you would find on the set of *Jurassic Park.*

"It's okay," he says taking my hand and leading me toward the large double gate. On the other side, I can hear loud music and people yelling and laughing. I start to feel anxious the closer we get to joining them.

After our first date and what happened when we were at dinner, the way he completely forgot I was around when his friend showed up, I know if he did that to me tonight it would be the end. There would be no coming back from that. And the idea of that happening after the amazing day we had causes my feet to freeze in place.

"You okay?" he asks, and I turn to face him, the light from the street lamp bouncing off his handsome features.

My eyes drop to his mouth then meet his gaze again when he growls my name.

I have never asked to be kissed, and I'm not sure I can do it now, but I don't want to miss out on the opportunity to kiss him at least once. He takes a step toward me and his arm wraps around my waist, tugging me until my body is flush with his.

"What do you want, July?" he asks as his lips hover over mine. My eyes slide closed and I swallow, not sure how to say the words. "Look at me," he demands, shaking me slightly.

My eyes flutter open and I whisper, "Please kiss me."

I feel his breath against my mouth as one of his hands moves up my back and his fingers fist into my hair, causing a whimper to climb up my throat.

"Jesus," he breaths against my lips, making me gasp, giving him the perfect opportunity to lick into my mouth. The first swipe of his tongue against mine causes my belly to dip and my hands to fist into his shirt, anchoring me to him.

His taste courses through my system as his hand in my hair pulls, causing me to tilt my head, opening me up to him while his other hand moves down, grabbing onto my ass between my cheeks. He pulls me tighter against him, allowing me to feel his erection against my belly and his fingers so close to my pussy.

His tongue swirls against mine, making me whimper and squeeze my thighs together, trapping his hand as I feel another rush of wetness spread between my legs. I follow his tongue moving mine in sync with his then slowly pull away, giving one last nibble to his bottom lip as he sets his forehead to rest against mine.

It's not my first kiss, but it's *the* kiss—the one that makes my soul light up, the kiss you wait your whole life for, the kiss that changes everything you thought you knew. I place my fingers to my lips, trying to memorize the feeling, knowing I will never have that again with another person.

"Ruined," he rumbles, and my eyes open slowly and I blink, trying to clear my head. "I don't even really know you, and you've ruined me." He shakes his head and walks me backward until my back hits the concrete wall and his mouth crashes back down on mine again, this time stilling my breath as his body surrounds me. His hands go to my ass, making me moan.

"Wes." I dig my fingers into his shoulders and lift up on my tiptoes, wanting to get closer to him as his mouth travels down my neck. The moment his name leaves my mouth, his lips come back to mine, and my fingers slide up the back of his neck and into his hair. I could easily become addicted to his kiss and taste.

"Yep, fucking ruined," he mumbles, pulling his mouth from mine and looking down at me.

"Let me have some when you're done," I hear a deep voice say, and I rest my forehead against Wes' chest, inhaling a deep lungful of air while trying to clear my head.

"Fuck off, Neo," Wes growls, wrapping his arms around my back and holding me closer against his body.

"You always share, man," the guy named Neo states, and I feel my body freeze and my insides twist with jealousy.

"Not her," Wes says, and the guy mumbles something else before I hear him stumbling away, but my mind is still stuck on the fact that Wes shared women with other guys.

"You ready to go in?" he asks, and I pull my forehead away from his chest as my hands slide down his shoulders and come to rest against his chest.

"You share women with your friends?" I ask him, the words causing that feeling of jealousy to increase and wrap around my stomach, making it hard to breath.

"I did," he says, and his thumbs slide into my jeans at my hips. "Won't be anymore."

I take a breath then nod and bite my lip before digging my fingers into his chest. "If we're in a relationship, then there is no one else," I tell him.

He pulls me closer to him using his thumbs in my jeans to drag my body flush against his. "Are you asking me to be your man?" He smirks, and my hands in his shirt fist tighter then release and drop to my sides.

"Take me home," I tell him, and his arms tighten around me.

"I'm not taking you home," he growls looking angry. Good, I'm angry too.

"I don't play games, so if you can't give me what I want then I'll find someone else who will," I tell him, sounding stronger than I feel, but I know I need to do this. He has me and doesn't even know it.

"Do not ever fucking threaten me," he rumbles as his hand wraps around my lower jaw and his face dips closer to mine. "And unless you want to be responsible for someone's death, do not ever try to use another man to get back at me."

I fight the urge to apologize as his eyes search my face. His face dips and his lips whisper over mine, "I'm willing to explore this thing between us, and willing to give you me while doing that, but I expect the same from you."

"I don't share." I pause then lift my hands to fist into his shirt again, and lift my face closer to his. "Ever."

"Me neither," he says, and I raise an eyebrow. "Not you, not ever." He shakes his head and kisses me once. "Now, are you ready to meet my boys?"

I want to say no, but instead I tell him yes and walk with him towards a door that is next to the gate. As soon as we pass through it, I scan the wide-open space. Two sides are blocked in by tall concrete buildings that look like apartments from the outside, with stairwells and walkways that lead from one door to another. Along the back is a tall chain-link fence with razor wire along the top, and a million cars piled one on top of the other. The area seems almost like a fortress, with large barrels with fires going in them all over.

"Harder," I hear a woman moan, and my eyes go to a couch that looks like it had been picked up from the dump. The material is torn and shredded, and the foam from the cushions is coming out, but the fact the couch looks like a reason for a tetanus shot doesn't seem to be stopping the couple on top of it, who are going at it. The woman moaning is straddling a man, her jean skirt pulled up around her waist. I couldn't be sure, but if I had to guess, the guy's pants are down enough for his dick to be free. My stomach rolls and I immediately feel out of place.

I pull my eyes from the couple and look around. There is a large bar that has a few stools in front of it. Next to it are three tables with men playing cards or talking. Some of the men at the tables have women sitting on their laps. I look around, noticing there are men wearing vests then others who are dressed in regular clothes. I can tell without asking who are members and who are recruits. Thank God for reading and *Sons of Anarchy*.

"Do you want a beer?" Wes asks, pulling me from my perusal.

"Yes," I mutter, hoping if I get a good buzz going it will help take the edge off. He takes my hand in his and leads me to the bar, where a guy in a plain white tee is passing out drinks.

"Boss," he greets Wes as soon as we're near.

"Blaze." Wes dips his chin then pulls me closer by dropping my hand and wrapping his arm around my waist. "A beer and a shot of Jack."

Blaze nods and sets a beer in front of me and a glass in front of Wes, and then pours him a shot. I pick up my beer and down half of it without pulling the bottle from my lips. I have never been a big beer drinker, but I have a feeling I'm going to need it.

"Baby," I hear a woman call, and my beer drops to the top of the bar and I look around Wes. A pretty woman with long auburn hair, wearing close to nothing, comes to stand on the other side of Wes. Her shorts are so short they may as well be underwear, and the plaid shirt she has on is tied up under her boobs, the buttons not even buttoned, leaving her lace bra and cleavage showing. "You didn't call me," she tells him, and that anger and jealousy from earlier comes back full-force, making it almost hard to see.

She presses her body against the side of his and smashes her breasts into his arm, wrapping her arms around his neck. I feel my fingers press into the bottle in my hand so hard that I'm surprised it doesn't break.

"Off," Wes growls.

"What?" she asks confused, then her eyes move to me and she frowns. "You know I don't mind sharing," she whispers, kissing his neck while looking at me. My stomach rolls and that red haze grows darker.

"Lacy," he warns, stepping away, but her hands seem to hold him tighter.

"I suggest you get your hands off of him before I rip them off," I tell her, and her hands drop and she takes a step back, looking between the two of us.

"Lacy, come here," one of the guys at the table calls, and he pats his lap. Lacy looks from me to him then shakes her head and goes to sit on his lap.

I down the rest of my beer as Wes turns his head to look at me, and I notice he has lip-gloss smeared on his neck when his face comes toward mine, and I turn my head.

"July," he growls, and I shake my head.

"You have her mark on you," I tell him then look at Blaze, who's looking between the two of us. "Can I get another?" I ask, holding up my beer. He looks at Wes and I roll my eyes, but I take the beer he sets on the bar top then pat Wes' chest. "When you get that cleaned up, come find me," I mutter then walk off toward one of the barrels.

I have never been jealous in my life, but the idea of Wes even touching someone else makes me feel like I could actually kill.

"Come with me," Wes says, not giving me a choice. He takes the bottle out of my hand and tosses it into the barrel. His hand wraps around my elbow and he pulls me along with him past the bar and through an orange metal door.

He leads me down a long hallway and stops outside a door then reaches in his pocket and pulls out a set of keys. He unlocks the door and holds it open for me to go inside before him. Once I clear the doorway, the light flips on and I look around the room.

There's a queen-sized bed with a blanket bunched up on one side of it, along with two pillows. Clothes and things are scattered around the room and tossed on the floor. I watch Wes as he walks past me into a small bathroom that connects to the room. His hand goes to his neck and he uses a paper towel to wipe Lacy's lip-gloss off his skin.

"You should have a seat," he tells me sounding angry.

"I'm not sitting on a bed that you have probably had sex with other women in," I huff, crossing my arms over my chest.

His green eyes narrow and heat, turning a shade darker with anger and lust. He tosses the paper towel in the trash and stalks toward me, not stopping until I can feel the heat coming off his body.

"Let's be clear, baby. I'll let you get away with a lot of shit, but do not disrespect me in front of my men." His hand goes to my hip then slides back to rest on my ass. "That happens, and this ass," he squeezes my ass cheek, "will be red."

"Pardon?" I growl, not sure if I'm pissed off or turned on.

"We're not talking foreplay, baby. We're talking you won't even be able to sit."

"Are you insane?" I ask him, feeling my pulse speed up.

"No." He shakes his head as his free hand tangles in my hair. "You're hot when you're jealous, and it's cool if you want to claim me, but you get a smart mouth like you did earlier, we're gonna have words."

"You let another woman touch you or put her mouth on you, and we're going to have problems that no words will be able to solve. In fact, no words will be needed ever again. You get me, *baby*?" I ask, studying him, and his hand in my hair tightens and he forces my head to the side. He covers my mouth with his, biting my bottom lip hard enough to sting, my mouth to open and his tongue to sweep in tangling with mine. This time, when he's pulling away, I'm panting for breath and clutching onto him so I don't fall on my face.

"Don't test me, July. I will win," he says, standing me up then tugging my hand leading me back outside.

Chapter 6

I FEEL WARMTH and open one eye, then the other. They lock on dark stubble and a pair of lips I learned last night are perfect for kissing.

"Sleep," his deep voice rumbles as his hand on my ass and his arm wrapped around my shoulders pull me tighter against his warm body.

I feel the hair on his chest scrape against my nipples and my eyebrows pull together. "Where's my shirt?" I question, then sigh in relief when I realize I still have my panties on.

"You insisted we sleep chest-to-chest, something about feeling connected to me," he mumbles sleepily.

"Seriously?" I whisper, feeling like an idiot. *Who says crap like that*?

"You kept saying our souls are connected," he says, and I hear the smile in his voice.

"Shut up," I hiss, tilting my head back to look at him.

His head inclines and a smile forms on his lips. "True story, baby."

"I'm never drinking with you again." I shake my head then regret it when it starts to throb. I drank too much last night, but when we went back out to the party, more women had shown up, and I knew the only way I was going to make it through the night was by getting a good buzz going.

"You should be saying you'll never try to outdrink Harlen again," he corrects, and flashes of me and a guy who was *giant* taking shots filter through my head.

"That happened?" I question, biting my lip.

"Oh, yeah."

"And the dance-off?" I whisper, hoping I had just made that memory up.

"You've got moves."

"Right," I mumble, feeling my face heat in embarrassment.

"Go to sleep, baby," he says softly, tucking the top of my head under his chin.

"We didn't…you know, right?" I ask in a hushed tone.

His face moves until his lips are brushing my ear. "The first time I have you, the first time my mouth and cock get a taste of your pussy, you're not going to be drunk, and you're sure as fuck going to remember it and feel it the next day."

My breath pauses, my nipples pucker in anticipation, and the walls of my vagina contract.

"Now try to sleep."

"Sure," I agreed, even though I know I'm not going to be able to sleep, not now, not with the heat of his skin absorbing into me, his smell making it hard to think, and feeling his cock against my belly through his boxers. "Have you washed these sheets since the last time you had someone else in your bed?" I ask him as my mind registers that not only am I practically naked, but I'm practically naked with him in his room at the clubhouse.

"You're a pain in my ass, beautiful," he grumbles.

"I just don't want cooties." I smile, and his hand on my ass taps twice before grabbing a handful making my belly clench.

"Remember how I said that until I was in there, you needed to wear clothes?" he questions, his voice sounding deeper than before.

"Uh…"

"Until I'm in there, baby, you're gonna need to settle when I ask you, 'cause right now, I can't give you what you need to help you sleep."

I start to pant, and my nipples scrape against his chest with each inhale. I'm not sure I would be able to handle him; his intensity and rawness are something new to me. The feeling he causes within me from a few words is intimidating.

"Sleep." He gives me another squeeze.

"So annoying," I mumble, and I try to fight it, but my eyes slowly slide closed and I relax into his embrace until I fall asleep.

"C'MERE," WES SAYS, pulling me down into his lap at my kitchen table and kissing me.

"I thought you were going to get Capone?" I breathe when his mouth leaves mine. This morning when he woke me up at the clubhouse, he asked me to spend the day with him before we even got out of bed. I knew I needed to step back, but I just can't. He's like a drug I can't get enough of. So while he went to the bathroom, I found his shirt and slipped it on, along with my jeans and sneakers, and planned what I would make for dinner since it was already after three in the afternoon.

His hand on my thigh traveling up my side brings me back to the moment, and the breath I was about to release gets trapped in my lungs as his fingers come to rest under my breast. My eyes move from his hand to his eyes that are heated, the mint green looking wild and untamed.

"You…in my shirt…no bra…your dark nipples visible…" His eyes lift to meet mine and his hands move to my hips, where he lifts me swiftly to the table in front of him. His face ducks and he pulls one of my nipples into his mouth through the material of his shirt.

"Oh!" I cry as the roughness of the shirt scrapes against my nipple as he tugs. "Wes." I grab onto his hair as my head drops back, and his mouth moves to my other breast, where he delivers the same treatment.

When his mouth leaves my breast, my eyes flutter open to look at him. His hand wraps around the back of my neck and he pulls my mouth down to his. I tilt my head and my lips part as his tongue slides across my bottom lip. My fingers thread through his hair as I slide off the table and onto his lap, my legs hanging over each side of the chair, my core connecting with the large bulge in his pants.

"Fuck," he mutters as I rock against him. His head tilts further taking over the kiss before ripping his mouth from mine.

"What?" I ask in a daze.

His head is back, his eyes are closed, and his jaw is tight. "Off," he commands, and I frown out of confusion. "Off, babe," he growls.

I scurry off of his lap and go to stand near my fridge with my arms crossed over my chest. The wetness from his mouth on the shirt makes it hard to focus as it rubs across my nipples.

"I'll be back," he mutters and leaves without even looking at me. I stand there confused for a few moments, not understanding what the hell just happened then look down when Juice rubs against my legs and meows like he's confused as well.

I pick him up and carry him back to my room, dumping him on the bed before heading to the shower replaying everything that just happened while trying to figure out what I missed. Once I'm dressed, I head for the door when the bell rings. I expect it to be Wes, and my pulse speeds up when I see my mom standing on the other side of the door.

"Shit," I whisper swinging the door open.

"Hey, Mom." I smile.

"What's wrong?" she asks, frowning.

"What? Nothing, I just got out of the shower."

"You have never been a good liar, honey." She shakes her head and drops her purse onto the couch. "So what's going on?" She crosses her arms over her chest and taps her foot.

I'm just about to cave into her Jedi mind tricks and spill about Wes, when the door opens. I watch in slow motion as Capone barks and runs past me. Lifting my head my gaze collides with Wes'. His eyes drop to my mouth and his hand wraps around my waist as he dips me backward, kissing me hard and stealing my breath. "Hi," He says against my lips before standing me upright.

"That explains a lot," I hear my mom say, and I pull my stare from Wes and look at her.

"Um." I look from my mom to Wes.

"Wes Silver." He sticks out his hand that isn't wrapped around my waist and shakes my mom's hand.

"November Mayson, July's mother." She smiles, and Wes' head dips so he can look at me.

"I also have four sisters. June, May, December and April." I tell him, then press my lips together when I see him smile.

He shakes his head then looks at my mom again. "Nice to meet you, ma'am."

"Ma'am, huh?" Mom looks at me and raises an eyebrow.

"Wes is—"

"Her man," he cuts me off, stepping fully into the house and shutting the door behind him.

"Her man," my mom whispers, looking between the two of us.

Her mouth opens, but I cut in before she can say anything else. "Did you need anything else, Mom?"

She blinks like she's coming out of a daze then looks at me and smiles. "I was planning on having your dad's birthday get-together this weekend."

Oh, crap! My dad. I love my dad. My dad loves me. But I know my dad, and there is no way he will approve of Wes. No way.

"You should bring your man." My mom smiles looking between the two of us.

"Wes will be busy," I explain then narrow my eyes when hers light up, *I can tell she's loving this.*

"Will I?" Wes asks, and I turn to look at him. He raises an eyebrow as he searches my face.

I take a breath and look at my mom. "Can I call you later?" I ask pleading with my eyes and her face softens as she cups my cheek.

"Sure, honey."

I really do have the best parents. "Thanks, Mom."

"Well, Wes Silver, it was nice meeting you," my mom says, picking up her bag.

"You too, Mrs. Mayson," Wes replies.

My mom glances at me, and I see a look pass through her eyes that I don't quite understand, but then she turns to look at Wes and smiles again. "Call me November," she tells him, and when he nods, her eyes come to me and they go soft. "Call me, honey," she says softly, and I feel my throat contract with emotion and I close the distance between us as I give her a hug. "I'm always here," she whispers into my ear, and those words offer me a comfort I didn't even know I needed.

I nod and step away then follow behind her as she leaves, waving at her as she pulls out of the driveway. As soon as she's out of sight, I head inside, go to the kitchen, grab an onion out of the fridge, a knife and the cutting board, and begin chopping it up.

"You wanna talk about what's going on up here?" Wes asks, running a hand over my head while pressing into my back, wrapping his arms around my waist.

"Nope," I reply, taking a deep breath and letting it out slowly. I don't know why this is causing me so much stress. I have never hid a relationship with anyone from my family or my father, and if I'm honest with myself, the reason I'm afraid of my father meeting Wes is I want my dad to approve of him. Well, maybe not approve. I don't know that my dad will ever approve of any man I decide to be with.

"Your mom seems nice," he says, placing a kiss under my ear.

"She is."

"Were you serious about the names?" he asks, and I can hear the smile in his voice.

I turn and look over my shoulder at him, my stomach fluttering when I realize just how close he is. "My mom's mom named her November because she didn't want to even bother to look for a name for my mom, and it was November when she was born. My dad loves my mom and wanted to turn the memory of her name into something good, so he named all of us girls after the month we were born."

"Your dad sounds like a good man."

"He's the best," I agree then lower my eyes back to the cutting board.

"What can I help with?"

I look at him again, and Juice takes that moment to come wrap him self around my feet. "Can you feed Juice for me?"

"Sure, where's his food?"

I point to the cabinet where I keep his cat food then turn again, only to have Wes' hand slide along the underside of my jaw. He pulls gently until my eyes go to him. His lips wisp over mine softly, then he drops his hand and goes about feeding Juice while leaving me completely exposed.

I have watched my father with my mom since I was a little girl, watched the way he spoke to her, watched the way he watched her, and watched the way he kissed her without reason, doing so just because he wanted too I've never had that. I didn't even know I craved that for myself. Not until Wes.

"Babe, the door."

"Hmm?" I turn to look at him, his statement barely registering over the loudness of my thoughts.

"Someone's at the door. Want me to get it?"

My eyebrows pull together as I set down the knife. My mom

wouldn't have told my dad about Wes. She would wait until I was ready, and no one had called to tell me they were coming over, so I'm at a loss as to who would be here on a Sunday.

When I make it to the door, I look through the peephole then swing it open.

"What happened?" I say shakily, pulling Kayan into the house. Her eyes fill up with tears and I help her over to the couch, scarcely registering that Wes is talking on the phone behind me. "Talk to me," I prompt and she lowers her head.

"Wait 'til Z and a couple of the guys get here," Wes says, getting down on his haunches next to me, handing Kayan some tissue.

"Why do we need to wait for them?" I ask, looking at my friend, who now has a black smudge under her eye and a cut on her bottom lip.

"I only want her to tell us once, and then you're going to go clean her up," he says, rubbing my lower back.

I nod then move and sit down next to her so I can wrap my arm around her shoulders. It takes less than five minutes for the loud sound of pipes to vibrate my house. I don't know how many guys are coming, but judging from the sound, it's way more than a couple.

"Be right back," Wes mutters, heading out the door only to come back a few minutes later with Z.

"Fuck no," Z growls as soon as he sees Kayan. His jaw starts ticking and his hands at his sides lift to cross over his chest like he's trying to control himself.

"Are you going to be okay talking in front of them?" I ask her, and she nods, taking my hand in hers.

"I went out with Eric to get some food," she says, and a growl fills the room and my head flies up to look at Z with a glare.

"Can you control yourself?" I snap, and he lifts his chin, making me roll my eyes.

"So you went out with Eric, and then what happened?"

"Um." She shakes her head and pulls her eyes from Z to look at me. "He dropped me home and when I got inside my apartment, I was shoved into the door and someone grabbed me around the throat. They told me I needed to give you a warning."

"What?" I whisper, squeezing her hand tighter as fear creeps down my spine.

"They said if we don't stop sticking our noses where they don't belong, we will find out what happens to nosey little girls."

I look at Wes and his gaze travels from Z's to mine.

"What did they look like?" Z questions.

"All I saw was a tattoo of a spider on his forehead. Really, I was too scared to pay much attention," she says, and more tears fill her eyes.

"It's going to be okay," I assure her and look towards the front door as Z leaves, slamming the door behind him.

"Baby," Wes calls, and my eyes go to him. "Go get her cleaned up. I'm heading out with the boys. Harlen and Everret will be outside."

"Okay," I agree, and he bends double, wraps his hand around the back of my neck, and pulls me up, kissing me quickly, and then is gone before I realize it.

"So I'm guessing I don't need a new calendar?" Kayan asks, and I look at her and can't help but smile. "What a difference a few days makes." She laughs.

"You're hilarious." I roll my eyes. "Now, let's get you cleaned up before Z comes back," I say, knowing that statement will have her mouth slamming shut.

"You know I can't deal with scary hot," she whispers, but her eyes cloud over.

"So you've said." I take her hand and lead her towards my room.

Chapter 7

"YOU'RE HOME," I whisper, blinking up at Wes. His face goes soft as he gets down on his haunches beside the couch and runs his hand over my head. I look around, seeing his friends are gone, but Kayan is still asleep next to me on the couch.

"You got a TV," he remarks, and I smile then look around him at my new TV before meeting his eyes again.

"The first thing your friends said when they walked into my house was, 'Where's your TV?'" I say, making my voice deeper. "So I asked them to take me to Target to buy one, but they refused, saying something about women and shopping...*blaw blaw blaw.* So they took us to BestBuy." I smile and sit up. "Which is funny, 'cause we were at BestBuy for two hours looking at TVs. Did you know they have 'smart' TVs?" I question, tilting my head to the side and studying him. When he shakes his head, I continue, "They do, but I refused to buy one when I already own a computer. Why would I need a TV that is a computer?" I take a deep breath and he chuckles, running his fingers down my cheek.

"Were you able to find out anything?" I ask after a moment, and he shakes his head again.

I bite the inside of my cheek and look at my friend. I hate that I had gotten her hurt. "What now?" I ask as he sits on the couch next to me.

"I TALKED TO Jax. Between his boys and mine, we'll be able to figure this out." He pulls me closer to him with a hand behind my neck which

I notice that he does a lot. "I'm going to stay here with you and your friend until we can get some security in at her place and yours."

"Ugh, what—?" I whisper.

"That's not happening. Whoever did this isn't going to scare me out of my own home. I love you, but I'm not staying here," Kayan says, cutting in and sitting up from where she had fallen asleep.

"It's not safe for you to be there alone," I tell her gently, and she stands up, crossing her arms over her chest.

"They are not scaring me out of my house," she repeats.

"You're not staying alone," Z growls, coming into the house.

"You're not my dad," she replies, and my mouth drops open in surprise.

"You're not staying alone, Kitten," Z says, leaning forward and getting into her space.

"Fine, I'll call Eric." She shrugs.

"Think again," Z tells her, and I have no idea what's going on, but I would swear I'm missing something.

"You can't tell me what to do!" she shouts.

"Bet your sweet ass I can!" he shouts back, causing Capone to start barking at them.

"I'm going home," she cries, throwing her hands up in the air in frustration when he continues to glare at her.

"Okay, then I'm staying with you," Z says, sweeping his hand toward the door.

"What?" She stops, her body freezing, and I swear you could have heard a pin drop.

"I'm staying with you," he repeats.

"Uhh..." She looks at me like she just realized what she was doing and I smile.

"Maybe I'll just stay here," she whispers.

"Nope, walk your sweet ass to your car. I'll follow you home."

"Um…" She glances at me and I press my lips together to keep from laughing. I have never seen her act like she did moments ago. *Never.*

"Fine," she glares at Z then looks at me, "I'm quitting tomorrow."

"You were already fired," I remind her. I'm still upset about that damn cat suit.

"I hate you." She tells me as she stomps toward the door, past Z, who watches her ass as she leaves.

"Please be nice to her," I plea, and he gets this strange look on his face, lifts his chin, and then leaves, shutting the door behind him.

"That was so weird," I say, looking from the door to Wes, who's smiling.

"She'll be fine." He runs his thumb over the skin under my eye. "Are you tired?"

"Very," I affirm through a yawn. It's been a very long weekend, and not a relaxing one. My life has never been this exciting.

"Go on to bed and I'll make sure everything's locked up."

"Are you sure?"

"Yeah," he mutters, pulling me off the couch, kissing my forehead, and pushing me towards the hall. I stop in my guestroom and put an extra pillow and blanket out before heading to my room, stripping off my clothes, slipping on a tank top, and getting into bed I expect it to take awhile to find sleep but the moment my eyes close I'm out.

"I put an extra pillow and blanket on the guest bed for you," I mumble half asleep as Wes drags me across the bed and wraps his body around mine.

"Saw that." He kisses the skin behind my ear, pulling me deeper into him with a hand on my stomach. "I'm not sleeping under the same roof as you and not sleeping next to you."

"Oh," I breathe. My body begins to wake up as his hips press forward so that his cock rests right between the cheeks of my ass. He feels huge and thick, and just thinking about it causes a shiver to slide down my spine.

"Shhh," he hushes me when I whimper as he lifts my tank top and rests his hand against the skin of my stomach. Every nerve in my body is in tune with him, every one of them reaching out to him, waiting for his touch.

"Wes," I whisper into the dark as his fingers slide along the elastic of my panties, causing the muscles in my lower abdomen to contract.

His hips shift forward again, making my lungs freeze in anticipation and a rush of wetness to spread between my legs. Squeezing my eyes closed, I wait for his touch. His fingers move slowly down my pubic bone and over the bare lips of my pussy. I let out a harsh breath as the muscles of his body coil behind me and his fingers slip through my folds.

"I haven't even touched you and you're fucking soaked," he breathes against my ear while sliding a finger inside me, only to move it out again. His hand on my hip forces me to my back and he looms over me, the light of the moon making it possible to see him. His head lowers and his breath whispers against my lips. "Open your legs, baby."

My knees had bent and my thighs had somehow locked together, his fingers again playing along the edge of my panties. I fight myself for only a brief moment before sliding my legs apart. His teeth bite into my bottom lip, making me gasp. His tongue slips into my mouth and two fingers glide between my folds, over my clit, and into me, making my back arch and a loud moan to leave my mouth into his.

My nails dig into his shoulders as he slowly works his fingers in and out of me, each thrust creating a slow burn. He moves again; this time, he slips between my spread legs pulls my tank top off over my head then lowers his body causing the cold metal of the necklace he wears to slide between my breasts.

Sliding one hand down his chest under the edge of his boxers, I wrap my hand around him. My pussy convulses when I feel how wide and long he is. I know the first time he enters me he'll steal my breath.

He pulls his mouth away and places his forehead to mine. "I swear I know how you'll taste by the way you smell, like vanilla and citrus. Your pussy would be sweet and tangy."

"Oh, God," I whimper, lifting my hips and pressing into his hand while pumping him faster.

"Your pussy is greedy for my fingers and soaking my hand. I want inside of you." He groans against my mouth as my hand squeezes and pumps.

"Yes," I hiss, and he closes his eyes like he's in pain then opens again, making my breath pause.

"Not tonight, but soon." His thumb circles my clit in sync with my hand that's wrapped around him. I pump faster and his fingers pull up against my g-spot, making my legs shake and causing the slow burn to spread like wildfire until I'm screaming his name. His head drops to my shoulder and he groans my name against the skin of my neck as bright lights fill my vision, and my pussy sucks greedily at his fingers that are still deep inside of me as his hot cum shoots across my belly.

My eyes close and my body completely relaxes, his heavy weight cocooning me, making me feel complete.

"I'ma get you cleaned up," he whispers. I nod, unable to speak, not even able to open my eyes, because my body is completely lax from my orgasm. "You're gonna need to let go of my dick." I hear the smile in his voice and my hand drops. I feel him leave the bed only to come back a few minutes later with a warm cloth that he uses to wipe gently between my legs and over my stomach. I hear a splat near my bathroom and smile as he lies back down with me, his body wrapping around mine.

"Night," I murmur, snuggling deeper into his embrace.

"Night, baby." He kisses my head and I sigh before drifting off to Dreamland.

MY EYES TRAVEL over Wes, taking in his dark hair, tattoo-covered chest, and the necklace that is hanging around his neck…the necklace I felt glide between my breasts last night as he brought me to orgasm.

He leans back against the counter behind him and lifts the cup of coffee to his mouth, taking a drink, watching me over the edge of the cup.

I pull one leg up on the counter, wrap my arm around my calf, and take a bite of my bagel, ducking my head and trying to hide my blush. When I woke up this morning with his arms wrapped around me, his breath brushing against the back of my neck, I smiled. I have always been happy—my life is full; my family is amazing—but waking up wrapped in his arms was a different kind of happiness. It was something that was only mine.

"I'll be by the hospital to pick you up for lunch."

"Pardon?" I say when I'm finally able to swallow the bite of bagel I had taken.

"Lunch, today."

"You were serious about that?"

He closes the space between us and his hand cups my knee while his other hand wraps around the side of my neck. His thumb grazes the underside of my jaw and he lowers his mouth over mine, kissing me until I stop breathing.

"I'm very serious about this," he says when his mouth leaves mine and his thumb runs over my bottom lip.

"It's kind of hard to get away during the day," I explain breathlessly.

"I'll bring food. I'm sure you can step away for thirty minutes to eat."

"I'll try."

He smiles then steps back, leaning against the counter and crossing one bare foot over the other.

"So, um…" My lips press together when I realize I have nothing to say, he smiles bigger and runs a hand over his hair, causing his abs to flex, making me fight myself when all I want to do is launch myself off of the counter and tackle him to the tile floor of my kitchen.

"Babe, stop looking at me like that."

I take a large bite of my bagel to prevent myself from saying, 'Or what?' in hopes he will return with, 'I will give you endless orgasms.'

"Be back," he mutters when his phone starts ringing from somewhere in the house. I say a silent *thank you* to whatever god that is preventing me from acting like an idiot, finish my bagel, and hop off the counter to wash my plate and cup, then feed Taser and Juice.

"Is everything okay?" I ask when he comes back into the kitchen a few minutes later carrying his boots and shirt.

"That was Mic; he just got to the shop and someone broke out the front window," he says as his jaw clenches. He drops his boots to the floor and pulls his shirt on over his head then drops his ass onto my kitchen chair to put his boots on.

"Listen." He pulls me down to his lap and pushes the hair out of my face. "This is not on you, so get that out of your head and that look off your face."

"Isn't it though?"

"No," he states firmly, squeezing my waist, and I go to stand up, knowing it's pointless to argue with him, only to be pulled back down into his lap. His hand slides up into the back of my hair kissing me before standing us both.

"See you later, baby."

"Later." I say watching him shut the door behind him.

"I TOLD YOU I didn't need you to follow me!" Kayan yells over her shoulder at Z, who is sitting on his bike with his arms crossed over his chest, watching her with a smirk on his face.

"Have a good day, Kitten," Z tells her, and she shakes her head then storms over to me, stomping her feet across the gravel parking lot. When she reaches my side, she grabs my arm and starts to pull me with her towards the door of the building.

"Can I close the door to my car and get my coffee?" I ask her while trying to control my laughter.

"This isn't funny," she pouts, reading my face. "This is all your fault. Thanks to you, I had to have that guy in my house last night and this morning."

"I could think of much worse problems, honey," I tell her, slamming my door with my hip and grabbing my to-go coffee cup off the roof of my car.

"You *would* think so. He was shirtless in my house. Who gets undressed in front of people they don't know then struts around showing off their body?" She blows a piece of hair out of her face, which has turned a nice shade of pink.

"You like him." I smile, laughing at her.

"I do not like him." She frowns, watching as he pulls out of the parking lot.

"Sure, you don't."

"I don't," she says, stomping past me as soon as I get the door open. "And if he thinks he's staying at my house tonight, he has another thing coming!" I hear her yell as I go to my office. I shake my head and put away all my stuff before heading out front to see who my first patient is.

As I walk around the corner, I stop dead. The guy we followed to the bar is standing in front of the reception desk with his hands on top of it and his body leaning over the counter.

"Can I help you?" I ask then sweep my eyes over my friend to make sure she's okay.

"Like I was just telling your friend, you guys need to mind your business."

"I need to mind my business?" I step toward him and poke my finger in his chest. "You made whatever it is you're doing *my business* when you started dropping dead dogs off at my hospital."

"I was trying to do the right thing, but I won't be able to save your stupid asses again. They will kill you," he says, and I take in his appearance. He looks younger than I first thought. He's maybe twenty-one. His hair is covered with a baseball cap that is sheading on the brim. His eyes are a crystal blue that is almost startling, and you can see stress and exhaustion in his gaze.

"I know people who can help you," I tell him gently, but his eyes change and he takes a step back. "They can help; I promise."

"Just mind your fucking business," he shouts then turns around and pushes so hard against the door that the glass cracks as it hits the outside of the building.

"I wonder what we're missing," I say aloud as I watch him pull out of the parking lot.

"I don't know, but he seems scared," Kayan says, and I see her eyes are still on the door.

"Yeah," I agree, swallowing.

"Do you want me to call Wes or Z and tell them what just happened?" she asks, and I look at her and shake my head. I know the first thing Wes would do is track down the kid, and I don't think that boy could handle anything else right now.

"No, if anything else happens, I'll tell him," I promise.

She eyes me doubtfully, but nods her head anyways. The rest of the day passes without much drama, and I'm even able to stop and have a quick lunch with Wes in my office. I avoid telling him about the kid, and manage to find out from him that the window at his shop was broken with a brick. He believes whoever did it was probably young and dumb, so he didn't believe it had anything to do with me.

Chapter 8

"WHO STOPPED BY this morning?" Wes asks as he walks through the door to my house. I look at him then my front door and wonder how the hell he was able to get in. I'm pretty sure I locked the door when I came home.

"How did you get in?" I question, feeling my brows pull together.

"I have a key. Now tell me who stopped by the hospital this morning."

"Um...pardon?" I cross my arms over my chest, ignoring the fact that he somehow found out the dog guy stopped by to warn me off, while zeroing in on the fact he just said he has a key to my house.

"You heard me; don't play dumb."

"Yeah, I heard you." I lean forward and point at my front door. "You have a key to my house that I never gave to you."

"That shit doesn't matter. Now, tell me what the fuck you were thinking keeping that from me."

"No, you tell me how you think it's okay to take a key to my house that I never gave you."

"You think I don't know what you're doing?" He points a finger at me and a vein in his neck begins to pulse. "Answer my question before I take you into your room and spank your ass," he roars, and I take a step back.

"Do not threaten me," I hiss.

"Do you know what can happen to you? Do you understand the guys this kid and his father are involved with drug women until they have no idea what their doing and put them on the street, only letting them quit when they are broken and can no longer make them money? Do you want to be one of those women? Do you think I want to come looking for you, only to find out you have been kidnapped and sold into prostitution?"

"Stop," I whisper as tears fill my eyes and my bottom lip begins to tremble.

"Do you think your family will understand that it happened because you were so bullheaded?"

"Please stop," I tell him, taking a seat on the couch. "I didn't know, and he looked scared. I didn't want you to go after him."

"That is something you could've said when you talked to me about it," he says quietly.

"He looked scared," I repeat, lifting my eyes to meet his. "I don't know what happened to him, but he looked terrified, and I could tell he didn't want us to get hurt."

He nods and gets down in front of me, taking my hands in his. "His dad owns Mamma's Country. It was one of the first places me and my boys started going to when we moved to town. His dad is a good man, but over the last couple months, he's gotten mixed up with some bad dudes. We don't know what's going on, but my guess is he owes these guys money."

"Can you help them?"

His eyes search my face then he mutters a quiet, "Fuck," as he pulls his hands from mine, stands, and runs his palms over his head.

"He's been bringing me dogs, even if they're on their last leg. I know the person running the fights isn't telling him to drop them to me, so that leads me to believe he's a good person."

He gets back down in front of me and swipes away a tear I didn't know had begun to fall.

"Me and Jax are looking into what's going on. If I can help him, I will."

"Thank you."

"You're a pain in my ass," he says, shaking his head, but the words are soft, and so is the look in his eyes. I take a much-needed breath and then remember we were fighting about the key before he somehow turned this around on me.

"So, how did you get a key to my house?" I ask, and he stands back up and crosses his arms over his chest.

"I took it off one of your key rings." He shrugs.

"Do you think that's something I should maybe give to you willingly?"

"How long do you think it would take for you to give me a key?" he asks, looking down on me, so I stand up, wanting to have every advantage I can get. Even if the advantage is just a couple feet.

"I don't know." I shrug. I don't even know why I'm arguing with him about this. It doesn't even matter he has a key. I would have given him one if he asked me to. Even if we have only been an us for a few days this seemed like something bigger then I could ever even understand.

He looks me over and his eyes drop to my mouth. I cover it with my hand and he smirks.

"We're back there, huh?" he questions, taking a step towards me. I take a step back and my knees hit the couch, and I fall to my ass on the soft cushion. "Now you're caught." He smiles, putting his fist into the couch on each side of me.

"What are you going to do to me?" I question, and his eyes heat as they roam over me.

"I can think of a few things, but you're gonna need to uncover that hot mouth of yours."

"We need to eat," I tell him, uncovering my mouth and placing my hands on his shoulders.

"Eating is definitely on my list of things to do."

"Holy crap," I whisper, and he lowers his mouth over mine.

"July, open the door right now." Kayan yells from outside breaking into the moment.

"Goddammit," Wes growls, punching the cushion next to my hip and looking at the door.

"Kitten," is growled, and the pounding gets more frantic. I regretfully slip out from under Wes and go to the door, opening it up only to close it back again when I see that Z has Kayan in his arms, his hand tangled in her hair and his mouth on hers.

"My neighbors are going to sign a petition for me to leave the neighborhood," I tell Wes, shaking my head.

"You can't just kiss people," I hear my friend say breathlessly from the other side of the door, and I open it again and move out of the way as she comes tumbling into the house, Z catching her around the waist before her face hits the hardwood floor.

"What's going on?" I ask as he rights her and she swipes his hands away from her waist.

"I came to make sure you were okay," she tells me, looking between Wes and me.

"Why wouldn't I be okay?" I frown.

"I may have been frustrated about Z being at my house when I got home and told him about the guy coming to the hospital. I told him not to tell Wes, but no sooner did the words leave my mouth did this big lug call Wes." She points at Z, who is smiling at her. She glares at him in return, only to have his smile become wider. "You're annoying."

"You've said that, Kitten," Z tells her.

"You couldn't call?" Wes asks, and I look at him and narrow my eyes.

"Don't be rude."

"I'm hungry," he states, making my core tighten.

"I'm hungry too," Kayan says, and my eyes leave Wes when his head tilts back so that he can look at the ceiling.

"I was going to make tacos." I sigh.

"Do you have enough?" Kayan asks.

"No," Wes says as I say, "Yes."

"Yes, I have plenty." I narrow my eyes on Wes, daring him to say something else. "Why don't you help me make dinner, while Wes and Z do guy stuff."

"Guy stuff." Wes shakes his head, looking at Z.

"Yeah, drink beer, scratch your balls…guy stuff." I throw my hands up in the air then roll my eyes when Z laughs.

"I'm going to start cooking," my poor, distressed friend says, walking to the kitchen.

"I'm beating the shit out of you tomorrow," Wes says, looking at Z, whose eyes are focused where Kayan just disappeared.

"Brother." Z shakes his head then looks at me. "You got any beer?"

"Yeah." I nod.

"I'll get it," he says, walking off towards the kitchen.

"She's safe with him, right?" I ask Wes when Z is out of earshot.

"I've been friends with him since we joined the Navy at eighteen. He's one of the best guys I know." He wraps his arms around me and places a lingering kiss on my forehead. "Now, go make me dinner, while I go do guy shit." He tilts my head back with two fingers under my chin and I laugh into his mouth as he kisses me again before pushing me towards the kitchen.

"How much trouble did I get you in with Wes?" Kayan asks as we start to cook dinner.

"None. Well, he was pissed, but he got over it."

"I didn't mean to open my mouth, but when I got home, Z was there and it just came out."

"I kinda got that." I take the hamburger out of the package, put it in the pan, and begin to cook it. "What's going on with you guys anyways?" I ask her, handing her two tomatoes to slice up.

"Nothing." She ducks her head.

"Didn't look like nothing when I opened my front door and his tongue was down your throat."

"That was an accident."

"He accidently kissed you? Or you accidently kissed him back?"

"I don't know." She lets out a loud breath.

"He seems to like you."

"I don't know," she whispers, and I take a can of refried beans and dump them on top of the taco meat, along with some cheese I grated the other day.

"I just don't want you to miss out on something great," I tell her after a few minutes.

"He makes me crazy."

"I think that if you don't explore things with him, you're going to end up regretting it."

She chews on her bottom lip then looks toward the living room, where the guys are watching TV. "I know you're right," she whispers then looks at the pan in front of me and frowns. "I thought we were making tacos."

"These are tacos. They're 'I don't want to wash a million dishes' tacos."

She shakes her head then goes back to chopping.

It doesn't take long for dinner to be done, and even less time for the guys to scarf down every last bite. By the time dinner's done and Z and Kayan leave for the night, I'm asleep on my feet.

"WHAT ARE YOU doing?" I ask sleepily, opening my eyes and coming face-to-face with Wes, who's staring down at me. Turning my head, I look at the clock, seeing I still have an hour before I have to get up and ready for work.

"You were whimpering in your sleep."

"Whimpering?" I ask, still half unconscious.

"Whimpering," he confirms.

"That's strange," I say then notice his eyes have turned a darker shade of green, and my body begins to heat. I was so tired last night that the moment my head hit the pillow, I fell asleep.

"You made that same whimpering noise when my fingers were deep inside you."

"Really?" I breathe as his hand slides down my stomach and cups me over my panties.

"Oh, yeah, I'll never forget that noise." His fingers slide over the lips of my pussy through the material, making me whimper. "That's the noise I'm talking about."

"Oh," I breathe as he slides between my legs. His hands slide up my sides and he slips my tank top off over my head, tossing the shirt behind him. Then he lifts one of my legs and places it on his shoulder, doing the same with the other.

My breath starts coming in rough pants as his hands slide over my breasts then down my sides.

"Jesus, you're fucking perfection," he says roughly as his fingers slide around my waist and grip my panties. As he pulls them up, the material sliding over my ass and hips, he places both of my legs on one of his shoulders until the panties slide over my ankles and he drops them to the bed near my hip. Then he pulls my right leg back over to his other shoulder and looks down again.

"I don't think I'll be able to make it through another day unless I know how you taste. Can I taste you, baby?" he asks as his hands slide from my ankles that are near his ears, down the front of my legs, then farther down as his fingers wrap around my inner thighs. I swallow hard, trying to get my voice to work, but all I can manage is a jerky nod.

"Hmm," he breathes, lowering my legs from his shoulders. He places my feet on the bed and leans over me, causing his necklace to hit me between my breasts as his mouth opens over mine.

Sliding his tongue into my mouth, rocking his hips against me, I lift my legs, wanting to wrap them around him.

"No." He pulls my legs from around him with his hands wrapped around my ankles, then spreads them, holding my feet to the mattress, his arm muscles flexing as he spreads me wider and lowers his face, placing a kiss on my lower belly, making the muscles flex.

His nose runs across my pubic bone as he inhales a deep breath. My thighs start to shake as his hands slide from my ankles, up over my kneecaps, and down my inner thighs.

My breathing starts to feel rushed as I try to anticipate when his mouth will touch me. My fingers tangle in the sheets near my hips as his eyes meet mine. Even though I had been anticipating the touch of his tongue, my back arches, my head digs into the pillow, and my eyes close in bliss as his warm tongue runs over my clit then back down.

"Give me your eyes," he growls. My head tips down and my eyes meet his as his tongue spreads across my sex. This time he does this thing, flicking his tongue in quick bursts while his thumbs hold me open.

My hands grab onto his hair and my heels dig into the mattress near his shoulders as I lift myself closer to his mouth, and his thumb slides inside me. He hums against my clit before pulling it into his mouth. My hips buck in response and my hands in his hair tug hard as he sucks mercilessly, pulling an orgasm from me that I didn't even feel building.

His name leaves my mouth on a loud moan. My nails scrape through his hair as I hold him to me, feeling the orgasm wash throughout my body.

I relax into the bed and drop my hands to my sides as he crawls up between my legs. His tongue sweeps across mine, leaving my taste and his behind. I wrap my legs around him as he leans back, and run my fingers down his scruffy jaw.

"You are seriously hot," I blurt then close my eyes, feeling like a dork.

He chuckles and kisses under my jaw then runs a hand over my head before rolling off me to his back and pulling me over to his chest. I press my legs together as I feel how hard he is against my arm, which is resting across his abs.

I inhale a deep breath, letting the oxygen give me the courage I need, then move before he can stop me. I pull down the band of his boxers and stop dead as all the oxygen leaves my body.

"Holy crap," I whisper. I knew he felt big when I had him in my hand, but he is huge, long and thick, the veins pronounced, the head red and angry-looking. I swallow hard as my mouth fills with saliva. I look up and meet his eyes. His body is frozen in place. I pull my hair over one shoulder, wrap my hand around him, and pull up the heavy weight of him with my hand, causing me to have another surge of wetness. I lower my head and lick over the tip, moaning as his taste explodes on my tongue.

"*Fuck*," he growls as his hand fists into my hair at the side of my head. I lower my mouth completely over him, going down until he hits the back of my throat, making me gag. I lift up then down, keeping my cheeks hollow as I suck. When I reach the tip again, I release him from my mouth with a pop then use my hand, pulling up then down as I swirl my tongue around the tip.

His hand leaves my hair and lifts above his head so he can grab onto the headboard. The visual of him, his muscles taught as I bring him closer to release, makes me moan loud and slide down, causing him to once again hit the back of my throat. I move faster, working my hand along with my mouth.

"I'm going to come," he groans, placing a hand on the side of my hair. My eyes meet his. I know he's giving me a chance to release him, but I just move faster, with my eyes locked on his as he comes hard. I swallow him down then swirl my tongue around the tip again before releasing him from my mouth. "I almost lifted you up and impaled you on my cock, baby," he says, pulling me up his body with his hands under my arms. Once my mouth is near his, he places his hand on the back of my head and pulls my lips down to his, kissing me until my nails are digging into his chest.

"Sorry," I apologize breathlessly, not knowing what else to say.

"Don't apologize; that was hot. I just had to check myself," he says, tucking some hair behind my ear then searching my face. "A friend of mine from the Navy is coming into town from California on Saturday and we're having a party for him. I want you there with me," he states, dragging his fingers through my hair, removing the knots he caused.

"I have to go to my dad's birthday party Saturday, so I won't be able to," I say, tracing the tattoos that start at his shoulder and travel down to his wrist.

"That's fine. We can go after his party," he says, wrapping his hand around my neck to pull my face towards him.

I pull back and search his face then remind him, "My dad's going to be there."

"It's his birthday, so I would expect him to be there." He smiles, running a finger of his free hand down the center of my face.

"You want to meet my dad?" I whisper in shock. Everyone is afraid of my dad, and I have never had any guy, even just friends, willing to meet him.

"You're mine. I can't tell the future, but I don't think that's going to change, so I would like to meet him."

"My dad is very protective."

"I wouldn't expect any man with all girls not to be," he says softly, searching my face.

"Will you let me talk to him about us first?" I ask. I'm not sure if I'm ready for the only man I have ever loved to meet the man I'm falling in love with. This thing between Wes and me is still so new, and I don't want anything to ruin it.

"I can do that," he says gently.

"Thank you." I smile, kissing him once more before my alarm goes off and we're forced to get up.

Chapter 9

"HAPPY BIRTHDAY, DAD," I say, walking up to where my dad is manning the barbeque.

"Thank you." He smiles, wrapping an arm around my shoulders and kissing the side of my head. "Where have you been?"

"Oh, you know, working." I shrug then cringe, willing myself to tell him about Wes.

"You need to take a break every once in awhile and come visit your old man."

"Sorry," I tell him, and he kisses my head again.

"Hey, honey." My mom smiles then looks around, and I jerk my head side-to-side before she asks exactly what I know she's going to.

"You didn't bring a date?" she asks, and I take a breath and shake my head.

"You're not dating, are you?" my dad asks.

"Do you need any help inside, Mom?" I ask ignoring my dad's question. Not giving her a chance to answer, I take her elbow and lead her past the pool and into the house.

"Honey," she laughs, looking at my dad, who is still in front of the grill, but his body is turned toward the house, "are you still seeing that nice guy Wes?"

"Mom, really?" I ask, going into the kitchen and pulling out platters from the fridge.

"What? I thought you would bring him, or that he would insist on coming today."

"He wanted to, but I asked him to let me tell Dad about him first."

"You didn't tell your father about him, and right now, when you had the perfect opportunity to tell him, you pulled me away."

"I know." I cover my face in frustration.

"What's wrong?" she asks, and I feel her hand on my back and uncover my face to look at her.

"I'm worried Dad won't like him," I whisper, and her face goes soft.

"Honey, what happens if he doesn't like him?" she asks, searching my face.

"I don't know," I say, feeling my chest constrict.

"When I started dating your father, Grandpa was not exactly happy about it, but I knew your dad made me feel things I didn't even think were possible, and I also knew *my* dad loved me enough to know I knew what I was doing."

"I want Dad to like him," I whisper.

"Then you need to give him a chance to get to know him."

"I don't know if I'm ready, if our relationship is ready."

"My beautiful girl is falling in love," she whispers, and I close my eyes, not wanting her to see how true that statement is. I'm falling in love with a guy I barely know.

"I think I just need a little more time," I tell her, finally opening my eyes.

"Just don't wait too long, honey."

"Promise I won't," I say as my insides twist.

"He's hot." She smiles after a moment.

"What?!" I shriek, looking at her.

"He is, and that kiss he gave you when he walked into you house. "Very nice."

"Shut up."

"What? I'm old, but I'm not dead." She smiles.

"You better not let Dad hear you say that," I warn, and the smile slides off her face.

"Watch it, young lady," she says, and I wrap my arms around her waist.

"Love you, Mom."

"Love you too, honey." She kisses my hair. "Now," she pulls away, leaving her hands on my shoulders, "let's get this stuff done, and get outside and enjoy your dad's birthday."

"Right," I agree, pulling the rest of the platters out of the fridge and heading back outside.

"Bye, Mom. Bye, Dad!" I yell out my car window to my parents, who are standing on the front porch with their arms wrapped around each other.

"Bye, honey," my mom calls back as my dad lifts his chin as I back out.

After dinner, we FaceTimed my sisters while we sang him happy birthday before cutting his cake. I missed my sisters, but with all of them going to college out of state, it was hard for all of us to get together like we used to when we were all home. The good thing is over the next few years, all of my sisters will be moving back to town one-by-one as they finish college. I pull out onto the main road and press send on Wes' number when it pulls up on my call log.

"Hey, babe," he answers, and I hear music in the background then moving.

"Hey," I say when his side goes quiet.

"You on your way?"

"Yeah." I smile.

"Good, I miss you," he says, lowering his tone—not like he's trying to hide what he's saying, but like he is really happy I will be there soon.

"Me too." I smile again, turning onto another road.

"How did things go with your dad?"

Shit. I don't want to lie, but I don't want to tell him I never even mentioned him to my dad, and that I actually tackled Jax to the ground when he was going to say something about Wes to his dad.

"He had a great birthday," I say, playing dumb while hoping he doesn't ask anything else—at least, not yet, not until I've spoken to my dad, which I will do soon. Okay, maybe not soon, but sooner, rather than later. "I'm going to stop by my house and change really quick, and then I will be there."

"Why do you need to change?"

"'Cause I wore a dress to the party."

"Come straight here," he growls, and the space between my legs tingles.

"Wes—"

"Come straight here, July," he demands, causing the tingle to become a shiver of excitement.

"I'll see you soon," I say, and the phone goes dead. I drop it into my lap and attempt to focus on driving, not on the ache that the tone of his voice caused.

When I pull up outside of the compound, Wes is waiting out front. My mouth waters as I take him in. Wearing a white tank that shows off his tattoos, his cut over it, a pair of jeans, and his black boots, leaning against the building with a beer in his hand at his hip.

I shut off my car and check my face in the mirror, noticing that my eyes are bright with excitement and happiness. They travel from my reflection to Wes, and his eyes hold me in a trance as I unlock my seatbelt and fumble until I get my door open.

The moment my sandal-covered foot touches the ground, Wes steps away from the building. I clear the door and slam it behind me, and his eyes run over me from head to toe. I left my hair down after I got out of the shower this afternoon, so it dried with messy waves. The dress is the color of buttercups. It has wide straps, and the top of the dress is snug, with buttons down the front, the bottom flaring out at the hips, making it look like I have the perfect hourglass figure.

I let out a long breath and wipe my hands down the front, trying to settle my nerves.

"I don't know if I'm going to be cool with my boys seeing you like this," he places a hand on my waist and dragging my body close to his until we're hip-to-hip. "You look beautiful," he says as his eyes take me in.

"Thank you." I smile, placing my hand on the leather of his cut, sliding up to wrap around the back of his neck so I can pull him down to kiss me.

"I should just take you back to your house," he whispers as his mouth hovers just out of reach of mine.

"Then I wouldn't get to meet your friend," I tell him, pressing up on my toes, trying to reach his mouth.

"He's not important."

I smile when I finally get the kiss I had been waiting for, and somehow end up with my legs wrapped around his hips and my arms wrapped around his neck, my back pressing into the door of my car. When we finally end our make-out session, he leads me inside and straight to the bar towards a group of guys who are talking.

The moment we're close, the conversation stops and one of the guys turns to look at us. His hair is low to his scalp, his face ruggedly handsome, almost so much so that it's intimidating. His eyes sweep over me and heat slightly then drop to the hand Wes has wrapped around my hip. Then they travel up to meet mine again, and this time, the heat is gone and understanding is in its place.

"So this is her, huh?" he asks, looking over my shoulder at Wes.

"Baby, this is Tuck. Tuck, this is July," Wes introduces us.

"Tuck?" I ask, and Wes chuckles.

"You don't want to know how I got that nickname." He shakes his head and sticks out his hand. "It's nice to meet you. Seems you have my boy strung out."

"I don't think so," I tell him as I shake his hand.

"You wouldn't." He looks over my shoulder and smiles as he drops my hand. "So what's your poison?"

"Oh, I'm not going to drink tonight," I say, shaking my head as memories of the last time I was here come to mind.

"One shot?" he questions, and Wes squeezes my side then whispers in my ear, "I'll make sure you don't challenge anyone to a dance-off."

"Very funny," I huff, looking over my shoulder at him and smiling.

"SHOT, SHOT, SHOT," is cheered, and I shoot back a shot of tequila and slam the glass down on the table then cover my mouth with my hand, wincing as the taste floods my mouth.

"Gahhh, I hate tequila." I laugh then pick up another shot.

"Baby," Wes laughs, taking the shot from my hand, lifting it to his mouth and shooting it back then wrapping a hand around the back of my neck and pulling my mouth to his. He presses his tongue into my mouth until I moaned down his throat.

"Get a room," Tuck says, pouring another shot.

"Fuck off." Wes smiles, kissing me again, this time below my ear.

"So have you taken July to meet Mama Judy?" Tuck asks, sitting back in his chair and taking a pull from his beer.

"Not yet, I was thinking this weekend," Wes says, rubbing my shoulder.

"Uh…what?" I wheeze out.

"She has next weekend off, so I figured we could take a ride up to Nashville."

Holy shit.

"Where is Z?" I ask, changing the subject before the conversation can turn to family and parents.

"He and your girl were supposed to be on their way when you called."

I frown then pull out my phone and check the time. "I got here over an hour ago," I say, and my frown grows deeper as I dial her number.

"Hello?" Kayan answers breathlessly then moans and I feel my face heat up.

"I…uh…later." I hang up and set the phone on the table, whispering, "I think they were having sex."

Wes and Tuck both start laughing and the music gets turned up, so I look around, noticing more people have shown up, and by more people, I mean more women, all of them wearing close to nothing.

"You good?" Wes asks, and I nod and look at the bottle of tequila when loud explosions fill my ears. Wes and Tuck both shove me under the table. My knees and hands hit the concrete hard, causing me to yell out in pain. Then the table is flipped to its side, blocking my view as women begin to scream, and the guys in the open court start yelling out at each other.

I tuck myself into a ball and cover my head with my hands when I realize they were gunshots. I don't know how long it lasts, but before I even think it's safe, Wes is picking me up off the ground and running, with me tucked in front of his body. My eyes are squeezed shut and my pulse is going haywire as I'm set down on a soft mattress.

"Baby, open your eyes." I shake my head, trying to clear the loud ringing in my ears. "Baby." I feel his hands hold my face and my eyes open, blinking a few times. "There you are," he says, pulling me forward and placing a gentle kiss on my lips.

"You good, man?" Wes pulls his mouth from mine and we both turn our heads toward the open doorway, where Tuck is standing, holding a gun.

"Yeah." His eyes leave his friends and come back to me and then flash, and he begins touching everywhere on my body until he gets to my knees, where they are scraped and bloody from hitting the concrete so hard. "Shit. Get me the first aid kit from the shop."

"It's okay. I'll just wash it with some water," I assure him then look towards the door, but Tuck is already out of sight.

"Who did that?" I ask, and his jaw clenches.

"No idea," he grits out. "I'm going to get you cleaned up then head out with the boys. Tuck will stay here and watch over you until I get back."

"Stay with me," I whisper desperately. No way do I want him out where he can get shot at.

"Here you go," Tuck says, coming back into the room and setting down what looks like a tackle box on the bed next to me, and Wes opens it up and starts to pull out supplies.

"You're going to stay here with July," Wes tells Tuck, wiping off my bloody knee.

"Fuck no, I'm going with you."

"You know you can't get in trouble when you're on leave, brother," Wes tells him, and I look at Tuck and see that his jaw is hard and his fists are balled at his sides.

"Please don't leave me," I plead, looking back at Wes, who gently cleans my wounds then covers them with some kind of ointment. If it weren't for the hardness of his jaw, I would guess he hadn't heard me. He closes up the box then pulls out a gun from under his mattress, drops his fist into the bed near my hip, and kisses me before standing up to his full height again.

"What are you going to do?" I ask, but he ignores me then looks at Tuck.

"Watch her," he tells him.

"Wes!" I cry, getting up from the bed and going after him, only to be grabbed with an arm around my waist that prevents me from following behind him. I kick out with everything I have, but my strength is no match for Tuck, who only holds me tighter against him.

"He's going to get himself hurt," I say, attempting to breathe.

"He'll be fine," Tuck argues, and my body slumps against him when I realize he's not going to help me. He walks backward two steps and sets me on the bed.

I look towards the exit and hear Tuck mutter, "Fuck," under his breath as he moves to the door and closes it.

"You're not going after him. He would kill me if something happened to you while I was on watch."

"You cannot expect me to just sit here and do nothing while he's doing God knows what!" I yell, standing up and looking around the room for something to throw at him.

"That's exactly what I expect you to do."

"This is ridiculous. I need to go out there. What if someone needs my help?"

"No one was hurt, and even if they were, you're staying here."

"I need my phone," I try again, hoping he will let me go look for it.

"Nice try." He shakes his head then mutters, "I see what he meant," while running a hand through his hair.

"Seriously, I need it. Can you call Z to ask if he and Kayan are okay?"

"Fine," he growls, pulling out his phone from his back pocket, pressing a couple buttons and putting his phone to his ear, then mutters a few things while watching me before putting his phone back in his pocket.

"Your friend is fine. She's home."

"Can I call her?" I ask, and he shakes his head.

"This is stupid," I murmur, flopping down on the bed. "You're lucky you have a gun or I would totally Kung Fu your ass and leave whether you liked it or not."

"Jesus." He shakes his head. I scoot back in the bed then lean back against the wall, crossing my arms over my chest and glaring at him.

"How is it I have been with my friend in some of the worst environments known to man, but after meeting you, I'm more concerned for his wellbeing than I ever was?"

"That's rude." I frown.

"No, it's the truth. I have never seen him mixed up over a woman. Even his ex-wife didn't affect him like you do," he says, and the breath I was going to take pauses in my lungs. I had no idea Wes was ever married. He never told me.

"Shit," Tuck says, sitting on the bed at my side. "Sorry, I thought you knew."

I turn my head to look at him and swallow around the lump that has painfully formed in my throat before speaking. "It's fine; we haven't known each other long," I admit with what I hope looks like a smile.

"He's going to kill me." He shakes his head.

"I won't even mention it," I assure him, leaning my head back against the wall and closing my eyes.

"JESUS," I HEAR and open my eyes then frown in confusion as I look at Wes, but I feel warmth under my cheek and the steady rise and fall of the chest I'm lying on with my arms wrapped over a hard stomach. I look from a pissed off Wes to Tuck, whose eyes are open, looking down at me.

I scoot back quickly and look at Wes again while trying to get my bearings straight. "I fell asleep," I say to him and myself.

"I see that, babe," he growls then looks at Tuck. "I need to talk with you."

"Brother, do not even fucking go there," Tuck says, and Wes' jaw grinds.

"What happened?" I ask.

"Nothing," Wes clips, not taking his eyes off his friend.

"You don't know, or you're not going to tell me?" I ask.

"It doesn't concern you," he says, causing my temper to flare.

"If it concerns you, it concerns me," I retort, crossing my arms over my chest when his eyes come to mine.

"Don't start your shit."

"What did you just say?" I ask, getting off the bed.

"I said don't start your shit, not right now."

"You're unbelievable," I hiss then look at Tuck. "I told you to let me leave, but no, you just had to listen to this jerk." I see the corners of his lips twitch, but I ignore it and walk past Wes towards the door.

"Where the fuck do you think you're going?"

I look over my shoulder to sweep my eyes over him then mutter, "Home, to bed."

"You're not leaving without me."

I snort in disbelief and head out the door, only to be pulled back. "Let me go," I hiss.

"Never," he replies close to my ear then growls, "If I ever see you touching another man, even unconsciously, I will kill him, friend or not."

"I was asleep," I whisper in disbelief.

"I don't give a fuck."

"Listen to yourself!" I shake my head.

"*You* have turned me into this."

"Don't blame me for you're insanity."

"I'd like to attest that my friend was never like this before you," Tuck says, and I look at him and glare. "Just saying." He holds up his hands in front of him.

"Unless you're going to tell me what happened while you were gone, let me go," I growl, and his arms tighten around me.

"You really think I would let my woman get involved in what went down tonight?" he asks, making it sound like *I'm* the crazy one.

"Did I ask you to take me along on a drive-by? No. I asked what happened, if you found anything out, if you know who shot up the building."

"I told you—you're not getting involved."

I'm just about ready to flip out, when I'm cut off.

"He's right. You're not getting involved. There is no reason for you to know what happened tonight," Jax says, standing in the open doorway of the room.

"You guys are so ridiculous." I shift out of Wes' hold and turn on him. "I was here when this place was shot up. I'm not asking you to go into detail about what went down; I just want to know I can go to bed tonight without worrying."

"You're safe," Wes tells me, and his voice gentles as his hand comes up so his fingers can run across my cheek.

"I don't like being shot at, and I hate that this is happening because of me," I say, pressing my cheek into his hand.

His jaw goes hard and his eyes leave me to look at the door. "This has nothing to do with what's been happening."

"It doesn't?" I ask, searching his face, then look at Jax when I notice Wes is still regarding him like he wants to kill him.

"I asked Wes to help me out with something," Jax cuts in. "The people his boys were watching must have caught wind of the situation and made it clear they knew we were watching them."

I look from Jax to Wes then back again. I want to strangle my cousin for getting Wes involved in whatever it is he's doing, but I know Wes well enough to understand the only way he would ever be involved in anything is if it was something he believed in. So what can I really say about that?

"Is it safe for me to go home?" I ask, as his jaw goes hard again and he glances at Tuck and then me.

"Can I trust you to take her home and wait for me to get there?" Wes asks Tuck.

"You know you don't even have to ask that shit," Tuck returns.

"Apparently, I do," Wes replies, and I throw my arms up.

"I was asleep!" I repeat again, which only makes his jaw tic harder.

"I found this outside," Jax says, breaking the moment by handing me my phone, which shows I have a few missed calls from Kayan.

"Thanks," I mutter then look at Wes. "Please, be careful."

"Just be good," he says, and his lips touch mine briefly before his hand goes to the middle of my back. Once we're outside, I look around and notice there are a few bullet holes in the building and one in my trunk, which I'll have to find a sticker or something to cover it with before someone in my family sees it and wonders why the hell there's a bullet hole in my car.

"We'll get it fixed," Wes says when he notices I have stopped to look at the hole.

I exhale a harsh breath then listen as he gives Tuck directions to my house before buckling me into the passenger seat with a kiss to my forehead.

"See why I'm worried about him?" Tuck says as we pull away from the building with Wes looking at us like he is going to run after us. I ignore his statement and put my phone to my ear.

"Oh, my God! I have been trying to get in touch with you. Are you okay?" Kayan says as soon as she answers.

"I'm fine; I just got my phone back. Are you okay?"

"Yes, I'm at Z's house. We were on our way there when someone called to tell him what happened, and he turned his car around, brought me here, and dropped me off before leaving."

"Did he tell you anything?" I ask.

"No, just that he would be back. Where are you now?"

"On my way home. Wes said he would be at my house in a couple of hours, so my guess is Z will be about that long as well."

"He let you go home alone?" she asks in disbelief.

"No, Tuck is my babysitter." I roll my eyes.

"Who's Tuck?" she asks, and I look out the window.

"He is one of Wes' friends from the military," I explain then yawn as the day catches up with me.

"Get some sleep and call me in the morning."

"I will. Be safe."

"You too, girl. All this drama is almost more than I can take."

"Sounded like you were taking it just fine when I called you earlier," I whisper and hear her giggle.

"Shut up. I'll talk to you tomorrow. Love you."

"Love you too," I say, hitting the end button on my phone just as we pull up to my house.

I get out of the car and head up to the front door with Tuck following close behind me. As soon as we get inside, I pick up Capone and scratch him behind his ears then let him go to the floor, where he runs circles around Tuck. Then I pick up Juice and give him some love before setting him back on the table and going to the couch, taking a seat so I can unbuckle my sandals and slip them off.

"Do you want a beer or something?" I ask Tuck, who has taken a seat on the couch.

"I'm good. You go on to bed," he says, picking up the remote and pressing the TV on.

"Are you sure?" I mutter, watching absently as the channels flip from one thing to another.

His finger comes off the remote, his head turns toward me, and his face goes soft. "Babe, go to bed."

"Right," I mumble, standing back up. "I'll see you tomorrow." He nods then turns back to the TV and begins flipping through the channels again. I head to my room and shut the door behind me then go to the shower, turning it on hot before stripping off my clothes and stepping in.

The moment the hot water rushes over me, I sigh in relief. I don't take long getting washed up before drying off and going to my room. Normally, I would just get into bed without putting anything on, but knowing Tuck is here has me pulling out a set of pajamas and slipping them on before crawling into bed.

"YOU'RE HOME," I sigh as Wes slides in behind me and his smell engulfs my senses.

"I like that you call this my home," he whispers, placing a kiss on the back of my neck. I try to reply, but sleep takes me away before I can get anything out.

Chapter 10

I LOOK OUT the front window of Wes' truck, watching as the rain beats mercilessly against the windshield, and my leg bounces in sync with the wipers.

"Babe, relax," Wes says as he takes my hand, placing it on his thigh. I look over at him and try to release, through a breath the stress that has been swarming in my stomach since he picked me up a half-hour ago.

We're going to meet his mom. I'm nervous…so nervous that I want to jump out of his truck and try my luck with hitting the road at seventy miles an hour.

"She's going to love you," he tells me, and I look out the window, wondering if he said that before to his ex-wife the first time she met his mom.

"Did she like your ex-wife?" I ask then kick my ass around in my head when I feel the muscles of his thigh contract. "Sorry, Tuck told me. He didn't mean to, and I promised I wouldn't say anything, but it just slipped out," I ramble, pulling my hand from his leg.

"I wasn't hiding it," he says quietly.

"I know. I told him we haven't known each other long. I totally get it," I reply just as quietly.

"My mom did like her," he answers, making me regret asking when that all too familiar feeling of jealousy begins to ignite in my stomach. "We met right after Hell Week. I was still on a high from making it through SEAL training." He pauses and pulls my hand back to his thigh and places his hand over it. "She had the whole girl-next-door thing going for her. I thought she was a sweet, beautiful woman, and I was gone so much that it took me far too long to realize she wasn't at all who I thought she was. She married me so she could say her man was in the military. The moment I started talking about getting out, things went to shit. She was more concerned about what her friends would say than how I was feeling going into work everyday."

"I'm sorry," I say, squeezing his thigh.

"Two years ago, right after I got out of the military, we got divorced. I know it may sound fucked up, but I don't even think about her," he confesses, and I have no idea what to say about that. I can't imagine being married and having the person I promised to spend my life with become nothing, not even a thought in my head.

"I don't know what to say."

"There's nothing to say." He clasps my hand tighter.

"Why did you get out of the military?" I ask after a moment, trying to fill the uncomfortable silence.

"Me and my boys had been on a rescue mission. One of our own had been kidnapped, and they were being held by insurgents who wanted us to give them back one of their men. The US doesn't negotiate with terrorist, but they will attempt to rescue their people if they think they can. We were sent in and found out too late that it was a setup. I lost three of my brothers when everything went to shit, and the rest of us barely made it out alive," he confides then runs his hand over mine, and I notice my fingers have dug into his denim-covered thigh. "Coming home from that solidified what I needed to do, and I knew it was time for me to leave the military and do something else with my life."

"I'm sorry you lost your friends," I say, feeling tears sting my nose.

"Me too, baby." He gives my hand a squeeze.

I look over at his profile and can tell he's not with me but back there, so I attempt to lighten the mood by asking, "So you decided to become a biker?"

"Smartass," he mutters, smiling at the windshield before bringing his eyes to me for a brief moment.

"Nah, me and my boys had always ridden on weekends when we were home, and we all did our own repairs and custom work on our bikes, so it seemed like fate was leading us down this path long before we moved to Tennessee."

"I'm glad it lead you here," I say softly, giving his thigh a pat.

"Me and you both, babe," he murmurs then takes his hand off mine to turn onto another road then another until we pull up outside a small light blue house with white shutters and a small porch that is covered with flowers.

"You ready for this?"

"No." I shake my head as a woman with long white hair wearing a pair of jeans, cowboy boots, and a t-shirt steps out onto the front porch.

"I've seen you face down a gang of angry bikers. This will be a walk in the park."

"Very funny," I mumble, and he kisses my nose and I watch as he gets out of the truck. I unhook my belt then find the handle at the same time he opens the door for me.

His hands go to my waist and he lifts me out of the cab, holding onto me until my ballet flat-covered feet hit the ground. Then he moves me out of the way, slams the door, puts his arm around my waist, and leads me up to the house.

The moment we hit the top landing of the porch, his mom wraps her arms around him, whispering something in his ear before releasing him, turning to look at me.

"Mom, I want you to meet July. July, this is my mom, Judy."

"It's so nice to meet you." I stick out my hand and she surprises me by pulling me into an embrace that fills me with warmth.

"Sorry." She smiles then laughs, patting my cheek. "I feel like I know you already. Every time I talk to my son, he tells me about you."

"Really?" I ask, feeling my cheeks heat in embarrassment.

"It's true. You have definitely woven a web around my son."

I look from her to Wes, unsure of what to say about that, but then don't say anything, because she is taking my hand and leading me into the house, leaving Wes on the front porch, shaking his head.

Once we get inside, the smell of cinnamon and apples touches my nose, reminding me of home. I follow Judy without choice through the living room and into the kitchen, where she leads me to the small island.

"Sit here," she says, dropping my hand. I hold back the laugh I feel and take a seat on one of her barstools to watch as she pulls a beautiful pie out of the oven and sets it in front of me.

"Pulling out the big guns, Mom?" Wes asks, kissing the side of my head before taking a seat next to me.

"You know I love to bake," she states, smiling and spinning the pie around slightly. I wish I had half the baking skills she does; the whole pie looks like it could be in a magazine.

"That would be true if you didn't leave the evidence of your baking skills in your garbage," Wes says, and I follow his eyes to the trashcan, where there is a box that once contained the apple pie sitting on top of it.

"You're such a know-it-all." His mom laughs, hitting him with the hot oven mitt in her hand, making me laugh. "Just so you know, honey, this is his favorite pie. They have it at every store and all you have to do is put it in the oven."

"That's good to know. I suck at baking," I tell her, and her face goes soft.

"Me too, but my boy didn't know I couldn't until he turned sixteen and found the first box from a frozen apple pie I had made him."

"I knew when I was ten," Wes confesses, and her eyes go to him.

"You did not!" she cries.

"I did; I had a sleepover at a friend's and his mom had bought one, and it looked and tasted just like yours. I just didn't confront you about it until I was sixteen."

She shakes her head, but her gaze on him is soft and so full of love that I feel it all the way down to my toes.

"So, how did you two meet?" she asks, going to a cupboard and pulling out three plates, setting them in front of us.

"Me and the boys were out riding when this biker swerved and tried to run me off the road," Wes says, and his mom's face pales.

"I swerved to miss a bird that was in the road," I defend, pulling Judy's eyes to me. "Its wing was broken, and I didn't want to kill it. After I swerved, your son and his friends chased me down on their bikes," I tattle, and she inhales a sharp breath.

"Why don't you tell her how you stun-gunned me?"

"Oh my…"

I turn my head and glare at him, then hiss, "You scared me and it was an accident."

"Oh lord," Judy whispers, and I turn to look at her. Her eyes go from him to me, and the same look I saw on my mom's face when she met Wes appears on hers. "That will be a good story for your kids one day," she cheers blissfully then turns around, leaving me sitting there like a fish out of water, with my mouth gaping while she goes over to a drawer, opening it up and pulling out forks.

"Close your mouth, babe," Wes chortles, pushing up on my chin. I turn to look at him, noticing he doesn't even look slightly taken aback by his mom's comment. I double-blink then snap my mouth closed.

"So, you ride a bike also?" Judy asks while cutting a piece of pie and placing it on the plate in front of me.

"I do…well, not a Harley, but a sport bike," I tell her, smiling.

"My ex used to ride, and I hate that my son rides. I worry about him everyday, but I know it's something that makes him happy. I'm glad you guys have that in common," she says, and Wes' hand wraps around the back of my neck and he pulls me closer to him so he can place a kiss above my ear.

"My mom rides, and it was always something we did together."

"How does your dad feel about it?" Judy asks.

"The first bike I ever had, I was constantly having to refill the tires with air, and I couldn't figure out why. And I wouldn't ride it, because it was too risky. Then one day, I went to the garage and found my dad taking the cap off the nozzle on the tires. He hated that I was riding, so he was sabotaging my bike."

"Well then, I don't feel so bad." His mom smiles and I smile back, taking a bite of the pie, and I have to agree; even if it was frozen, it is seriously delicious.

By the time we leave, I have completely fallen in love with Wes' mom, and I know that if the time ever comes for our parents to meet, my mom and dad will both love her too.

"I love your mom," I tell Wes as we head back to my house.

"Told you." He smiles, squeezing my thigh.

"Do you want to stay at my house tonight?" I ask, not knowing why I even bother asking, 'cause he has stayed with me every night since the first time he crawled into my bed.

"Babe," he starts, and I can tell he's trying not to laugh, "I haven't even been to my place in three days."

"It's weird how this thing has been happening between us," I say quietly.

"What do you mean?"

"Everything has been at warp speed since our first date, or what would have been our first date, if you hadn't ruined it."

"Thought you forgot about that," he mumbles, but I can hear the smile in his voice.

"Nope, I still remember, and will probably use it as leverage for the rest of your life."

"You plan on knowing me that long?"

"I hope so," I reply, wondering why the hell I just said that.

"Glad to know even in warp speed we're on the same page," he says, and I pull my eyes away from him and look out the window.

I don't know if it's possible to fall in love in such a short time, but if it is, I'm in love with Wes Silver. Now I just had to figure out how to tell my dad about him.

Wes

"SILVER," JAX CALLS, walking into the shop through the open bay's door. I lift my chin and step away from the bike I'm working on while wiping my hands on a greasy rag. "I have some news about Snake," he says, and my jaw grinds at the mention of his name. As much as I don't want to be involved with this shit, I know I have to be. It's not in me to sit by while good, innocent people are hurt. "He was seen leaving a meeting in downtown Nashville this afternoon."

"And?"

"And the meeting was with Franco Demitrez."

"Is that supposed to mean something to me?"

"He controls one of the largest sex trafficking and prostitution rings this side of the Mississippi," he says, and my gut twists. I had known for a while that what was happening with Snake and his boys was bad, but this takes this shit to a whole different level.

"You know I hate asking you for any favors," he starts, and my eyes narrow. Since the first moment we met he has been asking my crew to help him with shit. "I need you and your boys to help me secure some girls their moving soon."

"Then what? Do you even know the level of fucked-up you're dealing with right now? You can't just sweep in and you sure as fuck need to have a plan in place for when it's all over."

"I understand that, I also understand that Landon came to talk to me." He says pulling his hat off and running a hand over his head.

"What did he want?" I ask, Landon's dad owns Mamma's Country; he's the kid that was dropping off dogs to July, the same kid July asked me to help.

"Did you know Landon has a sister?"

"No." Ronnie never mentioned having another kid, not to me and I never saw a girl around.

"He does but Snakes boys took her and that's the leverage they have been holding over Ronnie that's why things went to shit at Mamma's Country.

"Christ."

"Landon heard one of Snake's boys talking about some girls that they were holding and Landon thinks his sister will be with them.

"Jesus," I grunt, disgusted. "Let me talk to the guys. I'll call you so we can meet up and figure out what we're going to do." The boys and I have never made a move without each of us agreeing, and I'm not going to start doing that shit now.

"I'm in," Z says, coming to my side.

"Me too," Mic chimes in.

"I'm down," Harlen mutters.

"I was getting bored anyways." Everret shrugs, walking up to the group.

"Looks like we're in," I sigh. "We'll meet tonight and go over the details.

"Until tonight," Jax says, heading out.

"We're going to need to get some weapons," Z says.

“I know a place,” Harlen tells us. “If I head out now, I should still be able to make the connect.”

“Mic, you go with Everret. Harlen, you find out everything you can about this situation.”

“On it,” Mic says, walking away, followed by Everret and Harlen.

“We’re going to need someone to watch the girls when we can’t,” Z states, and I run a hand over my head then look at him.

“Jax and the boys will help.”

“Would they kill to protect them? Die to protect them?” he asks, and I think about Jax, Talon and Sage and I know they would. “They would do whatever is necessary,” I assure him.

“I wasn’t going to tell anyone, not yet, ’cause it’s so early, but Kayan’s pregnant,” he confides, and all I can do is stare at him. “We weren’t planning on this happening. Hell, I wasn’t even planning on her.” He scrubs his hand down his face, and when his eyes meet mine, I notice for the first time in years that he looks happy.

“Jesus, you move fast,” I mutter, smiling.

“When she told me she was pregnant, I thought I was going to fucking pass out. I have never been so scared in my life.” He shakes his head and looks out the bay door then back at me. “I never put much thought into the future until her,” he says, and I get that. Even when I was married, I didn’t think about the future or having children. I didn’t think about anything but my next mission. Seeing July changed all of that. I want tomorrow and seventy years from now with her.

“I’m happy for you, brother.” I pull him in for a one-arm hug then lean back just enough to see his face and wrap my hand around the side of his neck, smiling. “You ever think two years ago this would have happened?”

“Fuck no.” He shakes his head and I let him go.

“Me, neither.” I didn’t expect to find a woman who fits me perfectly, a woman who makes me want to slide a ring on her finger just so I can show everyone she's mine, a woman who brings out every possessive and protective instinct I didn't even know I had. But that's what I found the day I met July Mayson. "You okay?" I ask Z, who suddenly looks worried.

"Never been in love. You know my family's fucked up," he says, and I nod. "I don't even know what love feels like."

Fuck…

"I worry I won't do her justice," he admits, rubbing his chest.

"That's love, brother. Knowing you're not good enough, but keeping her anyways—that's love."

"That's fucked up."

I laugh and agree, "Yep."

Chapter 11

"HEY, YOU," I greet, seeing Wes standing in the doorway to the bedroom.

His arms cross over his chest and his eyes drop to my breasts as I straighten the straps of my bra.

"You're so fucking beautiful," he says as he pushes away from the door.

"I thought we were leaving soon," I tell him, reading the look in his eyes. He doesn't say anything, just walks me backward until the backs of my knees hit the bed and I'm falling, landing with him on top of me.

"You smell good." His tongue licks up the column of my throat.

"Yeah?" I question, wrapping my arms around his neck and my leg around his hip.

His mouth lands on mine, and his tongue slides across my bottom lip as I open up for him, tilting my head to the side. The moment his taste floods my mouth, I moan and let my hands travel down his back then up his shirt, feeling his hot skin under my palms. I pull his shirt up until he's forced to release my mouth, and he sits back, pulling his shirt off over his head then comes back to me. His hand slips behind my back, and the bra I had just put on is quickly unhooked. He slips it off first one arm then the other before pulling it away from my chest, returning his mouth to mine as his hand runs up my side, stopping at the underside of my breast.

"Wes," I mewl, and his thumb sweeps over my nipple. That one swipe has my core tightening and wetness flooding between my legs.

There is nothing I want more than him inside me, but every time we get close to going there, he pulls away, and that thought has my nails scratching down his back and my head digging into the pillow as his mouth travels down my jaw and neck.

I tilt my head down to look at him as he shifts, palming my breast in one large hand then licking over my nipple before kissing down between my breasts, down my stomach, teasing around my belly button.

"Lift your ass, babe," he commands as he unsnaps my jeans. I lift my hips off the bed as he pulls them over my ass and down my legs. My hands go to the bed near my hips as I begin to pant. The thought of his mouth on me has my body lighting up in anticipation. "You're swollen and wet, baby," he breathes over my core, using his thumbs to spread me open.

I tilt my head down, and the moment our eyes meet, he licks up my center. My head falls back onto the bed, my eyes squeeze closed, and I lift myself higher then run a hand over his head. "I want to touch you," I hiss as his tongue licks back and forth over my clit, causing an ache to fill my lower belly.

He grunts and my hips stir as his fingers play just outside my entrance, torturing me.

"Wes, please stop," I cry, needing more than he's giving me, but instead of filling me with his fingers like I want, his hands go to my thighs and he holds me open, pulling my clit into his mouth. My head presses harder into the bed and my legs lift me higher to his mouth then slam closed around his ears as that ache in my lower stomach explodes.

"Wes!" I scream as my head thrashes against the pillow.

"Jesus," he growls, climbing up between my legs, taking my mouth in a deep kiss that makes that unfulfilled throbbing below burn. His fingers run between my legs again, but I can't take anymore. I roll him to his back, sit up with my hands on his chest, and look down at him before lowering my head and kissing him, pressing my tongue into his mouth then moaning as his hands wrap around my breasts, his fingers pulling on my nipples.

"You're soaking my stomach, baby," he says, and I lean back then scoot down his body enough to pull him free of his boots, jeans, and boxers. The moment my hand wraps around his width, my core tightens and his hips buck up. Blinded by want, I adjust, straddle him, and impale myself.

My breath hisses out, my head flies back, and my hands scratch down his chest and abs as he fills and stretches me.

"Fuck," I hear him grunt, and my head lowers, our eyes connect, and my body stills. I watch him swallow, the look in his eyes unlike anything I have ever seen. One of his hands goes to my ass, the other splaying over my lower stomach, his thumb pressing down on my clit as he starts rocking me back and forth.

"I'm never going to get anything done. All I'm going to think about is this pussy, how hot it is." He circles my clit. "How wet it is." His hand on my ass comes down hard, the pain and heat making me whimper. "How tight it is." He rocks me harder while lifting his hips up. I feel every single inch of him, all of them hitting the places deep inside me that make it hard to even think.

"Wes," I moan, lifting my hands to my breasts and pulling my nipples. My head falls back as I drop myself down, meeting each of his upward thrusts, that unfulfilled ache full and overflowing, expanding through my body.

"Fuck, baby, you're squeezing me so fucking hard," he growls, thrusting faster, each upward assault causing my breath to pause. Then, it happens. I scream out, stars light behind my eyes, and my body implodes.

He flips me to my back, lowers his mouth over mine, and kisses me as his hips pound into me. My legs wrap around his hips and my hands hold onto his shoulders as his mouth leaves mine. He nips and kisses down my neck until he reaches my breast, where he pulls my nipple into his mouth and bites down, causing another orgasm to light through my body.

"I want one more," he says, and my head rocks back and forth against the pillow. "Yes," he growls as his hand slides between us and his mouth latches onto my other nipple, pulling it into his mouth. He bites down hard as he thrusts twice more then stills, pressing deep inside me as I feel him become even larger. My arms and legs wrap tighter around him as his forehead drops to my shoulder. Our heartbeats beat rapidly against each other as we both fight for breath.

"I knew the moment I got into you I was screwed. Fuck, I was right," he breathes against my sweat-soaked skin. My body stills, and he lifts his head and looks down at me. "Never had anything sweeter than your pussy, baby." I smile and feel him jump deep inside me. "You have my dick thinking it's sixteen again." He kisses me before pulling out. "I know you're on birth control, and I know I'm clean. You good with us not using something every time I slide inside you?"

I can only nod. He felt so amazing I can't imagine having something separating us. "I want to take you again, but we're going to need a shower and food." I lick my lips as my eyes travel from his to his cock that is at half-mast, then my eyes fly up to meet his when he starts to laugh, making me frown. "Cat got your tongue, babe?" he asks, and I sit up, ducking my head and blushing. My body is still on sensory overload right now. I can barely keep my thoughts straight, let alone talk right now.

"That's one way to keep you quiet," he mutters, and I take a pillow and throw it at him. He ducks as it flies over his head then prowls towards the bed. He picks me up under my arms, my legs wrap around his waist, and his mouth steals my breath as he leads me to the bathroom, where he takes me up against the shower wall before carrying me back to bed, where we spend the rest of the night. Our plans of meeting up with his friends forgotten.

"BABE, WHAT THE fuck are you doing?" Wes asks, looking at me under the table.

"I dropped something," I lie, feeling around on the floor like I really did drop something, but then regret it instantly when my hand runs over a piece of chewed-up gum. *Eeewww!* I wipe my hand on my jeans, cringing at the thought of what I just touched.

"Get your ass up here," he growls, and my heart, which was already beating hard, begins to beat erratically at the idea of my Uncle Nico who had walked into the clubhouse moments before seeing me once I get out from under the table that I hid under.

Wes' eyes narrow and I reluctantly get out from my hiding space, and he wraps his arm around my shoulders and places a kiss on my hairline that has me closing my eyes, only to open them and come face-to-face with my uncle.

"July?"

"Hi." I smile and give him a little wave while pleading with my eyes for him to not say anything.

"What the fuck are you doing here?" he asks, looking between Wes and me.

So much for wishful thinking.

"You may want to watch how you're talking to my woman," Wes growls, making me cringe once again.

"Your woman?" Uncle Nico says, and I see something flash through his eyes, but I don't want to get my hopes up.

"My woman," Wes replies, and my body freezes and my lungs compress as I wait to see what's going to happen.

"Does my brother know his daughter is your woman?" Uncle Nico asks, crossing his arms over his chest, looking between the two of us, and all I want to do is dive back under the table and hide.

"I'm sure he does," Wes says, and I press my lips tighter together, because no way does my dad know about Wes.

"You sure about that?" he asks, and Wes looks from him to me, where he searches my face. I know the moment he sees what I'm trying to hide, because disappointment fills his eyes.

"I—" I start to explain, when he pulls his eyes from me, looks at Uncle Nico, and pulls his hand from behind my chair, crossing his arms over his chest.

"Is there a reason you're here?" Wes questions through gritted teeth.

"I told my nephew he needed to back off, but he and my sons are hard of hearing. Like I told them, I'm telling you. Stay out of it and let the authorities handle what's going on," my uncle says, setting his fists on his hips. His words barely penetrate over the fact that even though Wes is right next to me, it feels like he's miles away.

"You'll have no problems from me or my boys."

"Appreciate that," Uncle Nico mumbles, and I'm sure his eyes are on me, but mine are locked on Wes. I set my hand on Wes' thigh, and his muscles flex under my palm and his jaw goes hard at my touch.

"Sorry," I whisper, wishing he could understand.

His eyes come to me and I see pain flash in their green depths before he stands. "I'm heading out. Did you need anything else?" he asks my uncle, and my chest compresses under the pressure as a completely consuming pain slices through my body.

"Nah, we're good."

"Mic," Wes calls, and Mic, who has been watching everything play out, looks from me to Wes.

"What's up?"

"Make sure July gets home okay."

"Got it," Mic says, nodding his head.

"What?" I wheeze out, still stuck in place. This cannot be happening. I look at my uncle, who is watching me, looking concerned, and then his eyes go to Wes and so do mine, but all I'm able to catch is his back as he walks out the door.

"July," Uncle Nico calls, but I shake my head and place my hand to my throat as I attempt to fight for a breath. "I'll take my niece home," he says gently, but before he can reach me, I stand and run towards the door Wes just left out. I slam through, causing the large metal door to bang loudly against the brick exterior. The moment the cool outside air hits my face, I see Wes straddle his bike. He stops, looks over his shoulder, and then turns back around, and the loud roar of his bike fills the air.

"I know you don't believe me, but I'm sorry. I just couldn't tell him. No matter how many times I tried, I couldn't do it."

I see him shake his head and his boots leave the gravel as he takes off. "Oh, God," I whimper as pain explodes through my chest and I fall to my knees on the gravel.

"July," Uncle Nico says, picking me up like he used to when I was a little girl. I hold onto him as tears stream down my cheeks.

"I was so stupid," I whisper.

"Love makes us stupid," he says gently.

"I'm so in love with him."

"I see that, beautiful."

"He hates me."

"I promise you he doesn't." He sets me in his truck.

I inhale a few deep breaths then shake out my hands, trying to get myself under control enough that I can figure out what my next move needs to be. "I'll drive myself home," I tell Uncle Nico while hopping down from his truck.

"I don't think that's a good Idea."

"I'm not crying right now, and my house is five minutes away. I'll be fine."

His eyes search my face for a moment and he shakes his head. I know he doesn't want to let me go, but he knows he doesn't have a choice. "I'll follow you."

"Sure," I agree, pulling my keys from my pocket and getting into my Jeep. I turn down the music so I can focus on driving. It takes only a few minutes to get home, and I wave Uncle Nico off then look at my house. The windows are dark, and I know when I get inside I will be greeted by emptiness, and that thought brings a fresh wave of tears to my eyes.

I let out a ragged breath, pick up my cell phone out of my cup holder, and dial.

"Dad," I sob like an idiot when he answers the phone.

"July?" he asks, and I rest my forehead on the steering wheel of my car and will myself to calm down enough to talk.

"Dad, I need to tell you something."

"If you tell me you're pregnant, I'm killing someone."

"I'm in love," I cry then sniffle, covering my face. "Dad?" I pull the phone from my ear and look at the screen when the phone stays silent.

"I'm here," he says softly, and I hear shuffling. "Why are you crying?"

"Oh God, Dad. I'm so dumb…so, so dumb."

"You are not dumb. Now tell me what's wrong."

"I was supposed to tell you about Wes, but I never did, and tonight, Uncle Nico came to the compound, and it came out that you don't know who he is. He told someone to make sure I got home and took off. I don't want to hurt him. I love him, Dad…like really, really love him." I cry harder, my breath hiccupping with each gulp of air.

"What do you mean 'compound'?" he asks.

"Bike compound," I explain then shake my head. "That doesn't matter, Dad. Are you even listening to me?"

"Bike compound?" he asks, and I can hear the frown in his voice.

"A place bikers hang out, Dad. Focus."

"I hope you mean bicyclist, and not an MC."

"Dad!" I yell, becoming more and more frustrated.

"Fuck," he clips, then I hear more shuffling. "I'm on my way."

"What?" I freeze.

"I'll meet you at your house in twenty minutes max."

"Dad?"

"See you soon," he says and hangs up.

I pull the phone from my ear and look at it for a long moment while wondering just how stupid I am. "Oh, shit!" I scream, getting out of the car and coming face-to-face with Mic, who's standing with his arms crossed over his chest.

"Was gonna knock on your window, but you were on the phone."

"I was talking to my dad," I tell him, drying my eyes.

"I heard." He puts his arm around my shoulders and leads me up to my house.

"Have you talked to Wes?" I ask him, and he shakes his head, making a fresh wave of tears fill my eyes. I shake my head and open my front door, crying harder when Capone begins to jump around at my feet.

"He'll be back; just give him a chance to cool down," Mic says, and I nod. I know he's right, but I hate the idea of him somewhere pissed off at me. Not that he doesn't have a right to be pissed. I have continuously changed the subject or made excuses for why he and my dad haven't met, and because of that, I hurt him. I just hope that when Wes does come home, he will be willing to let me plead my case.

"You can go back to the compound. My dad will be here in just a few minutes," I tell Mic while going to my kitchen and grabbing the roll of paper towels off the counter.

"I'll just wait until he gets here, if that's okay?" he asks as I take a seat on the couch, wiping my face. Then I start to think about the last week and the fact I haven't been alone at all. I pull the paper towel away from my face and look at Mic.

"What's going on?"

"Just doing a favor for my brother."

"No," I shake my head, "I haven't had a moment's break over the last week. If Wes isn't with me, one of you guys is. Why is that?"

"Just being cautious. You know Wes is protective of you," he states. I know he's lying, but he pulls his eyes from me, looking at the front door when a car door slams outside, so I know that's the end of the conversation.

"It's my dad," I say when a knock sounds on the door that causes Capone to start barking. Mic nods and goes to the entrance with me. I glare and he just shrugs.

"Hey, Dad." I open the door and tears pool in my eyes as he pulls me in for a hug.

"This him?" he asks, lifting his chin at Mic.

"No, this is Mic. Mic, this is my dad, Asher."

"Nice to meet you, sir," Mic says before his eyes come to me and go soft. "I'm gonna step outside." He chucks me under my chin before he walks out the door.

"So that's not him?"

"No, he's Wes' friend." I sigh, going to the couch and sitting down.

"Why's he here?" he asks, and I hate that I have to lie to him, but there is no way I can tell him what is going on, even if I don't know all the details.

"Wes is protective," I say, hoping he will accept that explanation.

"Huh…" my dad grunts, taking a seat. The moment his body folds into my couch, he takes my hand in his, and then his eyes go soft as he searches my face for a long time before he speaks. "So, you're really in love?" he questions quietly in the same tone he used to talk to me in when I was little, when he would find me crying or upset.

"Yeah." I nod and swallow through the lump that has formed in my throat then wipe my eyes with the paper towel I still have in my hand.

"Why didn't you tell me?" he asks, squeezing my hand.

Sheesh! Why didn't I tell him about Wes? There are so many reasons, but now I feel like none of them make sense. None of them were good enough reasons for hurting Wes.

"I don't know." I cover my face with my hands. "Wes is like no one I have been with before; even Jax said that." I close my eyes, trying to get my thoughts in order before speaking again. "I want you to like him," I say when I open my eyes. "I love you, and I want you to like him, because I love him."

"You're my baby girl." He smiles and his hand comes up to hold my cheek. "From the moment your mom told me she was pregnant with you, my world changed, and you became one of the most important things in my life. When you took your first breath, I knew I would do everything within my power to make sure that each breath you took was easy. You will always be my baby girl, and I can't promise you I will like any man you're with."

He pulls me forward and kisses my forehead. "Your grandfather gave me a chance with your mom, and I swore that when my girls told me they were in love I would find a way to make peace with that, so they would never have to choose between me and the man they wanted to share their lives with," he confesses, and I cry harder, sobbing into his chest as he wraps his arms around me.

"I love you, Dad," I hiccup.

"Love you too, more than anything in this world."

"What should I do about Wes?" I ask, pulling away and wiping my face.

"Just talk to him. If he's a man worthy of you, he'll understand your reasoning."

"What if he doesn't?" I whisper my biggest fear.

"Then he doesn't deserve you," he states, standing. I follow him up and walk him to the door. He gives me a hug, and a kiss on the forehead, before stepping out onto the front porch. "Call me tomorrow," he orders, walking to his Jeep, passing Mic on the way and shaking his hand. I give him a small wave as he backs out of my driveway then look at Mic, who is standing near his bike, talking on his phone.

"Is that him?" I ask hopefully.

"No, babe, go back inside," he tells me, and I frown but step back into my house and shut the door.

The moment the door closes, I realize how quiet it is. Since the moment I met Wes, there has been a loudness in my life that wasn't there before. Not the kind of noise that is annoying or that you want to get away from, but the kind of noise that lets you know you're alive and that the life you're living is full. I didn't know my life was missing anything until Wes…until now. Closing my eyes, I take a few deep breaths then pick up the remote and turn on the TV, hoping the sound will help chase away the feeling that has settled in my gut since I watched Wes ride away.

"You did this to yourself," I whisper, going to the kitchen and getting a bottle of water before walking to my room and changing into a pair of sweats and a t-shirt. Afterwards, I head out to the living room to watch some TV.

"YOU'RE HOME," I murmur as I'm lifted off the couch and tucked close to Wes' front as he carries me to my room.

"Sleep," he mutters, laying me down then pulling the covers over me. I chew on my bottom lip, watching him, trying to gauge where his head's at.

His back is to me, and he lifts his shirt off over his head and drops it to the floor, and then the sound of his belt coming off fills the silence, making that coiled ball of energy in my stomach unravel slightly with the knowledge that he's not leaving.

"I'm sorry." I reach out to him and run my fingers down his back as he takes a seat on the side of the bed. The moment I touch him, his muscles contract and he looks over his shoulder at me.

"We'll talk about it in the morning."

"I told my dad. He was here earlier." I close my eyes, hating the distance I feel between us. "I know you will probably think it's idiotic, but the idea of you and my dad not getting along is one of the worst things I can imagine." I open my eyes back up, seeing he's still watching me. "I love my dad; he's my best friend, but since the moment I met you, that has changed. You have become important in a way that I know if I had to choose between the two of you, I wouldn't be able to without it ripping me apart."

"You think I would make you choose between us?" he growls, and his brows shoot together.

Okay, said out loud like that makes it sound stupid.

"I...I don't think you would," I shake my head. "I don't think he would either, but how could I choose between two men I love?"

"Love?"

"What?" I ask, confused.

"You said you couldn't choose between the two men you love." He crawls over me, pressing me into the bed with his weight, his face inches from mine. "You love me?" he asks softly, and I shake my head and close my eyes. "July, open your eyes and look at me."

I shake my head again and his hands go to each side of my face. "Baby, open your eyes and look at me." The tone of his voice has my eyes opening to look at him. "I love you too," he says, and my eyes slide closed and I let his words wash over me before opening them again. "Loving you means I want what's best for you and that I want you to be happy. You think I don't know what your family means to you?" He pushes my hair away from my face. "You don't think I see the way your face lights up when you talk about your dad, or the love you have for him?" He kisses my lips then my chin. "I see it baby, and regardless if we get along, I would never make you choose between us."

"I can't believe you love me."

"That's all you got from that speech?" he asks, smiling.

"Uh basically…"

"I have no idea what I'm going to do with your crazy ass," he mutters, looking over my head.

"Hey," I smack his side, "you telling me you love me is kinda a big deal."

"No more keeping shit from me," he demands as his face goes serious.

"Promise," I agree.

"Next time, I'm spanking your ass."

My body freezes under him, and the space between my legs tingles from the thought of him spanking me.

"Interesting." He smiles, and I pull my bottom lip into my mouth before I blurt out something completely inappropriate.

"Ruined," he says, biting my chin, making me gasp as he pulls one of my legs around his hip.

"What are you doing?" I moan as he runs his hand down my stomach into my sweats.

"Make-up sex, baby," he whispers against my mouth as he slides two fingers inside me.

Chapter 12

"OH, MY GOD. I'm coming!" I yell, rolling over to get out of bed when the doorbell rings for the tenth time in less than a minute.

"I'll get it, baby," Wes says, tugging me back down into bed and kissing the side of my head before getting up. I turn my head and watch as he pulls on his jeans, leaving the room without a shirt. Wondering who it is, I get up and follow him out of the room then stop in the hall, looking at his back as he opens the door. His body freezes, all of the muscles in his back going taught as he says something to whoever is at the door.

I pad to where he is then duck under his arm, coming face to face with my parents. *Oh, crap!*

"Morning, honey." My mom smiles.

I blink, looking at my mom then at my dad. "What are you guys doing here?"

"Figured if he was here, that would mean he's who I thought he was. If he didn't come back here last night, I knew you would need some of your mom's famous French toast to get you over him," my dad says as Wes wraps his arm around my waist, pulling me out of the way.

"Uhh..." I mumble as my dad tugs my mom into the house, shutting the door.

"You wanna put a shirt on?" my dad queries, looking at Wes. Then his eyes drop to my legs and he frowns. "And you some pants?"

"Asher Mayson!" my mom snaps, hitting my dad's chest.

"What?" he asks, frowning down at her.

"This is your daughter's house, not yours. You can't tell her or her guest to get dressed in her own house."

"The hell I can't," Dad growls then looks at Wes. "You think I'm gonna let him sit across from you shirtless while we eat breakfast? Fuck no."

"You're so ridiculous." Mom glares at him, crossing her arms over her chest.

"Call it what you want, baby," my dad says, glaring right back at her.

"We'll be back after we get dressed," I murmur, pulling a chuckling Wes with me to my room.

"My parents are here," I whimper, closing the door and pressing my back to the wood, closing my eyes.

"Saw that, babe," Wes says, and my eyes open and I watch him pull a clean shirt out from the dresser.

"We're going to have breakfast with my dad and mom." I tell him something he already knows as I watch him go into the bathroom. I follow behind him, watching as he pulls his toothbrush out of the holder next to mine and begins brushing his teeth. And I wonder how he's so cool about this.

"Get some pants on." His eyes meet mine in the mirror and he cups his hand under the flowing water to rinse his mouth. I look around the bathroom. The shower curtain is open, and Wes' body wash and shampoo are next to mine on the shelf. My eyes go back to him when he puts his toothbrush next to mine in the holder once again. My eyes drop to his clippers, deodorant, and man products that have taken up half the counter, and I shake my head and remind myself to get dressed.

I leave the bathroom and go to the closet. When I open it up, I notice Wes' clothes have filled up a whole side of my closet, and then my eyes drop to the ground and I see that his boots and sneakers are mixed in with mine on the floor. I grab a pair of sweats then go back to the bathroom, suddenly feeling overwhelmed.

I swallow hard, watching as he pulls his shirt on. "I…uhh…when did we move in together?"

"Babe, get dressed," he says, ignoring me, and I wonder if I'm thinking too much into it. I pull off my shirt, put on a bra and a tank top, and then slip on my sweats before brushing my teeth. When I come out of the bathroom, Wes is completely dressed and sitting on the side of the bed.

"Are you okay?" I ask, going to stand in front of him. He tugs me forward until my hips are settled between his then slides his hands up my tank, running along the skin of my sides.

"Whatever happens out there doesn't effect what we have. When your parents go home, we will still be us, and nothing will change that."

I lean in, and press a kiss to his lips.

"You ready?" I lick my lips and nod, he takes my hand, leading me out of the room towards the kitchen, where I hear my parents talking.

When we walk around the corner, I see my mom at the stove and my dad standing at her back with his arms around her. I clear my throat then tug Wes' hand when their eyes come to us.

"Dad, I would like you to meet Wes Silver. Wes, this is my dad, Asher Mayson," I introduce them.

"Nice to meet you, sir," Wes says, and my dad's eyes narrow and I hold my breath, almost afraid to watch.

"You military?" my dad asks, and Wes nods.

"Eight years in the Navy SEALs."

My dad grunts then shakes his head. "Marines," he says pointing to himself, then takes Wes' hand and gives it a firm shake. I let out a breath I didn't know I was holding and go to my mom's side to kiss her head then wrap my arm around her shoulders.

"Told you everything would be okay, honey," my mom whispers

softly, giving me a squeeze. I smile and walk to my dad's side and slip under his arm as he talks with Wes. He kisses my hairline and I hug his waist then slide from his grasp and go to Wes, wrapping my arms around him and resting my cheek on his chest. I stand there until my mom finishes making her famous breakfast of French toast, and we all move to sit around the table. "You guys should come over for dinner this weekend," my dad suggests as we walk my parents to the front door.

"Got some stuff going on this weekend," Wes says, and I look at him and frown; he hasn't said anything to me. "Should be able to work something out for next week though."

My dad nods and pats his shoulder then looks at me. "I know you guys are together, but I don't want to be a grandfather yet, so make sure you're being careful."

"Dad!" I hiss.

"No," he shakes his head then points at Wes, "If my girl tells me she's pregnant before she has a ring on her finger, we're gonna have issues. Hell, you shouldn't even be having sex."

"Dad, stop. I lost my virginity on prom night." I shake my head and his swings my way. His eyes narrow and I can see the wheels in his head turning.

When the hell will I learn to shut my big, fat mouth?

"You went to prom with Bobbie Evans. He still works at the car dealership in town," my dad growls and his jaw starts to tic.

"Um…" I look at my mom for help, but I can see that she's upset as well.

"I'm going to kill him," Dad seethes.

"I'll help you," Wes says. I look at him and narrow my eyes, and he shrugs.

"I haven't spoken to him in years," I say, tossing my arms in the air then crossing them over my chest, glaring at him.

"Keep it that way," Wes commands.

"Can you keep your caveman in your pants?" My eyes go from Wes to my dad, who is looking between Wes and me with a strange look on his face.

"Dad?" I say, and it's almost like he's frozen in place.

"Love you, honey," my mom says, cutting in and giving me a hug.

"Love you, Mom."

"Asher." My mom grabs his hand and his eyes go to her, and he shakes his head then looks at me.

"Be good," he mutters, giving me a hug and kissing my forehead. Then he looks at Wes and lifts his chin before heading towards his Jeep with his arm around my mom's shoulders.

"That wasn't so bad," I tell Wes. His arm wraps around my waist and I feel his lips on my hair as we watch my parents drive away.

"I like your parents," he says, leading me back into the house.

"They like you too." I smile then walk towards the bedroom once we're inside, but don't make it far, because the back of my shirt is grabbed and I'm tugged backward into his hard body.

"Where you going?" He wraps his arms around my waist and kisses down my neck.

"I was going to shower." I moan, tilting my head to the side.

"That sounds good." He bites my neck, lifting me and walking towards the bedroom, making me laugh.

"Where in that did you hear me invite you?" I ask as he reaches around me, turning on the shower.

"The part where you were going to be naked." He pulls my shirt off over my head and unhooks my bra, letting it drop to the floor before palming my breasts, pulling on both nipples, which makes my core tighten with want. His hands travel down my stomach and he slides my sweats down my legs, commanding, "Step out," against my neck before biting into my skin.

When his hands leave me again, I turn to look at him over my shoulder and watch as his hands go behind his back as he pulls his shirt off over his head, dropping it to the floor with mine. When his arms wrap around me again, I moan, feeling the denim of his jeans scrape against the skin on the back of my thighs as one of his hands slides down my stomach, the other wrapping across my breast. His foot spreads my legs farther apart and his fingers slide through my folds, making my hips buck forward. Turning my head, I pant into his neck as two fingers slide on either side of my swollen clit.

"My mouth is watering." He lets me go, making my eyes that had slid closed fly open. I turn and watch as he pulls a towel off of the shelf and sets it on the vanity. Then he pulls me by my hips and lifts me, placing me on it. "Show me your pussy, baby," he says, unbuckling his jeans. My eyes are glued to the outline of the budge the V of his hips is pointing to.

"Spread your legs, July." My eyes glide up to meet his and I swallow, slowly spreading my legs open. "Touch yourself how you want me to touch you." He pulls down his jeans and his cock bobs against his stomach, the veins pronounced, the head so red it looks painful. I bring two fingers down my stomach and pause just over my pubic bone, feeling unsure.

"Touch it, baby. Show me how you like it," he encourages while wrapping his hand around his length and pumping. I lower my fingers between my folds and rub circles around my clit then slip one finger inside of myself, taking the wetness of my arousal and sliding it up and around my clit.

"Fuck," he clips, and my eyes that had slid closed open and meet his. I swallow, keeping a slow pace, the ache in my core telling me that when I do come it's going to be huge. Like he can't stop himself, he steps towards me, circling my entrance with one finger then pulling his finger, covered in my arousal, out and swiping it across my bottom lip.

He crashes his mouth down on mine, pulling my bottom lip into his mouth and sucking hard, causing me to cry out and my fingers to move faster, circling my clit. Then he pulls his mouth from mine and drops his face between my legs, burying his tongue in my pussy taking long strokes as his fingers enter me, making me scream his name. My orgasm crashes over me suddenly; the walls of my vagina contract, pulling at his fingers as I float away, my body breaking out with cold bumps as he wipes his chin on the inside of my thigh. He stands, grabs my ankles, holding them out to the sides as he slams into me hard. My hands go behind my back to keep myself up.

"Watch," he growls, pulling out and slamming back in. "I love the way I look disappearing into you." His words make me hotter and I lower my eyes, watching him enter me in long, measured strokes. Each of his thrust hits something deep inside me that causes a sharp pain that simmers out into pleasure.

"I'm going to come," I whimper, and his mouth crashes down onto mine, causing the sound of my orgasm to slide down his throat. He pulls and wraps my legs around his hips, puts his hands under my ass, and then lifts me up, taking me into the shower, where he presses my back into the tiled wall. I use my legs wrapped around him as leverage to bring myself to orgasm again. "Fuck, baby, squeeze me," he groans, planting himself deep and dropping his forehead to my shoulder.

"I WANT TO follow Z tonight," Kayan says as I lock up the doors to the clinic.

"Follow him where?" I ask, watching as she pulls out her keys from her bag.

"I don't know," she mutters then lifts her eyes to look at me. "I feel like maybe he's cheating. He's been hiding something," she whispers, and I feel my eyebrows pull together.

"I don't think Z is cheating on you."

"Tonight, I'll find out for sure," she says, and I know there is no convincing her. When we were in college, she dated a guy that was cheating on her. The whole time, everyone knew except for her and me, or we didn't know until we went to a frat party and walked in on him while he was having sex with our other roommate Lynn.

"I'll go with you." I tell her seeing the look on her face.

"Thank you."

"I always have your back, even if I think you're crazy," I tell her.

"We're going to have to find some way to ditch our tail." She nods her head towards Harlen, who is sitting on his bike across the parking lot.

"*Fifty Shades of Grey* is coming out tonight. We will just say we're going to watch it."

"Perfect," she whispers.

"Call me and we'll make plans for the movies," I shout loud enough for Harlen to hear.

"I can't wait to see Fifty's ass!" she shouts back, and I can't help but laugh.

"SO WHAT ARE you guys doing tonight?" I ask Wes as I pull on my jeans.

His eyes lift from his cell phone and he looks at me. "We're helping Jax with something then going to ride up to Nashville and check out a club Harlen found. The boys are thinking about buying it."

"What kind of club?" I ask, pulling my hoodie out from the closet.

He pauses like he's not going to say, and I raise a brow with my hoodie paused over my head. "Strip club."

I nod once then pull the sweatshirt on. "You should talk to my uncle and mom. They've been running Teasers, now that my grandpa retired."

His head goes back like I hit him and his brows pull together. "Your uncle and mom run Teasers?"

"Yeah."

"What the fuck?"

I smile and pull my black Converse out of the closet. "Babe, your mouth." I laugh, tapping his chin as I sit down next to him on the bed.

"How did I not know that?" He kisses my neck.

"I guess it never came up, but I'm sure my mom and uncle would be happy to talk to you and the guys."

"I'll keep that in mind. So you guys are going to the movies?"

"Yes, and we don't need a bodyguard."

"You don't have a bodyguard." He shakes his head. "We're just being cautious until we know things have quieted down." I fight the urge to roll my eyes and just nod in agreement instead.

"Sage is going to be with you tonight," he tells me, standing.

"Sage is helping you out now?" I ask, wondering how my Uncle Nico's son got put up to this.

"No, Harlen heard you guys were watching some chick flick, so everyone drew straws."

"It's *Fifty Shades of Grey,* not a chick flick, and you may think Sage's the unlucky one, but I hear there's a lot of boobs," I inform him.

"I don't need to watch a movie with boobs, baby. I have the best tits I've seen in my life at my disposal twenty-four hours a day."

"Awww, you say the sweetest things." I laugh, tying my shoes.

He pulls me up off the bed, slapping my ass once before pushing me towards the door, muttering, "Smartass," as the bell goes off.

"Hey, man," he greets Sage when he opens the front door.

"What's good?" my cousin replies, stepping into the house, doing that guy handshake thing with Wes before pulling me into a hug and lifting me up off my feet.

My cousin Sage is mixed. His dad is black and his mom is white. Uncle Nico and Aunt Sophie adopted him and his twin sister when they were three. He's handsome in a way that my aunt asked Uncle Nico to buy her a gun to keep the girls away when he turned sixteen. He's really tall at almost six, six, and his skin is a few shades darker than mine is in the summer. His hair is curly and low to his head, and his eyes are a light hazel that stands out against his complexion.

Even though he's not my aunt and uncle's biological kid, you can see them in him. He's sweet and soft-spoken like Aunt Sophie, yet a badass to the core like Uncle Nico, which is why he works with Jax.

As soon as my feet touch the ground, Wes pulls me to him. "Be good," he says against my mouth. I don't say anything; after all, it's only a lie if you acknowledge it, and if Wes never finds out what I'm doing, he will have no reason to be mad.

"All right, let's go," Sage says, holding the door open. I grab my bag from the table and wave goodbye to Wes as he pulls away from the house on his bike.

"Kayan is meeting us at the theater. Z said he would follow her there and wait for us," I tell Sage as we get into his truck.

"Cool," he mutters, getting behind the wheel.

"I wish Nalia was here," I say, and Sage's eyes come to me for a moment before going back to the road.

"She'll be home soon," he says, but I can also hear the doubt in his words. When Sage and Nalia turned eighteen, they were able to talk to their biological parents. Sage wanted nothing to do with them, but Nalia got close with their mom and moved to Colorado to be nearer to her. I understand her reasoning, but I know it's hard on my aunt and uncle and her brother. I just pray she finds whatever it is she's looking for.

"Well, I'm happy she'll be home for Christmas."

"Me too. I just hope she'll decide to stay home after that," he says.

"Maybe." I shrug. I know Aunt Sophie has been torn up about her being gone. She feels like she did something wrong, but I also know that sometimes you have to do stuff for yourself, even if it's hard on the people you love.

When we pull into the parking lot of the movie theater, I see Z and Kayan standing near his bike. I look around for her car and sigh in relief when I see it parked over on the side of the building.

"Hey, Z, are you sure you don't want to watch the movie with us?" I ask, hopping out of Sage's truck and walking toward Z's bike.

"Thanks, but no, thanks." He smiles then turns and kisses Kayan, then whispers something to her before letting her go mussing my hair and getting on his bike starting it up and pulling out of the parking lot.

"Ready?" Kayan asks, wrapping my arm around hers and heading into the theater, with Sage following close behind us.

"Ready." I mummer wondering if there is a way that I can talk her out of this then I look over my shoulder at my cousin and ask "Are you sure you don't want to come in?"

"Nah, I'll wait here," he says, and we pay for our tickets and stop to get popcorn and candy, giving Sage a wave before heading into the movie.

"What's the plan?" Kayan asks as we head into the theater.

"This is your idea." I remind her.

"Yeah but you're the planner." She smiles and I roll my eyes and lead her towards the front of the theater, where I push through the door marked *Exit*. The moment we clear the door, I head towards the parking lot.

"What are you doing?" She shrieks as I start to toss the food we got into the garbage that is on the corner of the building. "You cannot throw that out," she pulls the popcorn from my hand, causing half of it to land on the ground, "or this." She hands me the keys to her car and takes the soda from me.

"Are you good now?" I ask. She shrugs shoving a hand full of popcorn into her mouth after making it to her car. I make sure Sage isn't anywhere around, start up the car and head out of the parking lot towards the compound.

"So much for this plan," Kayan says through a mouthful of popcorn as we pull up in front of the compound fifteen minutes later.

"Yeah," I agree then shove her head down and duck as well when I see a bike pull up. The moment the roar of pipes dies, I lift my head and watch as Harlen swings off his bike and heads inside, coming back a few minutes later carrying an envelope.

"We need to follow him. He'll be with Z." She says from her still bent position then takes a drink of her soda.

I look at her for a long moment then shake my head and take off after him following him for about ten minutes down some back roads. When he pulls into a parking lot, I park a block away and watch as he rides right to where the rest of the guys are waiting including my cousin Jax. When Harlen gets off his bike, he says something to Wes then hands him the envelope. Even from this distance, I see Wes' jaw go tight and I wonder why he's pissed. Then he puts his phone to his ear, and I watch his mouth work and wonder what he's saying.

"I wonder what they're talking about."

"I don't know," I say, watching Wes go to Z and say something. When Z's body goes tight, a ball of anxiety forms in my chest.

"We're busted," Kayan whispers. I look at her, put the car in drive, and take off. The moment I hit the road, the sound of pipes fills the air. My hands start to sweat and my heart starts to pound. "Oh, my God. Z is going to kill me."

"Maybe we can get back to the theater," I say, not believing it for a second.

"Yeah, maybe," she agrees, and I push down on the gas and take every back road I can until I reach the parking lot of the theater. The moment I turn off the car, we get out and rush toward the door of the theater we left out of, then stop dead when we come face-to-face with a very pissed-off Sage.

"Hey, what are you doing out here?" I ask, and his eyes turn even angrier.

"Are you fucking kidding me?"

"What? I came out to smoke. You know…the scenes were so hot I needed a cigarette," I say and hear someone chuckle. I turn to look over my shoulder as Mic, Wes, Z, and Jax walk up to where we're standing.

"This shit's not funny," Wes growls, looking at Mic, who holds up a hand in front of him.

When Wes' eyes come back to me, they do one sweep then he looks at Sage.

"You mind taking the girls home? We'll be there in an hour."

"No problem, man," Sage says, and Wes lifts his chin then his eyes drop to me.

"Do not fucking leave the house." He points at me, and my heart skids in my chest from the amount of anger I see on his face.

"Give me your keys," Z tells Kayan. She grabs my hand and I turn to look at her, seeing tears in her eyes. I hand over the keys and watch as Z storms off towards the parking lot.

"We—"

"Do not fucking talk," Wes says, and my mouth slams shut. "I'll deal with your ass when I get home." Okay, I knew he was mad and had a reason to be, but this was a little too much. My hand not holding my friend's balls into a fist at my side. It takes everything in me not to flip out.

"Let's go." Sage tugs my elbow and leads us away from the guys and towards his truck.

"Sorry about leaving," I mumble, looking out the window, trying to catch a glimpse of the Wes.

"You know we wouldn't be watching you guys if there wasn't some fucked-up shit going on," Sage says, and I can hear the anger and concern in his voice. The moment we arrive at my house, Sage shuts down the truck and follows us inside. "Both of you, sit here," he growls, pointing at the couch when I start to lead a still crying Kayan back to the bathroom.

"First, we're not going to leave again, and second, I'm older than you and this is my house. Now, if you don't mind, I'm going to take my friend back to the bathroom so she can splash some cold water on her face!" I reply and tug Kayan with me to the hall bathroom.

"Sit here," I tell her, closing the lid on the toilet so she can take a seat, and then I gab a washcloth and run it under cold water before handing it to her.

"Thanks," she murmurs, pressing it to her face.

"He's not cheating," I remind her, and she nods but doesn't say anything, making me feel worse than I already do. When we go back out to the living room, Sage is watching television. His eyes come to us and go soft.

"The guys are on their way back."

"Great," I mumble as the ball of stress in my stomach expands. When the sound of pipes rumbles the house, I close my eyes, trying to get myself under control. Having both Wes and me mad isn't going to fix anything.

The front door flies open, making me jump. I turn my head, expecting it to be Wes storming into the house, so I'm surprised when it's Z. "How the fuck do you think it's okay to take a pregnant woman on one of your crazy-ass adventures?" he roars at me, and I sit back on the couch, surprised by his words. I have no idea what he's talking about. I look at my friend, the girl I have been best friends with since our first day of kindergarten, and my mouth drops open when I see the truth in her eyes.

"You're pregnant?" I whisper in shock. "How did that happen? I mean…when, shit…I mean, why didn't you tell me?" I shake my head, completely flabbergasted.

"I don't know. I'm sorry; you know I love you," she says then looks up at Z. "And you had no right to tell her, you big, fat jerk. I'm pregnant, not incapable of making my own fucking decisions." She stands up and pushes past Z, whose glare has softened. "Fuck!" she screams when she gets to the front door, and I stand when I see her chest heaving up and down. "You have my keys. Either give them to me, or take me the fuck home."

I look from her to Z and blink, because I have never seen my friend like this, and Z doesn't even look a little bit fazed by her outburst.

"I'm gonna head out," Sage says, and I nod absently, my eyes still on my best friend.

"Are you coming, or am I walking?" She raises a brow, and I look at Z and hear him mumble something about his kitten having claws before he moves to the door. "I'll call you tomorrow," she says, looking at me before disappearing through the door.

I flop down on the couch and close my eyes, wondering what the hell just happened. Suddenly, the door slams so hard that the walls shake and I jump, my eyes flying open as I look towards the entryway and my eyes lock with Wes' angry ones.

"You wanna tell me what the fuck you were thinking tonight?" Wes roars. My brain is screaming to say, *'Not really,'* but judging by the look in his eyes, I don't think he would find me funny. "Jesus!" His fist clenches then he picks up an empty glass from the side table and pulls his hand back, throwing it full force at the wall across the room, causing glass to explode everywhere. My pulse speeds up and I press back into the couch. "This is not some fucking game. People's lives are on the line," he thunders, coming to stand in front of me.

He pulls out his phone, and I wonder what he's doing until he shoves the phone into my face and an image of a woman not much older than me is on his screen. She's tied up. Her nose is bleeding, one eye is swollen shut and black and blue, and her hair looks like it hasn't been washed in a few days. Her clothes are dirty, and there are bruises on her arms in the shape of handprints.

"This is Mellissa Hornel. She's twenty-five and a college graduate. She went missing three weeks ago. She had a date with a guy she met online. She never made it home." He flips to another picture, this girl younger than the pervious one. Her blonde hair is tied back in a ponytail, her lip is swollen, and you can tell they tried to use makeup to cover the bruise under her eye.

"This is Stacy, Landon's sister the kid that dropped the dogs to you. Tonight, I was going to go help him by getting her away from the slimeballs that have been keeping her and Mellissa" he says, and my eyes fly up to meet his and my chest starts to heave with anxiety. "Baby, I love you. I love that you're crazy, I love that you're fucking wild and untamable, but if I say or do something, it's for a reason. I—"

"We have to go get her," I say, cutting him off as tears cloud my vision. "We need to go help them." I stand up, but he pushes me back down onto the couch.

"Your uncle was able to get all the girls out before they moved them again."

"Oh, God," I sob, covering my face in relief.

"No more bullshit, baby. No more crazy antics. No more doing shit, just 'cause you feel like causing me headaches."

"No more," I agree, leaving out the part that this was all my crazy best friend's fault. The idea of those women being stuck in that situation will haunt me for a long time. I knew there were evil people in the world, but what was happening to them is sickening.

"I don't know what the fuck I'm going to do with you."

"I don't know, either," I breathe, crawling into his lap where he holds me until I stop crying.

"Go on to bed. I need to make a few calls," he orders on a squeeze.

I place a kiss on the underside of his jaw then head to the room, where I strip down quickly before getting into bed. I lay there for a long time thinking about what Wes said. The kid that was bringing me the dogs name is Landon and he had a sister, obviously the people that had her were using her as leverage over him and probably his dad. I couldn't imagine what they have been going through, what she was going through. Then I thought about the fact that Wes was helping rescue them and that brought more questions then I couldn't think any more because I fell asleep.

"WES?" I QUESTION as I'm flipped to my stomach and long fingers run over my clit.

"Up on your knees, baby." The sound of his voice causes a shiver to run down my spine as he wraps his arm around my stomach and lifts me up on my hands and knees.

"Please," I beg, grabbing onto the sheets in front of me while pressing back into his hand.

"You'll get what I give you. Get your shirt off."

I whimper in distress and feel myself soaking his hand as his fingers bring me closer to the edge while I struggle with my sleep shirt until I'm able to slide it off over my head.

"The idea of someone taking this from me makes me fucking furious," he growls, removing his fingers, lining up his cock, and then slamming deep while simultaneously smacking one cheek of my ass hard. My head lowers to the bed and I whimper, feeling myself tightening around him.

"I would kill for you, fucking die for you," he snarls, smacking the other cheek even harder than the first one, and a ball starts to coil in my lower stomach. "You belong to me. You are not allowed to risk what is mine." He pulls me up with an arm under my breasts. "Whose pussy is this?" he asks while holding his hips still, impaling me on his cock.

My breath hitches as my body tries to adjust to his length and girth.

"Who does this body..." His hands slide up my sides, over my stomach, then up, cupping my breasts where he tugs hard on my nipples, making my back arch and causing him to slide impossibly deeper, "...belong to?"

"Please."

"I'll give you what you want, but tell me who you belong to."

"You," I hiss.

"Yeah, baby, this body and this pussy are mine, and if you jeopardize my goods, you will be punished." He pushes me back down in front of him and smacks my ass hard, over and over, in rapid succession, each smack bringing me closer to orgasm. Then he pulls me back up and I turn my head just in time for his tongue to slide into my mouth as his hand slides down my stomach and over my clit, where he circles.

"I'm going to come," I say on a hitched breath.

"Give it to me, baby." He kisses down my neck, working slowly in and out of me as his hands slide over my body, like he's memorizing each exposed inch of flesh.

"Jesus, I love you," he says like he's talking to himself. "Come for me," he demands, rotating his hips on each upward thrust. His hands wrap around my hips and I slide my fingers between my legs, first feeling our connection then rolling one over my clit in fast circles.

My orgasm hits quickly; the top half of my body drops to the bed, Wes being the only thing keeping me up as he takes three more strokes before planting himself deep. My breath pauses and the walls of my core tighten around him. He stays rooted like that for long moments until he rolls us to the side, him still deep inside me.

Moving the hair off my neck, he kisses the skin behind my ear and wraps his arms tighter around me. There is no place I would rather be than with him just like this, sweaty and breathing hard from amazing sex while being safe in his arms.

"Love you, baby." He slides out of me rolls me to my back, kisses down my stomach, and then climbs out of bed. I listen absently as the water comes on in the bathroom. Seconds later, he comes back, sliding a warm cloth between my legs, then dries me off before coming to lay half-on me again. His thigh lays over both of mine, his arm is under my breasts, and his lips rest close to my ear, where I listen to his breath even out, and I let my body do the same, so I can follow him off to sleep.

Chapter 13

I PULL OFF my shirt and put my phone back to my ear. Then I reach behind my back with one hand and unhook my bra.

"Babe," Wes answers on the second ring, and a smile forms on my lips.

"Hey," I mutter, letting the sound of his voice wash over me.

"You good?"

"Um, yeah, my sisters and cousins want to go out tonight," I tell him, holding the phone to my ear as I start up the shower.

"Where are you going?"

"We'll probably get dinner then go have a drink at Daniel's bar," I tell him, slipping off my panties.

Yesterday was Thanksgiving, and Wes and I celebrated with his mom in the afternoon and my family that evening. I was so happy to see my family all welcome Wes with open arms. My mom and aunts adored him, or they just liked looking at him—I couldn't quite figure out that one yet—and my uncles all seemed to respect him, especially after the way Uncle Nico spoke about him in regards to what Wes and the guys did to help him get those girls out of the situation they were in. I never expected them to all get along, but I was very happy they did.

"Call me when you need to be picked up," he says, bringing me back into the conversation.

"I don't need you to pick me up. I don't plan on drinking that much."

"I love when you drink, baby," he says. I can hear the smile in his voice and I roll my eyes. "Call when you need to be picked up," he repeats more firmly than the previous time.

"Fine." I sigh, knowing there's no point in arguing with him. "Love you."

"Love you too, baby," he says, and I click the phone off, set it on the counter, and get into the shower. It's been a month since the night Kayan and I went to spy on Z, things have cooled down. The guys who had taken Landon's sister were arrested by Uncle Nico and are awaiting trial. I was definitely looking forward to them getting what they deserved, and hopefully that came in the form of becoming the bitch of some scary inmate in the state pen. I found out through Wes that Snake had taken Landon's sister and was using her as leverage over Ronnie the owner of Mamma's Country Landon also confided in Wes with the information about the dogfights that were being held. He said that when the guy Snake and his boys had taken over a few times a week they would hold fights but he didn't know where the dogs came from. He said that when he was forced to remove the loosing dog he would take them to me in hopes that I could save them. I hated that there were probably still dogs suffering somewhere but I was thankful that Snake no longer had a hold over Landon or his father.

Kayan also opened up about being pregnant. She was afraid I would have the same reaction her parents had. They were disappointed in her for having a baby with someone they didn't approve of, but her parents had always been part crazy, so I was glad she was finding a way to get over what they thought. She also admitted to me that she and Z had been seeing each other since their first encounter, but she wasn't sure then where their relationship was going until the night they came over for tacos. He made it clear then that he wanted to be with her and that he wasn't taking no for an answer.

She also said that half the things she said I needed to ignore, because the hormones were making her partly crazy. That, I had to agree with her on. If it weren't against the law, I would have fired her already. The other day, someone called about having their dog fixed, and she freaked out on them, questioned them on how they would feel if their balls were chopped off.

After that outburst, it took me a good hour to get the person calm enough to continue using me as their Vet, and the whole time I was talking to them, she was crying, apologizing about how she acted. I don't know if I'm going to be able to deal with her for the next few months. I feel bad for Z, but I swear every time I'm around them and she freaks out about something or another, he gets a weird smile on his face, like he thinks it's the most adorable thing he has ever seen in his life. They are both insane, and I guess a perfect match.

I finish getting washed up, get out, and wrap a towel around my head. I go out to the kitchen, grab a bottle of water before feeding both Juice and Capone, and then go back into the bathroom to blow out my hair, using a large round brush so the volume is at full capacity. Once I have my hair dry, I put large rollers into my hair with clips.

Going out with my sisters and cousins is different than going out with my normal girlfriends. Even in high school, we would all compete with each other for the most over the top look, even if we were just going to a bonfire. I think part of the reason we did it was no one else could ever really understand our fathers, and the extreme competitiveness in which they raised us.

We are all daddies' girls, and we all fought tooth and nail to get our way, some more than others. My cousin Ashlyn has had it the hardest of any of us. Uncle Cash is overly protective of her, so when we were younger and she would go out with us, it was the one time he didn't fight her on her outfit or makeup, because he, my dad, and my other uncles would get together, drink beer, and complain about us, while our moms rolled their eyes and insisted we have our time. I don't regret the way I grew up. Having the father I have has shown me how a man is supposed to treat not only his wife, but also his children.

I start my makeup with a smoky eye that causes my eye color to pop, and then add bronzer and blush that define my cheekbones. I use a lip liner to make my lips look even plumper than normal then find the perfect shade of light pink lipstick that gives me a nice, pouty mouth. Wes has never seen me this dolled up, so I have no idea what his reaction is going to be tonight when he comes to pick me up.

After my hair and makeup are done, I go to my closet, pull out the dress I bought a few weeks ago, and set it on the bed. Going to the dresser to pull out a black strapless bra and a seamless black thong, I put both on and look at myself in the mirror. The bra gives me the perfect amount of cleavage, and the thong sits just above my pubic bone, the fabric black but sheer, letting you see everything.

I step into the dress, the strapless ensemble ending just above my knees. The fabric covering my breasts is tight, and then the waist poofs out where there are pockets. The bottom is tight again, showing off my hips and ass. After struggling with the zipper for a few minutes, I slip on a pair of five-inch heels that wrap around my ankles and have a slim strap across my toes. Once I'm completely dressed, I step in front of the mirror, unroll my hair, toss the rollers onto the bed, and then fluff my hair. I look hot and am glad Wes isn't home, 'cause I have a feeling that he if he was here to see me, I wouldn't be allowed to leave the house.

I touch up my lipstick then head to the front room and grab my coat from the closet before going to the garage, which Wes cleaned out for me so I could actually fit my jeep inside without having to climb out the trunk.

Once I pull out onto the highway, I call December to let her know I'm on my way to my parents' house. My sisters normally stay with me when they are in town, but since Wes is basically living with me, they decided to give us our space and have been staying at my mom and dad's.

After I park and get out, not even knocking before going inside, the moment I cross the threshold, I see my sisters all standing in the kitchen, each of them defending themselves against my dad. My sister June has on a navy blue dress that is the same length as mine, but the outer shell is a lace material. Her long brown hair is tied back in a straight ponytail.

December is wearing a dress similar to mine, only hers has one long sleeve, and her long dirty-blonde hair is down each side of her breasts. May has a dress with cap-sleeves. The top is tight then it flows out at the waist, making her waist look perfectly curvy and her long white-blonde hair is pulled over one shoulder, showing off the curve of her neck. April has on a dark purple dress that swoops down, showing off her cleavage and tattoos. Her bright red hair that she colored weeks ago is hanging in waves down her back. I have seen my sister with every color hair you can think of, but she always looks beautiful. June smiles looking at me instead of wearing a dress she has on a black strapless romper with a chunky gold necklace that somehow accentuates her cleavage the bottom of the romper flares out at the ankle showing off a pair of gold heels that I may have to steel from her. Her hair is short but the cut stylish, which fits her almond, shaped face perfectly.

"Oh, great, you too?" my dad mutters as I join them. "Where is that man of yours? I have a hard time believing he let you out of the house wearing that getup." he says then his frown grows deeper. "And where is the bottom part of that dress?"

I roll my eyes and kiss his cheek. "Wes is working."

"Figures that I'm left to deal with this on my own," he grumbles then shakes his head, looking at all of his girls.

"When did you all grow up?" he asks softly, putting one arm around June and one around me, kissing the side of my head.

"You all look beautiful," my mom says, coming into the kitchen, wearing a pair of khaki capris and a cute tank that has ruffles along the sleeve, with a big chunky necklace and simple black sandals. She wraps her arm around December's waist, who is a few inches taller than her with the help of her heels. "My girls are so gorgeous." My mom smiles then looks at my dad, and her face goes soft the same way it has my whole life, and I swear I know exactly what she's thinking. My dad gave my mom everything she didn't even know she needed or wanted.

"They take after their mama." My dad smiles, and June mutters, "Gross," making me laugh.

"So, what are you girls doing tonight?" my mom asks as Dad wraps his arms around her waist and sets his chin on her head a pose I have seen them in more times than I could count.

"We're meeting the girls for dinner then drinks."

"I'll drive you guys."

"We don't need you to drive us, Dad," May says, and he just glares at her.

"I wasn't asking," he says, kissing the side of my mom's head before moving her aside and grabbing his keys. "Let's go; just let me know when you want to be picked up."

"Wes is picking me up," I say, and May comes over and wraps her arm around my waist.

"Does your hot biker man know any hot biker friends?" she asks, and my dad swings his head to look at us. I shake my head no while saying, "Yes," without moving my lips.

"I can't wait to move home," she says.

I look at her and smile, whispering, "Wait 'til you see Harlen and Everret," while getting into my mom's SUV.

When we pull up in front of the restaurant, we each kiss Dad's cheek before heading inside. The moment I walk through the doors, squeals ensue as we all greet each other. My cousin Ashlyn is Uncle Cash and Aunt Lilly's daughter. Hanna is Uncle Trevor and Aunt Liz's daughter. And Willow, Harmony, and Nalia are Uncle Nico and Aunt Sophie's daughters.

"How hard was it getting out of the house in that dress?" I ask Ashlyn, and she rolls her eyes.

"Between my dad and Jax, I might as well go live in a nunnery."

"Jax isn't even my brother and I want to kill him," I tell her, and understanding flashes in her eyes.

"Where's the hot boyfriend?" Hanna asks.

Okay, maybe my cousins were all watching my man, and not just my mom and aunts. "Working, he will be here later to pick me up."

"Is he bringing any friends?" Nalia asks, and I laugh. I'm so glad she came home for the holidays.

"Oh, yes, please tell me he has friends," my twin cousins Harmony and Willow say as we make our way to the table.

"When you guys all move home, I'll set up a meet and greet, or maybe I can host speed dating." I laugh again, taking a seat at the table and they all giggle too.

"I can't wait until you guys are all home. I miss these dinners," I say, taking a sip of wine.

"I don't know if I'm going to be moving home," Nalia confesses, and all eyes go to her. "I like being with my mom and brothers in Colorado. I miss you guys, but I'm happy there." She lowers her face.

"You have to do what makes you happy," April says, and all of us nod in agreement, even if we want her here with us.

"I just wish I wasn't hurting Mom and Dad," she replies, looking at Harmony and Willow.

"Mom gets it. She's sad, but she understands," Willow says softly.

"We all love you," Harmony adds, "and it's not like you're never going to come home. We will always be sisters."

"We will all always be family," December chips in.

"I'll drink to that." I smile. The rest of dinner is quiet, with all of us sharing stories of the last few months after we finish eating. We pay the bill and then walk a few blocks down to the bar we have been going to since we were old enough to drink.

"Find a table and I'll get us some drinks," I say, and Nalia wraps her hand around my elbow.

"I'll go with you." She smiles and I giggle, 'cause we're both already tipsy. I'm not sure if it will hurt or help having her with me. We make our way to the bar and get there in one piece without knocking anything or anyone over.

"Two pitchers of beer!" I yell at the bartender while holding onto Naila.

His eyes come to me briefly and he yells back, "Got it," then goes to pour the pitchers. The other bartender says something to him, and his eyes come to me and sweep me from hair to chest. I try to place him, but the alcohol in my system is making it hard to figure out where I know him from.

"Do you know him?" Nalia asks.

"I'm not sure," I shout over the music.

"He's cute," she says, and I look at him. No, he is not cute; he is *hot.* His arms are covered in tattoos, he has small gages in his ears, his skin is the color of chocolate, and his torso is covered in muscles that are shown off by his tight t-shirt.

"What did that guy say to you?" she asks him when he places the beer in front of us.

"Pardon, bebe?" he asks, leaning closer to Nalia over the bar. His voice is rough, and he has an accent I have never heard in person before, but it sounds Jamaican, and the look on his face as he looks at my cousin is one of awe. I don't blame him; my cousin is model material.

"Uhh..." Nalia sputters then looks at me.

"What did that guy say to you?" I ask him, taking pity on my cousin.

"Not fee. No charge you."

"Why?" I frown, and he shrugs then looks at Naila again and smiles.

"Seeya 'round, bebe," he says, running a finger over her cheek, then turns and walks to another customer. We each grab a pitcher of beer off the bar along with cups and take it to the table the girls are sitting at.

"What was that hottie saying?" Willow asks, looking towards the bar.

"Nothing," Naila mutters, frowning, and I smile at my cousin. Maybe there's hope of Naila moving home after all.

"The other one is hot too," December says, and I follow her gaze towards the bar and see the guy who said something to the bartender, then it clicks into place who he is. I met him at the first club party I had gone to. He was working behind the bar with the other guy. That's when I know Wes probably told them we were going to be at the bar and they should look out for us.

"Enough about guys." June rolls her eyes, grabbing a pitcher of beer and a glass.

"Just 'cause you're off the market doesn't mean everyone else is," April says, and I look at June and frown. I didn't know she was dating anyone.

"For your information, I haven't dated in a year," June retorts.

"Why?" Harmony asks, and June takes her glass of beer and chugs it then pours another glass and drinks that one as well.

"This must be bad," Nalia says and gets up. She goes to the bar, coming back a few minutes later with a bottle of tequila and a nice pink hue to her cheeks. She pours us each a shot and tilts the bottle back against her lips and takes a chug. "Spill it, bitch," she mutters, wiping her mouth.

"I was married," June blurts, causing the table to go silent and us all to look at her.

"I swear you just said you were married," December says, taking another shot and giggling.

"Oh, God." June starts to cry. Hanna, who is sitting next to her, wraps her arms around her, and I sit back in my chair, completely stunned.

"What happened?" I ask when I'm finally able to speak.

"His name is Evan. We got married in the spring before he went away to boot camp." She shakes her head and I watch tears fall onto her lap, so I go to the bar and get a stack of napkins and hand them to her when I return.

"He came home two weeks ago after going to Afghanistan, and served me with divorce papers." She laughs and it sound hollow, and then she lifts her glass to her mouth and takes a large drink.

"Well, he didn't actually serve me with them. I haven't even seen him since he's been home. He had his mom bring them to me. Can you believe that crap?" Actually, no, I couldn't. That was horrible.

"I wasn't even married for a year. I had sex one time the night we were married, the night before he went away to boot camp." She cries harder.

"Oh, my god," I whisper, feeling tears fill my eyes.

"Why didn't you tell us?" December asks.

"I don't know. I think deep down I knew he was done with me. I was humiliated." She shrugs, and I stand and walk around the table to wrap my arms around her.

"What do you mean?"

"When he first went away, he would call every night, but then things changed, and the phone calls became less and less frequent. I knew he would have a hard time keeping in contact, but I felt like he just never tried to call me. Eventually, he stopped calling at all. His mom would call me once a week to ask how I was. I started dreading those calls, and resenting him. Then his mom stopped calling, and two weeks ago, a friend of ours said he was home. He had gotten out early, and he was going to be moving to Tennessee. The next day, I got the divorce papers." She sobs, and I look around the table, at a loss for words.

"You have nothing to be embarrassed about. He is obviously an asshole," Harmony says, and I nod, agreeing with her.

"What is his last name?" Ashlyn asks, looking white as a ghost.

"Baristea," June mutters, and Ashlyn looks at me.

"What?"

"You're not going to believe this."

"What?" Hanna asks, sitting forward like this is a soap opera.

"Jax just hired a guy named Evan. He was in the Marines and his convoy was blown up. All of his friends were killed; he was the only survivor. He is supposed to start in two weeks."

"Oh, God," June whimpers. "So he's moving here." I cannot even believe this is happening.

"Yeah, since Jax's case load has been building up, he wanted to hire some new guys, and this guy, Evan, was recommended…by one of Wes' friends actually."

"Tell Jax he can't hire him," Harmony says.

"No," June whispers. "If it's true he lost all of his friends and all that happened to him, then he needs this. Don't take that from him," she breathes, and more tears fill my eyes. That is love—caring about what the other person is facing, even if they don't care about you.

"You're moving home next year," December reminds her softly.

"Then I have a year to get over him."

"We will help you, whatever you need," I tell her.

"I need to get drunk," June states.

"That, we can do," Willow says, handing her the bottle of tequila.

"I NEED TO call Wes," I slur when the girls start saying they are going to head home.

"You're not going to ride with us?" my sisters ask.

"No, Wes wants to pick me up." I smile.

"Wes is so hot and nice," December mumbles, leaning on my arm.

"I know," I agree, pulling out my phone to call him.

"Can he bring his friends?" Willow asks.

"I don't know. I'll ask him." I shrug and put my phone to my ear.

"Babe," Wes answers.

"I love that," I tell him while looking at my lap.

"What's that?"

"When you call me babe," I clarify, and December mutters, "I love it too," making me giggle.

"You drunk?"

"Just a little," I mutter, holding my fingers in front of my face an inch apart.

"Just a little, huh?" he chuckles.

"Can you bring your friends with you to come get me?" I ask, twirling my hair around my finger.

"Why?"

"Um…'cause they're hot."

"Pardon?" he growls making me giggle.

"Are you going to spank me for that?" I giggle louder.

"Jesus," he mutters that one word, making me squirm on my seat. "I'm on my way."

"Yay." I smile, hanging up.

"Wes is on his way," I tell the table.

"Is he bringing his friends?" Willow asks.

"I don't think so."

"Bummer," December mutters.

"One more shot," June murmurs.

"Dad, Uncle Trevor, and Jax are outside," April tells everyone, taking the shot glass December hands her.

"To a sisterhood that is more than just blood," Willow says, holding up her shot glass, and we all clink our drinks together then shoot the shots back. I can't wait until all of my girls are home; I miss this.

When we stumble out of the bar, I see Wes getting down from his SUV and a frown forms on my mouth.

"Where's your bike?" I pout, and his eyes sweep over me and his jaw goes hard.

"Where's the rest of your dress?" he asks.

"That's what I asked," my dad mumbles while opening the door to my mom's SUV for my sisters.

"You're supposed to say how beautiful I look," I tell him, putting my hands on my hips.

"Oh, you look beautiful, baby, too beautiful to be in a bar without your man."

"Oh, my God," I hear and look over at Harmony, and when her head turns, our eyes meet and she mutters, "What? That was hot." She shrugs, and Wes wraps his arm around my waist and leads me to his SUV.

"Where's your bike?" I ask again.

"Baby, you're not riding on the back of my bike sloshed," he says as I stumble, and he pulls me back into his body just before I hit the pavement.

"Thanks," I murmur while admitting to myself that it's probably best he didn't ride his bike.

"Come on. I'm taking you guys home," Jax says gathering Willow, Harmony, Nalia, and Ashlyn.

"Hey, Dad," Hanna says, stumbling over to Uncle Trevor, who is frowning at her. "Oh, turn that frown upside down. At least there are no boys here," she tells him, and he just shakes his head and looks at my dad, who shuts the door, cutting off the sound of my giggling sisters.

"Was one boy too much to ask for?" my dad asks.

"Aww, Dad, I'll give you a grandson," I say then cover my mouth and look at Wes, who has a funny look on his face, and then to my dad, who just shakes his head.

"Love you," Dad says, coming over and giving me a hug.

"Love you too." I hug him back then let Wes lift me up into his SUV.

"You gonna be around tomorrow?" Wes asks my dad, and even in my drunken state, I can see something flash in my dad's eyes as he nods. Wes slams my door and says something else before walking around and getting behind the wheel.

"What was that?" I ask Wes, watching Dad get into his car and take off.

"Nothing, baby," Wes says, pulling my seatbelt across my lap before putting his on and pulling out after Jax. "What do you got on under that dress baby?" he asks, and my breath hitches as his fingers skim up my thigh.

"Nothing," I breathe, and his finger pauses.

"Pardon?" he asks, but there is a hint of anger in his tone. "Let me see how you left the house with my goods." I start panting and slowly shimmy the tight bottom of the dress up and over my hips. "You're lucky, baby." His finger slides up my core, over the sheer material of my panties, making me gasp. "Pull that skirt back down," he says, and I hold my breath a moment then pull it back down over my hips as his hand slides back and forth over my thigh in soft, smooth strokes, not giving me anything, while at the same time, letting me know he's with me.

When we pull up to the house, he clicks the button for the garage and I'm reminded my Jeep is at my parents. He pulls in and parks then shuts the door to the garage, leaving only a small bit of light available to see with. My pulse spikes higher as he gets out without saying anything and comes around, opening my door and unhooking my belt, turning me with my feet out the door.

Without warning, his hand fists in the top of my dress, tugging it down, causing my breasts to spring free. His head lowers and he pulls one nipple into his mouth, while pulling, pinching, and tugging on the other one with two fingers. My head falls back and my legs try to wrap around his hips, while my hands grab onto his shoulders as he moves to cup the other breast, licking around the nipple before biting down on it.

"Wes," I moan, and his hands move to the back of my knees as he pulls me roughly towards him, shoving my dress up over my hips.

"Fuck, baby, your smell makes my mouth water, knowing when I bite into you, you're gonna gush into my mouth," he says, taking my mouth in an aggressive kiss.

Then his fingers slide up my center again, making my hips jerk forward. "Hmmm," leaves his mouth as his mouth leaves mine. He pushes me back gently with a hand on my chest then lifts my foot, placing it on the open door while placing a hand on the inner thigh of my other leg, spreading me out for him. He pulls up on the top of my panties causing the material to slide between the lips of my pussy and a moan to leave my mouth. My nails dig into his scalp as his mouth lowers and he pulls my clit into his mouth, sliding my panties to the side, and slips first one finger, then two inside me, lifting up, causing a deep burn to build inside me then ignite as he lifts my leg to his shoulder and sucks my clit, flicking it with his tongue.

His name leaves my mouth on a loud cry and my body lights up, every cell of my body buzzing. As I come back to myself, I feel Wes enter me. My arms go around his shoulders and my legs around his hips as he pulls me from his car with his hands on my ass then presses me into the cold metal of his truck.

"I like the idea of you having my son," he tells me, causing the walls of my vagina to contract around him. "Seems you like it too, baby." He smiles, lifting me higher with his hands around my thighs. My heels dig into his ass and my nails grasp into his tee-covered back.

"I'm going to come," I moan then clamp down on his shoulder with my teeth, coming hard.

"Fuck!" he roars, pulling me down hard on him, making the orgasm already flowing through me reignite as I feel him get bigger as warmth floods my insides. His hips still and my mouth releases his skin as he gathers me close to his chest.

"Love you," I mumble, wrapping myself tighter around him, and he gathers me impossibly closer, carrying me through the house and setting me on the bed. He pulls my dress off, along with my bra and panties, and then goes to the bathroom, coming back a few minutes later with a makeup wipe. He gently takes of my makeup then lays me down, unstrapping my shoes.

"You wanna shirt, or you wanna sleep like that?"

"Chest-to-chest," I mumble then watch as he slips off his clothes and turns out the light. When his body compresses the bed, I snuggle into his side, and he pulls me up and over until I'm lying on top of him with my legs between his.

"Love you, baby." His hand runs down my back, but I'm too out of it to reply, so I just kiss his chest and give him a pat. His body shakes and I know he's laughing, but I ignore it and fall asleep.

Chapter 14

I WAKE UP and look at the clock then down at the warm, sweet woman that's asleep on top of me, closing my eyes. I couldn't imagine not waking up to her everyday for the rest of my life.

I kiss her hair and roll to the side, fighting myself from sliding back inside her as I adjust her on the bed. These moments are the hardest. If I could spend my days with my mouth on her or my cock inside her, I would, but I need to get up and feed the boys then go over and meet her dad.

I never thought I would be asking a father for permission to marry his daughter, but with July, I know her dad's approval is important, and if I'm honest with myself, it's important to me as well. It would mean he thinks I'm good enough for his daughter.

"Stay with me," she mumbles in her sleep, burying her face in my chest and making me smile.

"I gotta get up, baby," I tell her, sitting up.

"I don't want to get up." She pouts, making me chuckle.

"You don't need to get up; you can sleep."

"Okay, good," she sighs, then tugs my pillow down, hugging it to her chest. I run a hand down my face and pick up my sweats off the chair, pulling them on, and then head to the kitchen.

"Hey." I pause to give Capone a scratch then go to the kitchen and set up the coffee pot before getting the boys their food and feeding Taser, who just tweets when he sees me. I still laugh when I think of his name and the fact if it weren't for him, I wouldn't have met July. Once

I finish a cup of coffee, I grab a bottle of water, the bottle of aspirin from the cabinet, along with a glass of orange juice, and take them with me, setting them on the side table, so when July wakes up, she will see them.

I pull out a pair of jeans and a thermal shirt, taking them with me to the guest bath so I don't wake her up.

Once I'm done showering, I dress quickly, put on my boots, grab my wallet and cell, and then head to my truck. When I open the door for the garage, the light comes on and I smile then laugh, going back into the house to grab a rag so I can wipe down the side of my truck, where July's ass-print is. *I don't think her dad would be cool with me showing up with proof on the side of my truck that I'm trying to get his daughter pregnant,* I think, then pause and lower my head, trying to breathe as I realize what I just thought. I know deep down it's the truth; I would be happy if she had my kid. Fuck, I would be over the moon about it, and my mom…hell, my mom would be fucking thrilled to be a grandmother.

"One thing at a time," I tell myself as I finish wiping down the truck.

By the time I pull out onto the highway, I feel like I'm preparing to go to war. I know that no matter what her dad says, I will still have July as my wife, but I want his approval, not for myself, but for her. I bought her ring two weeks ago, and I can't wait to put it on her finger.

When I pull up to her parents' house, I get out and November opens the front door, meeting me on the porch. "Hey, Wes. Where's my daughter?"

"Still in bed. She had a little too much fun last night with her sisters," I tell her on a chuckle.

She starts laughing and gives me a hug once I reach the front door. "The girls are still in bed, and when I offered them breakfast, they started throwing stuff at me. So would you like some breakfast? I have plenty." She smiles, and I can plainly see where July got hers from.

"I'd like that," I agree, following her into the house and to the kitchen, where she has a whole buffet of food prepared.

"I got a little carried away, but I like having the girls home, and I know one way to keep them coming back is by keeping them full while they're here," she says on a grin.

"I have no doubt they would continue to come back, even without your food," I assure her, seeing a lot of my mother in her.

"You hitting on my wife?" Asher asks, coming into the kitchen, and I hide my smile. These two have most likely been together for a good twenty years, and you can tell he is still possessive and protective of his wife.

"Don't know if that would bode well with you agreeing to let me marry your daughter," I tell him, and his eyes flash with respect, the same look he has given me since the first time we met, and some of the anxiety about this moment leaves me.

"Don't suppose it would," he concurs, patting my shoulder then kissing his wife, whispering something to her that makes her snap out of her daze.

"Coffee?" he asks me, holding up the pot.

"Yes, sir." I nod, and he fills a cup for himself and one for me.

"Do you think you deserve my girl?" he asks, and I'm actually impressed that's his first question. I take a drink of coffee and look at July's mom, who is watching me closely, more closely than she has any other time I've been around her before.

I swallow and set my cup on the counter. "No." I shake my head. "There's probably someone out there who can give her more than I can, but I would kill that guy before I gave him the chance to prove me right." I look at her mom then her dad. "I love her with everything in me. Since almost the moment I met her, I've felt a pull to her unlike anything I have felt before. I don't deserve her, but no one will ever love her like I do or will."

"Oh my," one voice says from behind me, but I don't take my eyes off Asher.

"If we're voting, my vote is yes," another voice says.

"He has my vote too," comes a third.

"I love my sister, but if she says no, I'm here."

"April!" November snaps, making me chuckle.

"All right, son, you have my blessing. Now you just have to ask my girl," he says, and the word *son* fills me with a sense of pride.

"Thank you, sir."

"Don't thank me; turn around and look at the girls behind you," he tells me, and I do as he says, taking in July's four sisters. "I didn't have any boys. I had five girls…five beautiful girls I swear to Christ were put on this earth to torture me." There is a lot of yelling, "Hey!" from the girls, all of them glaring at him. "You're the first man, which means some of this weight has been lifted off me, and you now have the responsibility of helping me look out for my girls. Welcome to the family," he says, lifting his cup to me then to his mouth and taking a drink.

"Well then, let's eat," November says, and I look at her then the girls, wondering what the hell I just got myself into. July is a handful on her own, and with all her sisters coming home over the next couple of years, I have a feeling I'm going to need some back-up. I shake off the feeling, knowing I have a few years until I need to think about it, and go and eat breakfast.

"Hey, babe," I answer the phone as the girls pass around the ring I got for July. I step out of the room and stand in the hallway. All along the wall are pictures of the Mayson family, and my eyes land on a picture of July when she was a little girl. Her long blonde hair looked wild, like she had been rolling in grass, her dress wrinkled, and her tiny arms were wrapped around a giant dog's neck, her head pressing into his black and white fur. He sat looking regal, the look on his face one that said he would eat anyone who got too close to her. I knew instantly that was Beast; I also knew from the picture the bond they shared.

"You're not home," she complains, her voice still scratchy from sleep. I look from the picture to the ground and smile. Since the moment I first stayed at her place, she has been calling her house our home. I love that.

"I came to your parents' to get your Jeep."

"Oh," she says, sounding disappointed.

"You okay?" I ask after a long moment of silence, wondering if she has fallen asleep.

"Did my mom make breakfast?" she asks.

I laugh and mutter, "Yes."

"Can you bring me some when you come home?"

"Sure thing, baby."

"Thank you," she murmurs, still sounding tired.

"Sleep 'til I get home."

"Okay," she agrees, saying, "I love you," before hanging up.

"Do you mind making July a plate, and then following me back with the Jeep, so she doesn't catch onto why I was here?" I ask, walking back into the living room.

"No problem," Asher says, and November gets up, gathering some food together for July.

"Do you know how you're going to ask her?" December asks.

"No, I haven't thought much about it. Figured it would come to me," I confess, taking the ring back, putting it in the box then in my pocket again.

"I think however you do it, it will be perfect. She loves you," November says, coming back and setting down a plate covered in plastic wrap. "Just follow your heart."

"Thank you." I smile, and she pats my cheek.

"Thank you too, for loving my baby the way she deserves to be loved," she tells me, and those words echo in my ears as I make my way out to my car, and I watch Asher get in July's Jeep as November gets into her own SUV so they can follow me to the house. The first time I got married, I did it because I thought I loved her. Now, I know different. Now, I know what love feels like, and the way it doesn't change you, but makes you want to change yourself…to be worthy of the person you are with. I also know that no matter what I want to do in life, I will have a woman at my side to support me, and that says it all.

July

I ROLL OVER and look at the clock when I hear the garage door open, seeing it's a little after ten.

I get out of bed and find one of his shirts, slipping it on, and then find a pair of panties and pull them on before heading out into the living room, where I'm greeted by Juice and Capone.

"I thought you would still be sleeping," Wes says, wrapping his arms around my waist from behind as I stop to pick up each of the boys for a cuddle.

"I heard you come in," I tell him, and then my stomach growls. "And I was hungry."

"I just put your plate in the microwave." He kisses the side of my neck and I follow him into the kitchen, hopping up on the counter across from him.

"Thank you for getting my Jeep," I say, watching as he pulls the plate out of the microwave.

"No problem." He takes in my position on the counter and smiles, handing me the plate then opening the drawer to get me a fork. "Coffee or juice?"

"Juice," I reply through a mouthful of fluffy pancake, and he pulls out the jug of orange juice from the fridge, giving me a glass and kissing my forehead before leaning on the counter behind him, crossing his arms over his chest. The top collar of his grey thermal is unbuttoned, showing off the defined muscles of his chest and arms. Last night flashes through my mind. I love the way he is able to make me feel so small and feminine, the way it feels as he's standing, holding me up with his strength while fucking me.

"What are you thinking about right now?"

My eyes focus on him and I feel my cheeks heat, so I shove a forkful of food in my mouth again and mumble, "Nothing," causing him to smirk and my eyes to narrow, which only causes his smirk to turn into a grin. "What's the plan for today?" I ask, swallowing another bite of pancake.

"You wanna go on a ride with me?"

"Sure," I agree immediately; there is nothing better than being on the back of his bike.

"You're gonna need to dress warm."

"Where are we going?"

"Just for a ride," he says, shrugging.

"Okay," I agree slowly, wondering what he's up to.

"Also, we need to stop pretending I'm not living here, and stop wasting money on my apartment."

"Um…you were the one pretending like you hadn't moved in," I remind him.

"No."

"Yes. I asked you, 'When did we move in together?' and you acted like we hadn't," I tell him, hopping off the counter and rinsing off my plate before setting it in the drying rack.

"No, I just didn't want to have that conversation, with your mom and dad in the next room. Plus, you looked freaked when you asked that shit." Okay, so he may be slightly right. I was a little freaked about it, just because I had no idea when it happened. It was like one minute we were dating, and the next, he moved in. "Judging by the silence, I think you get my point," he says, and I roll my eyes. "So are you good with me closing my lease?"

"Yes," I agree, wrapping my arms around his waist and looking up into his handsome face.

"What's the mortgage on your house?"

"I don't have one." I shrug.

"You rent this place?" he asks as his eyebrows pull together.

"Maybe you should sit down," I suggest, walking him backwards until we reach the living room, where I push him onto the couch and straddle his lap.

"I like this idea." He smiles, palming my ass and lifting up, causing my core to rub across the denim of his jeans.

"Hold on." I place my hands on his chest and lift my hips. "Let me tell you about this, and then we can get back to this," I say, dropping my ass onto his lap.

"Get to it, baby," he commands as his eyes drop to my mouth, making me smile.

"My mom was left an inheritance. My dad wouldn't let her use it, so she put it into an account and it grew, and when each of us girls turned twenty-one, we were given an even share of it. I paid for my clinic and my house, and the rest is in an account that just collects interest.

"So, you're telling me you're loaded," he says, but I can't read his face. I don't know how to answer that question; I'm not loaded, but I'm comfortable, and will be until the day I die as long as I continue to work.

"Um..."

"I'm good with you having money, baby. All that means to me is if something happens and I leave this earth before you, you're good. That shit will help me rest easy," he tells me, and with that, he pulls my mouth down to his and kisses me until I'm riding him hard and fast on the couch, only stopping when I scream my orgasm into his mouth while he groans his into mine.

I WATCH THE open road and smile while wrapping my arms tighter around Wes' stomach, feeling his muscles flex under my fingers I slid under his leather jacket and t-shirt.

This morning, after our couch session, I got up and took a shower, and then got dressed while Wes did whatever guys do while they are waiting for women to get ready. I chose a pair of dark jeans that I tucked into my brown boots, a tank top with a sweater and my brown leather jacket, and a scarf that has the story of *The Secret Garden* by Frances Hodgson Burnett printed on it.

I tied my hair into a long braid that I laid over one shoulder and did light makeup of bronzer, a little blush, and mascara. I know nothing about our destination today, and that is okay by me. I just like being with Wes, and if I happen to be on the back of his bike, that is even better.

We turn down one road and then another until we're riding on the road I first came across Wes and his boys. I can't believe that was only a few months ago; it feels like I have known Wes much longer. I honestly don't know what things would be like anymore without him in my life.

I would probably still be eating cereal alone in bed every night while watching TV, and only going out when my sisters were home. Thinking about it now, I realize how boring my life was. I was actually a perfect match for my ex; I was absolutely as boring as him, but just wasn't seeing it, and on that thought, I wrap my arms tighter around Wes.

We drive for about twenty more minutes then pull over to the side of the road, where I instantly recognize as the place I tasered him. It's actually a beautiful spot. The road curves around a large bend, there's a forest along the side of the road, and on the other side, there is a drop-off that looks out at the lake.

"What are we doing here?" I laugh, sliding off the bike behind him.

He does the same then stands in front of me, not speaking as he unhooks my helmet along with his, setting both on the seat.

"You're kind of freaking me out," I tell him, not able to read his face.

"This is the place you knocked me on my ass," he says, and I smile. "The place I realized why I moved to Tennessee, and the place I found my future." I stop breathing as he puts his hand in his pocket, coming out with a diamond ring. "I want to share everyday with you, to grow old with you. Will you be my wife?" he asks, and I look down at the ring. The center stone is imbedded into the design of filigree work that runs around and down each side of the ring. My eyes go from the ring in his hand to his eyes, and my mouth opens and closes. I can't believe this moment is really happening.

"Are you sure about this?" I ask after a long moment.

"Baby, I wouldn't be asking you if I didn't know I want to spend the rest of my life with you."

"This is forever, as in for-ev-er," I sound out.

"Jesus, you're a pain in the ass," he says, grabbing my hand and sliding the ring onto my finger. "We're getting married," he states, and a bubble of laughter climbs up my throat, which he silences with a kiss.

"I love you," I mumble against his lips when his mouth leaves mine.

"Love you too, baby."

"We're getting married," I whisper, and his face goes soft and he kisses me again, murmuring, "We are."

"*Holy cow! I'm getting married!*" I scream and start jumping around while holding my hand up in the air, looking at the way the light bounces off the stones.

"I can't wait to tell everyone," I say, breathing heavily and pausing to look at him. "I'm so happy." I run at him and he catches me in his arms as I wrap my legs around his waist. He hoists me up with his hands under my ass. "I'm so, so happy." I rest my forehead against his.

"July Abigail Silver." He smiles, and my heart does a little flutter in my chest at the sound of his name with mine.

"I like the sound of that." I close my eyes and tighten my arms and legs around him.

"Me too, babe," he replies, kissing me again. This time, his mouth stays against mine for an extra long moment.

"Holy cow," I repeat, opening my eyes and looking at the ring on my hand that is resting against his cheek.

"So I take it you say yes?" he asks, and I look into his eyes and nod then press my mouth to his again.

"Yes, a million times," I say and he smiles. "Can we go tell my mom and dad?"

Chuckling, he mutters, "Thought I'd at least get lucky before then, but yeah, babe."

"Oh, you're gonna get lucky…very lucky, but the things I plan to do to you are going to take all night."

"Really?"

"Yes," I reply, and he slides me down his body, letting me feel his arousal, which causes me to whimper. "Maybe we can tell my parents tomorrow," I suggest, and he throws his head back laughing, which causes me to giggle.

"Your sisters will be excited. I wasn't sure when I was going to ask, and I know they are leaving tomorrow, so we can go visit with them then have the night to ourselves," he says then picks up the helmet off the seat, placing it gently over my head and buckling me in. My heart, which is already full of love for him, gets that much bigger.

I wait until he has his helmet on and lifts his leg over the bike before I do the same. Once I have my legs tight to his thighs and my hands on his abs, he starts up the bike, squeezes my knee, and then pulls off onto the road, going back the way we just came, and even though I just saw the same scenery moments before, everything looks more vibrant. The colors of the trees in yellows, golds and oranges that let you know fall is in full swing, and the air feels cleaner and I just feel happier.

It doesn't take long to reach my parents' house, and when we do, my dad is the first to step outside. His eyes go to Wes, and even though I was afraid of his reaction to Wes to begin with, I can't wait to tell him I'm getting married, that I found someone who loves me the way he does, completely without question, and honestly, I should have known better. That was all my dad ever wanted for any of his girls.

As soon as Wes shuts off the bike, I lift my hand in the air, and yell, "I'm getting married!" at the top of my lungs, which causes my dad to smile and Wes, who I was still pressed up against to laugh.

"Babe, hop off," Wes orders, squeezing my knee, and I get off the bike and start fiddling with the straps of my helmet, trying to get it off while my hands shake with excitement. Lucky for me, Wes pushes my fingers away and quickly removes the helmet from my head. As soon as I'm free, I take off at a run towards my dad, who is still smiling, only bigger now. I pause halfway, run back to Wes, kiss the underside of his jaw, and then take off back towards my dad, who is now laughing at me, but I don't care. I make it up the stairs to him and wrap my arms around his waist, feeling his go tight around me before I tip my head back and breathe, "I'm getting married," again, this time with tears in my eyes.

"I know, my beautiful girl," he says gently, bringing one hand up to cup my cheek, and I can see a deep happiness in his eyes. That one look tells me he's happy I found what he and my mom have...what my grandparents have.

"Where's mom?" I ask, swiping my eyes free of the tears that had filled them.

"She and your sisters were out back near the fire pit," he tells me. I give him one more squeeze then take off into the house, running through, and then out the back door, yelling once again, "Wes asked me to marry him!" only this time, my news is met with squeals of happiness from my sisters, who all come and hug me, each saying how happy they are. Then I look at my mom, who has her hand covering her mouth and tears in her eyes. I go to her, wrapping my arms around her waist then resting my head on her chest, like I did when I was young.

"I love you, honey," she whispers, running a hand down my hair and back, "more than you could ever know." But she's wrong. I do know how much she loves me. I know, because since the first moment I can remember, she has reinforced that love, always showing just how much each of us means to her. I'm lucky to have that, blessed beyond reason to know what it feels like to have that kind of love from my family. "Wes is a good man. Me and your father are both so happy for you guys."

"Thank you, Mom," I tell her as a lump forms in my throat and a sob escapes.

"No crying." Mom hushes me, and then I'm transferred to another set of arms, and this time, the smell of Wes sweeps through my system as I take in a shaky breath, muttering against his shirt, "I'm okay."

"If you weren't riding that damn bike with my baby girl on the back, I'd offer you a beer," my dad says, making me laugh and look up at Wes.

I turn my head to smile at my dad. "I love that damn bike," I tell him, something he already knows, and he just shakes his head, putting his beer to his lips and taking a pull before muttering, "One down, four to go."

Chapter 15

I LOOK DOWN at my phone and bite my lip when I see Wes is calling.

"Are you going to answer that?" Kayan asks, and I want to say no, but I know deep down that I can't avoid Wes forever. *Especially since we live together.* It's been a week since he asked me to marry him, a week of us living happily, and a week of getting all of his crap out of his old apartment and moving it to my house.

I'm happy, and I know he is too, but I have a feeling I may have stepped over my bounds as new fiancé today, when I walked the three blocks down from my clinic and went to the furniture store in town. We didn't need anything new; we're keeping my bed, but we changed out my couch for his, since his is newer, the leather soft and the cushions comfortable. Plus, it has the cool cup holders built into the armrests, and the seats lean back, so you can lay and watch a movies without taking up the whole couch. I love his couch, and my old couch is going into storage, along with anything else in good enough condition that one of my sisters or cousins could use it when they come home to live.

But that isn't why Wes is calling, and I know this, because when we discussed getting a new bed or keeping mine, it reminded me of his bed at the compound. I know he hasn't slept with anyone in it since meeting me, but I'm also not naïve enough to believe the mattress hadn't seen a lot of action prior to us. That thought made me sick. It also made me pissed, so I stomped three blocks over to Jem's Furniture Warehouse and ordered a new bed for Wes, which would be being delivered right now.

The phone went silent, and then started ringing again, and Kayan, who was looking at me, dropped her eyes to the phone and frowned.

"What happened?"

"Nothing," I tell her then bite the inside of my cheek, debating what I should do, but then my cell phone stops and the office phone starts up.

"Beast's Veterinarian Clinic, how can I help you?" Kayan asks, answering the phone before I can tell her not to or slide across the counter and pull the phone from her ear.

"Sorry, Wes, but she's with someone right now. Do you want me to have her call you back?" she asks as I jump around with my hands in the air, pointing at myself and shaking my head franticly. "I'm not sure I can tell my best friend that," Kayan says, looking at me with her eyes getting big then hangs up the phone then raises a brow at me.

"Umm…"

"So I guess your lunch break consisted of a shopping trip?" she prompts.

I press my lips together then ask, "What did he say?"

"You can ask him yourself. He's on his way down here." She smiles, and my heart starts to pound in my chest.

"Why are you smiling?" I hiss.

"'Cause what he told me to tell you didn't exactly sound like punishment."

"Oh, my God. Z has caused you to become delusional."

"If you want a head-start on getting away, I suggest you go now." She returns to looking at her computer, and I glare at her then jump when I hear the sound of a door slamming in the parking lot.

"I hate you," I tell her, watching Wes walk up to the front of the clinic.

"Run." She laughs, and I do just that. I take off towards my office, where I know I have a lock on the door, enter, and shut it behind me, pressing the button.

"Babe, open the door." Wes pounds, and I'm sure my ex-best friend told him where I am, because she would find it funny. "If you don't open it, I'm taking it off the hinges," he shouts, and I have no doubt he will do just that, so I take the two steps to the door, twist the knob, releasing the lock, and then jump back behind my desk, putting it between us.

I expect the door to crash open, but instead, it opens slowly and Wes fills the space, his hands resting on his hips. I didn't see him before he left this morning, because like most days, he went to work a couple hours before me. My eyes take him in, not for the first time thinking how lucky I am. He is hot, today and like always, and in anger, his features stand out and he looks even more handsome. His top-half is covered in a burgundy thermal, and a black jacket with a straight collar that looks good against his neck and jaw. Today's jeans are darker, and of course his black boots. My eyes travel from his boot-covered feet to his face.

"Hey." I smile, and his eyes narrow before he steps inside the office and shuts the door.

"Lose the clothes."

At his words, my body jumps and I whisper, "What?"

"Take off your clothes, 'cause if I do it, I can't guarantee you'll have anything to wear home."

"Wes—"

"Now, July."

"I may have a client."

"You don't I made sure."

My hands go to my jacket and I slip it off my shoulders then pull my shirt off over my head. As I remove my clothes with shaky fingers, he moves the stuff on my desk, setting it aside before taking off his jacket and tossing it onto my chair. Knowing what is going to happen—or *thinking* I know what's going to happen—is causing wetness to form between my legs and my breathing to pick up.

I stand there naked, and Wes' eyes move hungrily over me before he growls,

"Come here. I want your tits to the desk and your hands above your head."

"Wes—" I try again.

"No more talking; just do it."

I chew on the inside of my cheek for just a moment before stepping around to the side of my desk, bending over the side, and inhaling a sharp breath as my nipples touch the cool wood.

"Hands all the way up," he orders. I slide my hands out above me until I'm almost on my tiptoes. "Do you know why I'm pissed?" he asks, stepping up behind me, the feel of the denim of his jeans rubbing against my bare skin.

"Yes," I say, and his hand slides over my ass, his boot-covered foot spreading mine farther apart.

"Do you think you deserve to be punished for going behind my back, ordering a bed, having it delivered, and telling them they had to take away the old one or you wouldn't pay?"

"No," I tell him honestly.

"Figured you'd feel that way." He bent over me, nipping my ear. "You gonna apologize?"

"Sorry," I tell him, squeezing my eyes closed as his hand slides over my clit, then cry out as that same hand comes down hard on my ass.

"That didn't sound sincere, baby," he admonishes, placing that hand back between my legs. Each pass over my clit causes my back to arch and my ass to press into his groin. "Now, tell me you're sorry again."

"I'm sorry about the bed," I say, and his fingers slide inside me, out and around my clit, and then back in deep. His other hand slides under me, cups my breast, and pulls at my nipple.

"You're soaked, baby. You like pissing me off. Does it make you hot?" he asks against my ear, making me whimper. Then his hand moves from between my legs again, spanking me harder than the last time.

"N-no," I stutter out, needing just a little more. My body is on fire, every inch of me just waiting to see what he'll do next.

"Your pussy's so hungry you'd think I wasn't feeding it everyday," he tells me as my core tightens around his fingers entering me. He then steps back and orders, "Up." Confused, I look over my shoulder at him and swallow when I see the look in his eyes. "Up on your knees, baby."

Oh.

My.

God.

I can't believe I'm doing this in my office, even if my office is down at the end of the hall, too far away for anyone to hear anything.

"Up, baby," he says a little softer, and I lift one knee then the other onto the desktop, and then look over my shoulder at him.

His eyes travel from my gaze, over the curve of my back and ass, and then lock between my legs. "I wish you could see what I see right now. Wish you could see how fucking hot you look, how wet and swollen your pussy is for me…for my touch." He shakes his head, puts his hands behind his neck, and pulls off his shirt.

I lick my lip as his abs flex, and the outline of his cock in his jeans is so large that I know when he unhooks the buttons, the head will be red and angry, the veins down the length so pronounced when he slides inside me I swear I can feel each of them.

He steps back behind me and I lower my head, waiting to see what he will do. His hands go to my ass and lifts, and then I feel the wet warmth of his tongue sliding over me.

"Wes," I whimper as I feel my arms shake while attempting to hold myself up.

"Easy, baby." He licks again then swirls his tongue around. I feel his thumbs holding me open to him, bringing me closer and closer, and then my arms give out and my head lowers when my orgasm crashes over me. It takes a moment to come back to myself, but when I do, he's entering me swiftly in a hard, fast thrust.

I push back on him each time then lift up on my hands as my knees start to slide farther apart. My legs start to shake as his hand comes down hard on my ass, and then whimper as he flips me to my back and reenters me, one hand going to my thigh, the other going down my stomach, his thumb pressing against my clit.

"Oh, God!" I cry, my head tilting back, my hands going to my breasts, pulling my nipples.

"Give me your eyes." My head tilts down again and our gaze connects. Then his eyes travel down my body from my hands on my breasts to our connection, and his thumb swirls faster as he bends forward, puts his hand behind my head, lifts me up to him, and takes my mouth in a deep kiss, his taste and mine flooding my mouth. My hands move to his shoulders, clutching at him as my legs wrap tighter around his hips.

"Squeeze me, baby."

I do without needing to be told as my core convulses around him with my orgasm, pulling him even deeper. His hips jerk and he plants himself deep, groaning his orgasm into the skin of my throat as my limbs lock tight around him.

"I'm going to buy you a bed everyday," I say with a smile, and I feel his body shake against mine, letting me know he's laughing.

"You're a pain in the ass, baby." He pulls his face away from my neck and moves some hair out of my face. "Don't do that shit again."

I press my lips together to avoid telling him I won't, because it's already done; there is no need to buy another bed for his room at the compound. We don't stay there often, but when we do, I don't want to think about who was there before me. I can't handle that.

"I love you…only you," he says, reading my face. "My future will be with you. Nothing before you matters." Tears fill my eyes and I turn my head to the side to avoid his gaze while crying. But Wes, being Wes, places his hand on my cheek, pulling my attention back to him. "No crying." He wipes my tears and I nod, but still, the tears fall.

He slides out, fixes his jeans, and then gathers me into his arms and turns to sit on my desk, with his arms tight around me. I don't even know why I'm crying…probably the stress and excitement of everything that has happened. "I hate when you cry, baby," he says softly, and my face presses into his neck for a moment, taking in a deep lungful of his scent before tilting my head back to look at him. His fingers run under my eyes and he searches my face. "You okay?"

"Yeah, a lot has happened and I think I just needed to cry."

"You happy?" he questions, and that has me searching his face, seeing worry in his eyes. I never want him to worry about my feelings for him.

"When I was little, I told myself the guy I would marry would love to ride motorcycles, have a soft spot for animals, and be strong like my dad." I place my hand on his stubble-covered jaw and run my thumb over his bottom lip. "When I got older, I never believed I would find a guy like that. Then you chased me down on your motorcycle and gave me everything I could ever want. So, no, I'm not happy; I surpassed that the first time you looked at me like I was something you wanted to devour and protect, all at the same time."

"Jesus," he whispers, looking into my eyes before pulling me closer and tucking my face into his neck. "Never wanted much, babe, but knew the moment I looked into your eyes that I wanted you. Just didn't think I'd ever have a shot. I promise I'll find a way to make myself worthy of you."

"You're my everything," I tell him, then look at the clock and slide out of his arms to stand in front of him. "Sorry about the bed, but I'm not taking it back."

"Let me know what it cost and I'll give you the money for it."

"Why?" I frown, going to my chair and pulling on my panties then putting on my bra.

"Just tell me the cost," he says a little more firmly. "We won't talk about it now, but I also need to know the house cost, so I can give you that. Then we'll figure out the bills and shit, so we can get that worked out."

"I told you I own my house."

"I know that, baby, but I'm not going to be living there free and clear, knowing you paid for it and I didn't do my part."

"I thought we were getting married."

"We are," he says immediately.

"Then what does it matter?"

"It matters, because you're not my mother; you're my woman, and it's my job to take care of you," he says, but I'm still completely lost. I mean, I know whenever we go out he doesn't let me pay, not even for groceries, and I'm fine with that—not that I have a choice—but this is a house I paid for already, so getting money back on it, when that money would just go into an account, doesn't make sense to me. "I'm not loaded, baby, but I have money saved from the service, and work at the shop is good. I need to know that I do my part."

I can tell by his tone that he is serious and this means something to him, so I just nod while putting on my shirt. Once I have it on, I go to him and place my hands on his thighs. "We'll get it worked out."

"Appreciate that, baby. You got anymore patients today?"

"A couple."

"I gotta head back to the shop, but call when you're on your way home and we'll figure out dinner."

"Sounds good." I smile, leaning in and pressing my mouth to his.

"How much shit is your girl going to talk when I leave?"

That comment gets him a full smile as I mumble, "Tons."

"Figured." He smiles back and waits until I have on my pants and shoes before opening the door. I walk him out hand-in-hand, past a smiling Kayan, who laughs her, "Later, Wes." He doesn't reply, just gives her a chin lift and me a touch from his mouth before leaving through the glass doors.

"Maybe I should buy Z a bed," Kayan says as soon as the door closes behind Wes. I look at her and roll my eyes.

"What? You're not the only one with a scary-hot guy," she mutters.

"How are things with you and Z?"

"Great between us. My parents are still being dumb, and I think my dad may end up murdered if he tells one more guy to ask me out."

"He's doing that while you're pregnant?"

"Yeah, and Z is about to have a coronary because of it."

"I bet he is." Knowing Z and how protective he is over Kayan, I can't imagine he's even a little okay with what her dad is doing. Hell, if my dad was doing that to Wes and me, I'm pretty sure Wes would kill him.

"Last week, he asked Mark to call me and ask me to dinner. Z was there when I got the call, and spoke to Mark. He explained that even though my dad didn't want to believe I'm in a relationship, I'm very much taken and pregnant, and surprisingly, Z was very nice to him and asked if he could spread the word to anyone else he knows who might hear the same thing from my father. Mark agreed that he would and told us congrats on the baby."

"Your dad is an asshole."

"I know." I see tears fill her eyes, so I walk around the counter and hug her. "Z is perfect, amazing actually, and I worry this is going to push him away."

"He loves you, honey, and I have a feeling there is nothing that would ever keep Z away." And that was the truth. Even Kayan's overbearing parents were no match for Z, who had found a woman to spend his life with. "You're not allowed to cry. You know Z freaks out when you cry," I remind her.

"Z's not here right now."

"No, but like a damn dog, I swear he can smell when you've been upset, and I would rather not give him a reason to be pissed off at me."

"You're right," she agrees, and I pull out a couple of tissues and hand them to her while rubbing her back.

"It will all work out. When the baby gets here, I bet they change their tune."

"If they don't stop what they're doing, I won't let them see the baby."

"Really?" I ask surprised, not that Kayan has ever been really afraid of her parents, but they have been known to push her into things she really didn't want to do.

"Really. Z's the man I'm going to marry one day, and he will be the father of our children. He deserves respect, much more than they have given him, and if that doesn't change, I won't be allowing them to see our baby."

"You know, I think if you tell them that, they might come around a little quicker than you think," I tell her.

"Do you really think so?"

"How could anyone not want to be a part of your baby's life?"

"Why didn't I think of that?"

"'Cause I'm the smart friend."

"Whatever, that just means I'm the hot one." She shrugs, making me laugh before I head back to my office.

I LOOK AT the clock, see it's midnight, roll over, grab Wes' gift from under my side of the bed, and sit up. I turn on my bedside light then look at Wes, who is sleeping with his hand, which was wrapped around my waist, now over my thighs.

I run my hand over his hair, and his eyes open slowly and he looks up at me, looking sleepy and confused.

"You okay, baby?"

"Merry Christmas." I smile and he double blinks.

His eyebrows come together and he looks over me, glancing at the clock, then smiles as he lifts up and kisses me, saying, "Merry Christmas, baby," against my lips.

"Here you go." I hand him the box I have been holding onto for weeks, but then I want to take it back and rip the paper off for him when he just looks at it. "I know technically we open gifts tomorrow, but I just can wait any longer," I tell him excitedly. He sits up completely, the sheet landing at his waist, so the expanse of his chest is visible. I turn towards him, sitting on my calves with my knees tucked against his thigh. "Please, open it." I bounce a little, which makes his eyes drop to my breasts, which are not covered, since after he made love to me, I didn't take the time to put anything on.

"Not sure I can focus on this with your tits bouncing in my face," he says, and I roll my eyes, pulling the sheet up to cover my chest. "Should have kept my mouth shut," he mutters, and I cry, "Open the box!" which makes him laugh.

He pulls my face to his with a hand wrapped around my nape, and then he lets me go and drops his eyes to the box, ripping the paper off slowly. Finally, he opens the top of the box, moving the tissue paper out of the way and pulling out the leather wallet I had designed for him. When asked what he wanted for Christmas, he would repeat over and over that he wanted me in a bow, naked in bed, waiting for him. Since he could have that any day of the year, I gave up on asking him, and actually gave up on finding him anything at all until I was talking to my Aunt Liz, and she told me about a shop in town where the guy custom made silver jewelry and leather goods. So I talked him about what I wanted, and a little about our story, and he created a piece of art that Wes could carry with him always and add things to it as time went on.

"Jesus," he whispers, and I bite my bottom lip, watching the way his fingers travel over the designs in the leather, which if you're not looking closely, you would miss. I chose things I felt repressed us: the Taser and bird from the first time we met, the motorcycle that is a huge part of our lives and who he is, and then on the back, his name, Silver, in the shape of a motorcycle, and on the end, where the medal hook is that holds his chain, is the date he asked me to marry him.

"If you don't like it, you don't have to carry it—"

I'm cut off when his mouth crashes down on mine and he rips the sheet away, pulling me over to straddle his lap. The feel of his tongue and his taste work through my system as he adjusts me slightly, filling me with him. I rock against him slowly, wrapping my arms more tightly around him, our mouths never leaving the other as he brings me to a slow orgasm that doesn't explode, but burns, feeling like it never ends. Tears spring from my eyes and I taste salt in our kiss as his orgasm slides down my throat.

When he leans his head back, his hands hold my face gently and he whispers, "I love you, babe."

"I know," I reply, because I do know; I feel it all the time. Even when we're apart, I feel it.

"Gonna carry it always," he says while wiping away another stray tear, and I know he's talking about more than just the wallet. He's also talking about the love and connection we have. I cuddle closer to him as he leans over with us still connected and turns off the light, and then he adjusts us, with me still on top of him, him still deep inside of me as he pulls the covers over us. He rubs my back for a long time while I listen to the sound of his breath. When it evens out, I follow him off to sleep.

"YOU'RE GLOWING," my mom says, walking up to me and wrapping her arm around my waist.

"I'm happy." I smile at her and wrap my arm around her. I lean my head on her shoulder and look at my family and Wes, who are all sitting in my parents' living room, talking and laughing. When we got up this morning, we fed Capone and Juice then sat around our Christmas tree and opened the gifts we had gotten one another. Wes got me a beautiful gold necklace that is an exact replica of his dog tag he wears, just smaller. The small metal plate has the same information his dog tag carries, but unless you flip it over, you would never know it is just for me. He will always be pressed to my skin, the same way he's wrapped around my heart.

"Are you pregnant?" my mom asks, and my gaze immediately goes to her.

"No, Mom." I smile, then add, "Not yet."

"What?" she whispers in shock.

"I'm kidding, Mom. We're not even trying. I want to have a wedding and then take some time for just us before we start planning for a baby."

"Oh, God. I didn't know how I would be able to rein in your dad."

"If anyone could do it, it would be you," I assure her.

"Not sure about that one, honey. Honestly, I'm shocked your dad is so cool about Wes."

"There's a lot to love about Wes," I tell her, and she looks out at the living room at Wes and my dad, who seem to be in a deep conversation. Then my dad throws his head back, laughing and patting Wes on the shoulder as he chuckles. His eyes come to me and go soft, and then he turns his attention back to my man.

"You did good, honey."

"I know," I reply, taking a sip of coffee then laying my head against hers, laughing when I see my sisters dancing around in the matching pajamas my mom got all of us for Christmas. This is more than I could have ever hoped for, everyone I love in the same place, all of us together.

"What do you say we get the turkey in the oven and have a mimosa?" Mom asks, and I nod, giving her waist a squeeze, and then we get the turkey in the oven and go out to sit with everyone else, me tucked close to Wes' side, my sisters all gathered together, and my dad with my mom on his lap. We all stay like that most of the day, only taking breaks to cook then to eat. I couldn't have asked for a better Christmas.

Chapter 16

"BABE, WHERE THE fuck are you?" Wes growls as soon as I put my phone to my ear after digging through my bag to find it. It's a week since Christmas, and things have been good. I've been busy trying to plan a wedding, and Wes has been busy keeping me cool about it.

"I had to stop at the store to get chips and stuff for the party."

"We're not having a party," he says, and I know that if I were in front of him, he would be shaking his head with a smile on his face.

"There are more than ten people coming over to watch football. I think that's called a party," I explain, rolling my eyes while tossing some avocados in my basket.

"I got beer," he says like that's all anyone needs, and he may be right with his boys; as long as they have beer, they're cool. And that was fine before he had a woman, but not now. So I'll be making wings, seven layer dip, fresh salsa, and some puff pastries I'm sure the guys will complain are too girly, but will scarf down. I'm even getting two apple pies. No, I didn't make them from scratch, but they're Wes' favorite, so that's all that matters. "Did you hear me?" he asks, bringing me back to the conversation.

"I know you got beer, honey," I tell him, walking up to check out, and I do know he got beer, because last night, when I got home from work, there were five cases of beer on the back porch where he had put them, because it was cold enough out that he didn't have to put them in the fridge in the house. "I'm still getting snacks."

"You don't need to go all out."

"I like going all out."

"Pain in the ass," he mutters.

"You love this ass." I smile.

"Fuck yeah, I do," he growls, causing a shiver to slide down my spine as I put the groceries on the conveyer belt.

"I'll be home soon," I tell him softly while swiping my card through the credit card machine.

"See you then, baby," he says, and I smile at the cashier, pick up my bags, and head toward the doors.

"Love you," I say, hanging up and shoving my phone into my purse, then shuffle the shopping bag from one hand to the other so I can open the door to my car. Once the doors open, I lean over the driver's seat and set my purse and the bags down, then scream out when I'm pulled backwards. A hand covers my mouth and I kick my legs hard as I'm dragged into a van and the door slams shut. My knees hit the metal floor and I feel a sharp blade against my throat.

"Got you, bitch," is breathed near my ear, and the stench of cigarettes and leather hits my nose. "You scream, and I'm slicing your throat. Nod if you understand me."

I nod frantically, and my mouth is uncovered and I'm pushed over until my cheek hits the floor. My hands are pulled together and my wrists are tied behind my back with what feel like plastic ties.

"I'm going to fuck you just like this, at my mercy, nowhere to go, no one to hear you cry," the guy behind me says, pressing his hard-on against my ass, making me gag. I feel tears roll over the bridge of my nose onto the floor before a sharp blow to the side of my head, then nothing but black.

I OPEN MY eyes then slam them shut, not wanting to believe what I'm seeing is real. My heartbeat thumps rapidly, and my breathing begins to increase, so much so that I know if I don't calm down, I will pass out again. I take a moment, gathering courage, and when I open my eyes again, it takes a few seconds for my eyes to adjust to the darkness. I look around, seeing I'm in a small room. The walls are pitched, which makes me believe I'm in an attic. The sound of dogs barking is so loud it's almost deafening.

My eyes land on a small figure that is huddled in the corner. Her long brown hair is down, and her face is smudged with dirt, along with her clothes. I scoot closer to her and she begins to cower away.

"I won't hurt you," I whisper, going to her side, but not too close. "What's your name?"

"El...Ellie. Wh-what's yours?" she whispers in a hoarse tone after a long moment.

"July," I whisper back. "Do you know where we are?" I ask while looking around the space, trying to see if there are any windows.

"No," she whimpers, and I can hear the fear in her voice from that one single word.

"How did they get you?" I ask.

Her eyes close and she lowers her head as her body begins to shake, and I don't think she's going to answer, but then she says so low that I almost miss it, "My mom sold me to these guys."

"What?" I hiss, completely caught off-guard.

"I know," she whimpers, dropping my hand and wrapping her arms around her legs, resting her forehead on her bent knees. "She has my daughter. I need to get my daughter," she cries, and her body begins to shake with silent tears.

I wrap my arms around her and whisper, "It will be okay," even though I have no idea how I will make it okay. Not for her...not with this.

"You don't understand. There was another girl here before me. They took her out, and when they brought her back, she was strung out on some kind of drug. She didn't even remember her own name," she tells me, and memories of what Wes told me about these guys flash through my head, making me vow that I will get us out of here before they can hurt us.

"Did you hear anything? See anything?" I ask.

"No, I was unconscious when they brought me here. When I woke up, Claire was with me. She said she was kidnapped from outside her house. Not long after I woke up, they came and got her."

"What did they look like?"

"I don't...I don't know. They were big; one of them had a tattoo on his forehead of a spider," she says, and a chill slides over me, knowing that was the same person who threatened Kayan at her apartment.

"We need to look around and see if we can find anything to use as a weapon to protect ourselves when they come back. My fiancé will be expecting me home soon, and when I don't show, he'll come looking for me," I tell her, trying to comfort her and myself.

I just have no idea how long I was out, or how long it took for them to bring me here. I hate this. I can't imagine what Wes is going to do when he realizes I'm not on my way home.

"Come on," I whisper, and we begin crawling around on the floor, trying to be careful, because there seem to be some parts that are weak in the floor, like the structure is old. The floor is covered in a thick layer of dust, and my hand runs over a puddle of thick liquid, and when I lift my hand close to my face, my stomach turns as I see it's actually blood. Someone was hurt here, hurt bad. It's not a little blood; it's a lot of it.

"Oh, God," I whimper in fear as the weight of the situation crashes over me.

"I found something," Ellie says from across the room, and I wipe my hand on my jeans and go towards her. When I make it to her side, I see she has a two-by-four with a thick rusty nail sticking out of one side.

"This is good," I say, giving her a hug. At least we won't be going down without a fight. "Let's see if we can find anything else, and then we'll come up with a plan."

Wes

"WHERE'S JULY?" MIC asks, and I look from the TV to my phone and feel myself frown. I spoke with her fifteen minutes ago; she should be home by now. I put the phone to my ear and her phone rings and goes to voicemail.

"This is July. Leave a message…or not. Who leaves messages nowadays anyways?" She laughs, and a bad feeling settles in the bottom of my gut. I click off the phone then redial, and it rings then goes to voicemail again.

"What's up?" Harlen asks as I step out onto the front porch, where he's having a cigarette.

"Something's off," I tell him, waiting to see if her car comes around the corner. The store that we always go to is about ten minutes from the house, if that, and she was checking out when I hung up. "July's not picking up her phone."

"Maybe she can't reach it," he says, and I nod, but I know that's not the case. Something's definitely off.

"I'm giving her three more minutes, but then I'm taking off to look for her," I tell him, putting my phone back to my ear and trying her again.

"I'll ride with you," he agrees, going into the house, coming back moments later with his jacket and handing me mine.

"What's up?" Mic asks stepping out onto the front porch."

"Gonna ride out with Wes to check on July. You stay here and have her call if she gets back," Harlen tells him, and I pull on my jacket then try her number one more time.

"Fuck," I clip and head towards my bike, swinging my leg over my seat, and Harlen does the same with his. The rumble of our pipes fills the air as we pull out of our driveway. I ride ahead of Harlen onto Main, heading right to the store, where I know July was last.

The moment we get there, I see her car in the parking lot off to the side of the door, where no one would see it. My stomach drops and my adrenaline kicks in as I pull into the space next to it and look inside. Her purse and the groceries she had just bought are sitting inside on the passenger seat. I open the back door, knowing not to touch the front in case someone needs to dust for prints, and reach in to grab her bag, pulling out her cell to see if she had gotten a call from anyone else, and there are no messages or anything in her call log.

When I lift my head, I see Harlen is on the phone, so I head into the store to see if anyone had seen anything, which no one has, and they don't even have cameras, so that's out. When I get back outside, Jax, Talon, Sage, and July's uncle Nico are waiting near her car, with Harlen, Mic, Everett and two officers I don't know.

"Z's at the house with Kayan," Mic says when he notices me looking at him.

"They got any cameras?" Nico asks, and I shake my head while walking closer to them, instead of going to the building and punching the shit out of it to relieve some of the rage I have pumping through me.

"You gonna be able to keep your head?" Nico questions, and I glare at him.

"I find who took her, they're dead," I say, meaning that shit to my core. Not if, but *when* I find them, they will pay with their lives for taking her from me.

"Do I need to take you in?" Nico asks, and I fold my arms over my chest. Uncle or not, I will lay him out if he thinks he can take me anywhere.

"You gonna stand around all day asking dumb as fuck questions while my woman is out there somewhere?"

"I'ma let that slide, 'cause I know you're worried about my niece, but say some shit like that again and I will put you down," Nico threatens, and my body stills and expands, ready to tackle his ass to the ground.

"Brother," Mic says, and I turn my attention to him, "cool it."

I run my hands down my face, attempting to get myself under control. Lashing out at everyone isn't going to help anything right now. "What do we know?"

"Nothing." Nico puts his hands on his hips. "She had no enemies, and the man I would have thought had something to do with this is in prison awaiting trial."

"Fuck," I rumble, and then think about Landon. It's a long shot, but he may know something. "I'm going to ride to Mamma's Country."

"You think someone there is connected?" Harlen asks, straddling his bike.

"Not sure, but it's doing no good just standing around here," I mutter then look at Nico. "You call Asher?"

"Yeah, he and November are going to your house to wait and see if she showed up there."

"Thanks, man. Call me if you find anything, and I'll do the same," I tell him, and he lifts his chin. I straddle my bike, start it up, lift my chin, and take off. It takes fifteen minutes to get to Mamma's Country, and the parking lot is empty except for a few cars I'm sure are regulars at the bar during the week. I park close to the entrance, Mic on my left, Harlen on my right, and we get off our bikes and head inside. Tommy is behind the bar, and his eyes come to us.

"Where's Ronnie?"

"Office," he says, and I head back behind the bar and knock once, opening the door without waiting for an okay. As soon as the door opens, Ronnie is standing behind his desk with a nine-millimeter aimed at us.

"Jesus," Ronnie says, putting away his gun. "What are you doing here?"

"You know anything about my woman being taken today?" I ask him, and he sits back in his chair and his face goes pale. Knowing what happened to his daughter I'm sure he gets how fucked up this situation is.

"No, son."

"Where's your boy?" I ask, and he looks at the three of us. I'm sure we look imposing as fuck standing in front of his desk.

"I'm here," Landon says, coming into the office and walking around to stand next to his dad. "What's going on?"

"July was taken from outside the grocery store on 5th. You know anything about that?"

"No," he says, looking at each of us then his dad. "Since Snake got locked up, things have been quiet."

"You know a guy with a tattoo of a spider on his skull?"

He swallows and then looks at his dad again then back at me. "Snake's brother, River, has a spider tattoo."

How the fuck did I not know he had a brother? "You know where he hangs?"

"No, he used to work at the tattoo shop on Westend, but since that place got new management and they didn't much like the fact he had a history of being inappropriate to the women who came into have work done, they let him go. "If you go over there, they might be able to tell you some info," he suggests, and I know exactly who he's talking about.

Blaze and his boy Jinx just opened a tattoo shop in town and bought out the people who owned Daniel's Bar, where July, her sisters, and her cousins had gone to drink. Jinx was a recruit, and Blaze came to talk to us a week ago about wanting into our club. We were still talking about it. Our crew has always been small, but since moving to town, there has been an influx of new recruits, guys who have ridden solo, or who have crews that are into drugs or other shit we're not into, and they want to ride clean.

"I'll call Jinx and have him bring Blaze with him to the compound, and then we can go from there," Harlen says, walking out of the room.

"You want us to do anything?" Landon asks, and I know July's right; he's a good kid. He was just in a situation that was out of his hands, and he was doing the right thing the only way he could, by bringing in those dogs.

"Call around and see if anyone knows where he is, or if anyone knows who he's hanging out with."

"Sure, man, and sorry about your woman. She seemed cool," he says, and I lift my chin and head out the bar, meeting Harlen, who's standing near his bike.

"They're meeting us at the compound."

"Let's roll out," I mutter, getting back on my bike.

When we get to the compound, the street is littered with bikes and cars. I look at Harlen, and he shakes his head as we park our bikes and move towards the gate. The second we get inside, we see all the guys are there, not just the few we called to meet us.

"We know you guys don't know if you're recruiting anymore members, but we wanted to come and show our support and help anyway we can," Maxen says, patting my shoulder, and I look around the open area of the compound. There must be at least thirty guys standing around, some whom I know, and others I have never seen before.

"'Preciate that, brother," I tell him then move to where I see Z talking to Blaze and Jinx.

"Where's Kayan?" I ask Z as soon as I reach his side.

"She's with July's mom and dad," he says, and I nod then put my attention on Blaze.

"You know anything about a guy named River? He has a snake tattoo on his skull."

"Yeah, he was at Zero's before we bought it. Management was afraid of him, so even though he had a history of stepping over the line with female clients, they never fired him. Unfortunately for him, me and Blaze didn't hold that same fear, so as soon as we closed on the shop, we gave him his walking papers."

"Do you know where he went?" Mic asks, and Jinx shakes his head.

Blaze looks at me. "One of his clients came into the shop and said he moved to Chapel Hill. Said he bought an old church and was going to open a tattoo shop in it."

"Thanks," I tell him, walking towards my room with the phone to my ear.

"You got anything?" Jax asks as soon as he answers, and I unlock the door, go in, lift my mattress, and grab my gun, putting it in the back of my jeans, pulling my shirt out and over it.

"Not sure. Seems Snake has a brother, and I think he's the same guy who threatened the girls before. I'm gonna take a few of the guys to Chapel Hill to see if I can find anything out."

"Meet you at the gas station off the highway in ten and I'll follow you."

"See you then." I hang up, lock up my room, head straight towards my bike, and swing my leg over.

"Anything you want us to do here?" Blaze and Jinx ask, and I hadn't even realized they were following me.

"Ask around and see if anyone heard anything, if anyone knows anything. Right now, we're taking any lead we can get."

"Got it.," Blaze says, stepping back from my bike.

"Jax is meeting us off the highway and will follow us down," I tell Harlen, Everett, Z, and Mic.

"Let's roll," Mic says, and it takes just a few minutes to get to the gas station, and when we do, I don't even stop; I just circle the parking lot and let Jax follow me in his SUV. On the highway, I lead with my boys to my sides and July's cousins to my back. It takes less then twenty minutes to get to Chapel Hill, and when we pull into town, I stop at the first mom and pop shop I see.

"Don't really got time to stop and get cookies, Silver," Jax says, and I ignore him and head inside the small shop, and just what I thought, an older gentlemen is behind the counter.

"I was wondering if you know anything about a church in town being up for sale?" I ask him, and he nods.

"If you take a right out of the parking lot and go about four miles then go over the train tracks, past Lord's Jewelry, you'll see it on the left. Someone bought it about three weeks ago, and they've been having work done to it."

"Thanks."

"Anytime," he tells me, and I lift my chin then head out front.

"Church is down across the tracks on the left. I say one of us goes down and checks the area then comes back with intel, just to make sure we don't need any back-up."

"On it," Mic says, taking off towards the church.

"You got any info?" I ask Jax.

"Uncle Nico says River and Snake are not related. They grew up in foster care together, and that's why we didn't know about him. Seems like River is Snake's muscle."

"Jesus," I say, and I hear Mic before I see him. He pulls up close on his bike and doesn't even shut it down before he starts to talk.

"Church parking lot is empty, and the doors have chains locking them closed. Across the street are some houses, and I saw a woman out front in her garden. She said this morning a van had pulled up, and a couple men took some stuff inside, but it's been quiet since then."

"Let's go check it out."

July

I LOOK AT Ellie then at the piece of wood I'm still holding in my hands. We didn't find anything else, but I did find a hole in the roof. It's small, but I think that with how weak it is, we can chip away at it, hopefully making it large enough to fit through.

"Hold this," I tell Ellie, handing her the two-by-four. I go to where the hole is and peek through. The sun is setting, and I can see—at least from where I'm looking—it appears we're in the forest. I press on the wood, and it bends slightly at my touch. I don't know who has us, or if they are around so I don't really want to make a lot of noise. I hold onto the beams in the ceiling where the wall pitches downward and put my foot to the wood, pressing hard, and my foot goes through the roof.

"Oh, my God!" Ellie whispers, and I stop what I'm doing to look at her, wondering if she heard someone coming.

"What?" I whisper back.

"I can't believe I didn't try that," she says, and I almost want to laugh at the look on her face, but I don't; I just turn around and press my foot a little higher. This time, more of the roof crumbles enough that I can stick my head out, which I do cautiously then look around. We're about two stories up, but until we get out, we won't know if there is a way down.

"I don't know if there's going to be a way for us to get down, but I would rather be on the roof than in here waiting for them when they come back."

"Me too," she agrees, holding the two-by-four a little tighter in her grasp.

I use my sweatshirt over my hands to pull more of the roof off. I know that if this spot is so weak that I can do this, then there must be others in the same shape, so once we're out, we're going to have to be very careful not to fall through. "I'm going to get out first, then you're going to follow me and only put your body where I put mine. The roof is weak, and there is a chance we could fall through if we're not super cautious."

"Okay," she agrees, and I push out through the opening, using my arm strength to lift myself out. I look around to make sure no one's below then stick my head back in the hole.

"Come on." I hold my hand out to Ellie, and she hands me the two-by-four. I set it aside then help lift her out onto the roof. Once she's out, we both lean back against the shingles. I grab her hand and give it a squeeze. "If anything happens and one of us is able to get away, we go for help, okay?"

"I won't leave you behind," she says, shaking her head.

"It's not about either of us leaving the other behind, but about getting help if we need to," I tell her, and she looks away then squeezes my hand back.

"Fine," she says after a long moment. I nod, turn onto my belly, and start to slide across the roof. It's steep, and I know that one wrong move could have me tumbling to the ground. When we make it to the side of the house, I see there are wire cages set up. It takes a moment for me to realize what I'm looking at. Hundreds of dogs are stacked one on top of the other in two rows for about twenty feet. My stomach begins to turn with rage. I know these dogs are probably either fighting dogs, or it's a puppy mill.

"Can we use the cages to get down that way?" Ellie asks in a hushed tone, and I look at her, shaking my head.

"The dogs will all flip out if we try, and if someone's around, they will come to see what's causing the dogs to go nuts," I whisper, and she looks over me, down to the ground, then back towards the way we came.

"Maybe there is something on the other side."

"Yeah," I agree, and she leads us in the other direction. Halfway there, her foot goes through the roof, and she covers her mouth before a scream can leave it.

"It's okay; just go slow," I assure her when her body freezes and begins to shake. She closes her eyes then opens them before moving again, this time more cautiously. I follow behind her as she slides over the hole, and I do the same. The roof pitches at a steeper angle, almost like we're completely vertical. I look down and cringe when I see how far we are from the ground.

"Don't look down," Ellie hisses, grabbing my hand. I bite my lip then follow her to a ledge near where the roof changes angles. "Someone's here," Ellie says, peeking around a corner of the roof. "It's the guy who took me," she whimpers, with fear evident in her voice. I hold her hand and she scoots back toward me.

"What is he doing?" I ask, looking around and noticing we are surrounded by forest on all sides.

"Taking dog food out of his truck," she says, disgusted.

"Did you see a way down?"

"No, I didn't really look though, 'cause he's there and I didn't want him to see me."

"Our only other option is to wait until it's dark, hope they don't come to check on us, make our way down the side the cages are on, and then make a run for it," I tell her.

"Since I have been here, they have checked on me once in the morning, and once at night. They take me down to the bathroom and give me some water or bread then send me back up."

"So they will be coming back. Staying here isn't an option," I say then hear a vehicle start up, and Ellie stands, peeking over the pitch in the roof.

"He's leaving," she hisses, sitting back down next to me. "What if we go down over the cages and open them as we leave?" she asks.

I hate the idea they would hurt the dogs if we let them out, but I know we need to do something. If we stay put, we are sitting ducks, and that is not an option.

"Let's head over to that side of the roof. We'll find a safe way to get down then make a run for it."

She agrees silently and we make our way across the roof again as the sun sets in the sky. Once we reach the side of the house with the cages, I know we can get down, but I also know the minute we make our presence known to the dogs below, they are going to start barking, drawing attention to us.

"We're going to have to be fast…really, *really* fast," I whisper.

"If we make it out of this, I'm joining the gym."

"I'll go with you," I whisper back, making her smile, and even with the events of the day and how exhausted she looks, I realize how beautiful she is. Her smile is blinding, and I hope when we're out of here and she gets her daughter back that she smiles more.

"Let's get the hell out of here, and then go get your baby," I say, and a light fills her eyes right before she hugs me.

"Let's go," she murmurs, releasing me from her grasp. I take a few deep inhales and then lower myself to the shortest part of the roof. A fresh wave of adrenalin starts coursing through me as I watch Ellie get down next to me. It's about six feet to the top of the cages, which have pieces of plywood set on top of them. I hop down, and the dogs immediately begin to bark louder and snarl in the cages.

"Hurry," I tell Ellie, looking up at her. She hops down, and I hear someone off in the distance yell, "Shut the fuck up!" and my body freezes. Then I slide over the back of the cage, hitting the ground hard, and Ellie comes down next to me, her feet hitting the ground then landing on her ass.

"We can't let them out. They'll attack us," I tell her as she looks at the dogs. "Let's run back that way." I point towards the forest behind the house. "I don't know where the road is, but maybe we will see another house." We slowly make our way back into the woods, and the deeper we go, the darker it gets.

"What was that?" I pause, asking Ellie as I hear what sounds like a four-wheeler.

"I don't know." She holds my hand a little tighter, and we begin to run as the sound gets closer.

"You can't hide, you dumb bitches. This is five hundred acres of private property. No one is around for miles," I hear yelled from off in the distance.

"Oh, God," Ellie whimpers, and I stop and grab her shoulders.

"Listen to me. We got this far; we are going to get out of here," I tell her. Even as scared as I am, there is no way I'm giving up. Not now, not when we have come so far.

"I'm not giving up, but I'm scared," she says.

"Me too, but we need to keep moving. That's the only way we're going to be able to make it out of this alive," I say then begin pulling her with me again. We run forever without coming across any sign of life, and my body is beginning to shut down from exhaustion. I know Ellie is in the same shape, because we both start to stumble more. Then I see lights shine through the trees, as the sound of the four-wheeler gets closer than it has been.

"I have a plan," I whisper when I see the lights coming closer. "But you're going to have to be brave."

"What?"

"I'm going to stand out in the open for him to see me, and you're going to hide behind a tree. When he gets close, I want you to hit him in the head with the two-by-four," I say, looking down at that weapon both of us have taken turns carrying since finding it.

"I think you should hit him. I've been here for four days. I don't know if I'm strong enough to hit him," she whispers.

"Are you sure?"

"We have a better chance if you do it," she replies, and the lights get closer, so I know we don't have time to debate with each other who's doing what. I slip behind the tree, keeping my eyes locked on Ellie.

"I'm here, and we're not going down without a fight," I tell her, looking into her scared eyes.

The lights land directly on her, and she yells, "Please, the other girl is hurt. She needs help!" She starts to cry, and I see the four-wheeler move closer, driven by a guy I don't recognize.

"Where is she?" he growls, reaching out to Ellie, so I take that moment to run out from behind the tree. His head turns my way and his eyes grow with shock as I hit him in the side of the head. His body slumps forward and I push him off the four-wheeler.

"Let's go," I tell Ellie, who seems to be frozen in place. Her body startles then she jumps on behind me.

"Do you know how to drive one of these things?" she asks as I pull off quickly. Uncontrollable laughter bubbles out at her question, and I don't answer, just drive faster. "I hope so." She wraps her arms tight around me.

"I know it's stupid, but we need to go back to the house and follow the road. We stand a better chance of making it to safety if we do."

"You've gotten us this far," Ellie says, and I just hope I can get us to safety.

We drive for a good hour, and I'm actually really surprised how long it takes for us to get back to the house. When we get closer, I notice a figure standing outside. I zoom past him, fishtailing, then press the gas harder as we head down a long dirt road.

"He's coming!" Ellie screams right before the four-wheeler jolts forward. "Oh, God! He's got a gun!" she cries, and I yell, "Duck," getting down as low as I can while pulling back on the throttle. Then I see it, off it the distance—headlights. My pulse kicks up, and I know if these are his friends we are as good as dead. Shots ring out from behind me as I drive faster, and then I pull off the road and into the forest when the headlights coming from the other direction get closer.

"July!" I hear roared, and I'd know that voice anywhere. *Wes.* Then I hear gunshots, and my body begins to shake with worry. I turn, going back towards the road, and stop.

"Stay here," I tell Ellie.

"No." She grabs my hand, but I don't have time to fight with her. I need to make sure Wes is okay.

"I need to get to my fiancé," I tell her in a panic, and then we hear two more shots. I sob, trying to get to the road.

"July!" Wes roars again, and I yell back, "Over here!"

I step out of the clearing, my eyes landing on the truck that was chasing us. The door is open, and the guy is slumped onto the steering wheel. Mic, Harlen, and Z are standing next to him, and Jax, Talon Everett and Sage all look at us as tears form in my eyes.

"He's dead baby," Wes says, pulling my attention to him. His eyes meet mine then do a sweep over the rest of me. I run to him, pulling Ellie with me, only letting go of her when I throw myself into Wes. His arms wrap around me, holding me so tight that I feel myself molding to him. "Jesus." He lets me go and begins to look me over, his hands moving over my body.

"I'm okay," I assure him, putting my hands on his cheeks. He drops to his knees and his face goes into my belly, and I wrap myself around him for a moment. Then he stands, kissing me once more before looking to my side. "This is Ellie. She was here when they brought me," I tell him.

His face turns hard and he growls, "There was more than one guy?"

"Yes, he was in the forest. We knocked him off the four-wheeler and took it."

"Do a sweep of the forest. See if you can find the other guy. Your dad should be here soon," Jax tells my cousins as he walks towards us, carrying a flashlight. The light sweeps over me then Ellie, and his step falters for a brief moment, before he continues towards us.

"Let me have that, baby," Jax says, his eyes locked on Ellie, and she holds the two-by-four a little tighter to her chest then shakes her head, backing up almost until she's behind me. "I promise I won't let anything hurt you, but I need you to give that to me, and then I want to look you over," he tells her gently. Her eyes leave him and come to me. I look at her hands and see they are red, and I know why Jax is worried about her.

"This is Ellie," I tell Jax then say, "Jax is my cousin. He looks scary, but he's a big softy." Her eyes go back to Jax, looking him over. He is imposing; at a little over six feet, his body is honed from workouts and training, and his dark hair is buzzed close to his skull. And next to Ellie, he looks like a giant.

"Swear on my life I won't hurt you, or let anyone hurt you ever again," he tells her, and I watch his eyes go soft in a way I have never seen before, not from him. Ellie swallows then hands him the two-by-four. He drops it to the ground then takes her hands, making her cry out, causing anger to flood his features. "I won't hurt you, but your hands are in bad shape," he explains then looks at me. "You hurt?"

"No." I shake my head and Wes's arms wrap tighter around me.

"I'm going to put Ellie in my truck and look her over while I wait for Uncle Nico to get here," Jax says, and I watch, stunned as he swings Ellie up into his arms and carries her off to his truck.

"That was so weird," I mutter, looking at where Jax is standing in front of the open door of his truck, with Ellie in front of him. "How did you find me?" I ask Wes, and his eyes sweep over me again before his mouth lands on mine, kissing me so deep that when he pulls his mouth from mine, I have unconsciously wrapped myself around him.

"The place these guys were turning into a tattoo shop is about an hour from here. When we got inside, we found they left a computer, and the computer was hooked up to that guy's cell phone. We did a backwards trace and it lead us here."

"That's pretty smart," I mutter.

"That's all Harlen; he's good at that kind of shit." He says and I wiggle out of his arms when the guys walk over, I give them each a hug, telling them thank you before getting pulled back by the loop of my jeans into Wes' side, where I stay when Uncle Nico pulls up along with ten other cop cars. Ellie stays with me, and we both answer as many questions as we can, most of which we have no answers to.

After an hour of talking to the police, Wes gets fed up and tells them he's taking me home and they can talk to me the next day. Jax, who hadn't left Ellie's side, agreed, and Uncle Nico told me he would be around in the morning. I was okay with that, and hugged Ellie, who was going to the hospital before getting on the back of Wes' bike.

"I'm glad you're okay, honey." My mom kisses my head and tucks the blankets tighter around me.

"You worried the fuck out of us," my dad complains, running his hand over my hair then narrowing his eyes. "You're not allowed to do anything like that again," he says like I did it on purpose.

"Promise." I place my hand on his cheek while fighting my smile, which makes his eyes narrow further. "Can you find out how Ellie is doing?" I ask after a moment.

"She's good. She's going home," my mom informs me, and my heart drops into my stomach.

"She can't go home." I sit up, looking towards the door. "Oh, God, she can't go home! Her mom is the one who sold her to that guy. She can't go home."

"Jax is taking her to get her daughter," my dad says with a strange look on his face. "They were heading out as soon as the doctor said she could leave the hospital."

"Thank God," I breathe, plopping back down onto the bed.

"Careful," Wes snarls, walking into the room. I take a breath and let it out slowly. I know he's worried about me, so he's on edge, but he's been a snarling beast since he carried me into the room, stripped me out of my clothes put me in the shower, and then tucked me into bed.

"We're going to head out and let you guys get settled in, we'll be back in the morning," my mom says, kissing me then Wes' cheek. My dad does the same, but pats Wes' shoulder.

"Are you okay?" I ask Wes as he sits next to my hip.

"Fuck no, that guy is still out there somewhere. I don't know how the fuck I'm going to be able to deal with knowing you're still in danger. Meanwhile, you're acting like this is fucking normal."

I sit up then climb into his lap, holding onto his cheek gently. "I'm alive. I rode home on your bike. I'm lying in our bed. And tomorrow, I'm going to talk to the ASPCA and ask them to help me with all the dogs, and hopefully we can save some of them. Then I'm going with Kayan to pick out the kind of cake we will eat on our wedding day. It's not that I don't know what happened today; it's that I have this amazing life, and some asshole isn't going to take that from me," I say, wanting him to understand.

I'm scared about the guy being free, but I have a feeling he isn't going to be for long, and if he does happen to come after me again, I know Wes will find a way to keep me safe. But I was never going to go back to not living.

"Love you, baby."

"Love you too." I smile then lean up, kissing him and trying to make him understand that as long as we have each other, we're going to be okay.

Epilogue

Wes

6 Years later

"HEY, LITTLE MAN," I say, lifting my son to my chest and kissing his head. "Mama's sleeping, so you're going to have to hang with your old man until she wakes up," I tell him, taking him over to his changing table, where I lie him down and change his diaper before sitting in the rocking chair near the window so I can give him his bottle.

After four years of trying and two years of fertility treatments, I told July no more. I hated seeing her breakdown after each try, each negative test killing her slowly. It got to the point that when friends and family would share their happy news, she would have to battle her mind, knowing she was happy for them, but sad for herself. I hated what it was doing to her, so I talked to a buddy of mine and he got me hooked up with an adoption agency.

After our last fertility treatment was a fail, I came home and handed her the paperwork. She cried…she cried for a full day, and then my beautiful, strong woman pulled it together, and we sat down and filled out the paperwork. We had no idea of how long it would take to go through. That was seven months ago.

The adoption process happened a lot faster for us than it did for other families. The family that had been planning on adopting James decided they weren't ready for a baby. I have to say the day we went to meet our son I wasn't sure we were either, but then I held my boy in my arms and knew right then that it didn't matter to me how James came to be with us; he is my son.

I look down at him, pull the bottle from his lips, and a small pout forms at the loss. I lift him to my shoulder with a smile on my face.

"I thought I heard you in here," July says, and my eyes go to her at the door of the nursery. She is even more beautiful than she was when we first started dating. She still makes me question my luck.

"You needed to sleep," I tell her gently. Since the moment James came home, she has been on edge, trying to make sure to do everything perfectly.

"I'm okay." She smiles, walking into the room and bending over, kissing me then the top of James' fuzzy head. I take her hand and pull her down onto my lap, and she lays her head on my shoulder, tucking her forehead into my neck, placing one hand on James. Even after all these years, knowing this could have been taken from me causes a buzz of anger to sizzle through me.

"Thank you for letting me sleep," she whispers, moving her hand from James to settle on my jaw.

"Anytime, baby." I turn my head, kissing her palm.

"I love this chair," she says, making me chuckle. Two months before James came home, July had her dad go into the attic and bring over the rocker that had been in her family for generations. She and her sisters argued for days over who got what, and July finally pulled the 'I'm the oldest' card and got the chair.

"It's a nice chair," I agree, rocking the three of us until I feel her body relax and James' little body sink into mine.

July

I LOOK AT the pregnancy test in my hand and cannot believe what I'm seeing. Since we brought James home, I have been feeling ill. I honestly didn't think much of it until this morning, when I walked into the kitchen, where Wes was standing shirtless, flipping bacon, the smell touched my nose and I got sick. That had never happened before, not ever. They say it's possible when you adopt that sometimes something clicks into place, and voila—you end up pregnant.

"Holy cow," I breathe then look at myself in the mirror, bursting into tears. I never believed I would take a pregnancy test and have it come out positive. After so many attempts of IUI then IVF, I gave up. Now, I have James, and we're pregnant.

"Babe, you good?" Wes asks, knocking on the door, and I toss the test in a drawer quickly.

"Yeah, sorry, I spaced out," I say. I mouth, *I spaced out?* in the mirror to myself, shaking my head, then splash some water on my face to conceal my tears and open the door.

"James is sleeping. Why don't you lay down for a bit?" he asks, and I nod absently as he kisses my hair then tilts my head back to get my eyes. "You sure you're good?" he questions, making that panic from a few minutes ago disappear.

"I'm sure," I tell him, and he kisses me briefly then takes off down the hall. I head to the bedroom then pick up my phone and call my doctor, setting up an appointment for later in the afternoon.

"I'VE GOT TO head out," I tell Wes, walking into the living room, where he and James are sitting and watching TV.

"Where are you going?" he asks, looking concerned.

"I need to meet Kayan," I say the first lie that comes to mind.

"Come kiss me," he demands, and I go to him, kissing him then James, trying to avoid the look in his eyes as I make it out of the house.

When I get to my Jeep, I start it up and head into town. We sold our house in town a couple years ago, and Wes bought a piece of property from my dad and built a house on it. I love our house, but I loved it more, knowing Wes and my family had built it.

"You're pregnant," Dr. Marks says, then I turn my head when there is a pounding on the door of the exam room.

"Are you sure this isn't a fluke?" I whisper in shock. Dr. Marks has been with us since the beginning. He knows how much we have struggled with getting pregnant.

"I'm sure," he says, and the pounding gets louder.

"July," Wes says from the other side, and I feel my eyes grow wide in shock then look at Dr. Marks as he opens the door.

"Congratulations, Wes," he says as Wes steps into the room.

"You lied," he says to me, then looks at Dr. Marks and growls, "Congratulations on what?"

"You're going to be a dad, and actually, we can do an ultrasound today if you like, since you're both here."

"What?" Wes says, looking at me then stumbling over to one of the chairs sitting down. "Pregnant?" he asks then shakes his head. "How is that possible?"

"Sometimes, it just happens," Dr. Marks says, looking proud, like it was his doing. "I'm going to give you guys a few minutes and go get the ultrasound set up."

"Where's James?" I ask, seeing our son isn't with him.

"He's with your mom. When did you find out?"

"This morning. I took a test, one of the leftovers that had been collecting dust. I didn't think it would be positive, and when it said I was pregnant, I wanted to know for sure before telling you," I say, hoping he understands. I hated seeing the disappointment in his eyes every time I took a test. I hated that no matter what I did we weren't getting pregnant, and no doctor could answer why. Why couldn't we have a baby?

"You know how I feel about that kind of shit," he says, and I do know how he feels about me keeping things from him, but if it's tell him and have him hurt, or save him that, I would do it all over again.

"Sorry." I get down from the table, curling myself around him on his lap.

"I can't believe you're pregnant." His hand lies gently over my stomach, and tears form in my eyes and a sob climbs up my throat. I have wanted this moment forever, and to finally have it makes it that much more memorable.

"You guys ready?" Dr. Marks asks, coming back into the room.

"Sure." I nod and do as he instructs, getting back up on the table. He squirts the liquid on my belly then moves it around with the wand in his hand. Before I even know it, the sound of a heartbeat fills the room, and my eyes fill with more tears.

"Jesus," Wes whispers.

"You're about nine weeks along," the doctor says, and I absently find Wes' hand with mine and hold on tight. *James is going to be a big brother. I can't believe it.*

"I'll print you guys some pictures to show off to everyone, and when you go out front, just tell them you need to make your next appointment. I'll leave a prescription up front for prenatal vitamins," he says, wiping off my belly before leaving the room. I sit up, stunned, and look at Wes, who's looking down at the pictures in his hand. When his eyes come to me, the love I see there tells me everything I need to know.

Wes

One year later

I WALK INTO our bedroom and my eyes fall on July, who has both our boys tucked close to her waist. Her eyes open slowly, and the smile that lights her face makes me feel like I'm the king of the world.

"We fell asleep." She smiles, and I smile back then kiss her neck before running my hand over James and Dean's heads.

"Your mom and dad are coming to pick up the boys," I tell her, waiting for her reaction. I love my boys, but I miss being inside my wife without interruption, and I plan on fixing that tonight.

"Why are they picking up the boys?"

"Because I'm tired of being cock-blocked by my kids," I tell her, and she giggles. Shit, just this morning I was going down on her, and she came hard and loud, but before I could lift up and enter her, the boys woke up, leaving me to take care of myself in the shower.

"I've never been away from them for more than a few hours," she says, and my face goes soft then I remind myself of my mission, and my dick throbs, reminding me what it's missing, so I steel myself against saying, 'We can do it another time,' and tell her instead, "I know, baby, me either, but we need this. My dick needs this."

"I'm sorry." She searches my face then lifts up, giving me a shot of her cleavage, which causes my dick to press harder against my zipper. When her mouth touches mine, I pull her head to the side with my hand at her nape and take over until she whimpers when I pull away.

"Let me get their bags ready," she breathes, making me laugh.

"Already done."

"Sure of yourself, aren't you, Mr. Silver?" She raises a brow, and I flick one of her nipples through the thin material of her summer dress.

"Yes."

"Da." I look down at James, and he rolls over then crawls to me.

"Hey, little man," I say, picking him up and kissing his head as he babbles on about something, then turn just in time for Dean to reach his little arms up at me. Unless you know us, you would think my boys are twins. They both have dark hair and blue eyes. James is just bigger.

"You guys are going to spend the night with Grandpa and Grandma. How does that sound?" July coos, taking James from my grasp as he reaches out for her.

We walk out into the living room, and July smiles over her shoulder when she sees I wasn't lying. Both of the boys' bags are sitting by the front door, ready to go. "Thanks, mom," July tells November as she walks out of the house, carrying both diaper bags. Asher just exited moments before carrying both boys. James was more than excited to spend some time with their pop, while Dean grinned up at him toothlessly from his car seat.

"They will be fine, and we're just down the road," November says over her shoulder then mutters something under her breath. As soon as I see they have all gotten into their car, I shut the door after pulling July inside, pressing her back into the wood then lifting her up with my hands under her ass. As soon as her legs wrap around me, I groan, feeling the heat coming off her pussy.

"Unhook my belt, baby," I growl, bunching up the material of her dress and ripping it off over her head. Then I do the same with my shirt, using the door and my hips as leverage to keep her up.

She bites her lip as I strip my shirt off, and then her nails scrape down my abs before working my belt. She groans and her head falls back with a thunk as I pull down the cups of her bra then lower my mouth, pulling her nipple in with a deep tug.

"Wes," she moans, and I get down my jeans, just releasing my cock, pull her panties to the side, and impale her. "Oh, God, you're so deep," she whimpers, and I fuck her hard, watching as I enter her, then my gaze travels up, watching the way her tits bounce with each thrust.

"Whose pussy is this, baby?" I ask, wrapping a hand in the back of her hair, twisting my fingers until her half-mast eyes meet mine. "Whose is it?" I growl on an outward slide.

"Yours," she breathes, wrapping her legs tighter around me.

"That's right, baby, and tonight, I'm going to fucking imprint my dick in your pussy," I tell her, slamming back in, making the door bang loud throughout the quiet house.

"Please!" she screams as her orgasm pulls at my cock, sucking it deeper until I come so hard I'm not even able to hold us up. My legs start to give out, so I carry her to the couch, sitting down with her in my arms, my cock still deep inside her.

"Fuck, I missed this pussy," I confess, and she giggles, burrowing closer, then mewls as I stand, carrying her to the bedroom, never leaving the heat of her. I lay her on the bed and start to go again, and her eyes go wide then slide closed. We spend the rest of the night in bed…in the kitchen…in the shower…

"I love you, Wes Silver. Until the day I die, I will love you," she tells me when we're lying in bed later that night.

I let her words sink into my soul and pull her closer, resting my lips against her temple before whispering there, "Love you too, babe. You have given me everything." And she did. A man who didn't expect to have a woman or a family, a man who was okay with just living life day by day—one little woman changed all of that and made him want more. It's on that thought I drift off to sleep, with everything I ever needed right in my arms.

The End

Cut scenes

JUST AS WE begin down a dirt road with giant pine trees along both sides of the road, I'm about to ask where we are going, when the road opens up and a large parking lot comes into view with a lake just beyond it.

When the bike stops, I hop off and he follows, pulling off his helmet and setting it on the seat, then he pushes my hands out of the way and unclips mine gently, pulling it off my head.

"Where are we?" I ask him, looking around. I have grown up in Tennessee my whole life and never been to this place before, and that is surprising because my family spends most of the summer out on the lake tubing and water skiing.

"Just a spot I found a few weeks ago," he mutters, pulling a bag out of the saddlebag that is attached to the side of his bike, the same bag he put in there when we dropped Capone off at his work, which just happened to be right down the road from my hospital.

When we arrived, I found out that not only did he have a parts shop and car lot, there was a whole compound set up. When you walk down a short alley between the two buildings, you come to a high gate. Once you are through the gate, it feels like you are on the set of a prison show. There is a large open area with two sides blocked in by tall concrete buildings that look like apartments from the outside, with stairwells and walkways that lead from one door to another. Along the back is a tall chain-link fence with razor wire along the top, and a million cars piled one on top of the other. The area seems almost like a fortress.

Taking my hand, he leads me towards a trail. Tall trees line one side of the path, while the other has a small cliff that goes down to the lake.

"This is really beautiful," I whisper as we walk hand-in-hand down the dirt path. With birds singing and the sun shining through the trees, it makes for a gorgeous, romantic setting.

"So why did you clam up when Jax brought up your dad?" he asks, catching me off-guard. Looking at him out of the corner of my eye, I think about how to answer that question. "Are you afraid of your dad?"

"Afraid of my dad?" I ask, slowing down to look at him.

"Yeah, are you afraid of your dad?" he growls, narrowing his eyes.

I start laughing and pull my hand from his, covering my face to laugh harder. "Sorry," I breathe, trying to catch my breath and wipe the tears away from my eyes then lift my head so our gazes connect.

"I have four sisters and a mom my dad is over-protective of, but he's also my best friend," I tell him seriously, wanting him to understand I will always be a daddy's girl. "I call him and complain when I've had a bad day, or to laugh when something funny happens. He has known every man I have dated, and been indifferent to all of them." I look down at the ground and kick a pebble. "I'm not afraid of my dad, but I respect him and know he will have a lot of questions about you."

"Like what?" His brows pull together, and I fight the urge to step closer and run my finger over the ridges that have formed between his eyebrows.

"What I'm doing with a guy like you," I tell him simply then start to walk again.

"A guy like me?" he asks as his thumb slips into the back of my jeans and his finger hooks through my belt loop.

"A guy like you," I confirm with a nod, not looking at him.

"What kind of guy am I?" he asks, turning me to face him, and my eyes focus on his face, which looks gorgeous with the way the sunlight is shining through the trees.

"A guy who rides a motorcycle and has tattoos, a guy who doesn't seem to take no for an answer, but who can apologize when he's wrong," I say, knowing some of those are qualities my dad has, and that's what scares me.

"You don't believe he would like you dating a biker with tattoos?"

"It's not that you're a biker or that you have tattoos." I shake my head and look around. "Enough about my dad. What are we doing here?" I ask, changing the subject.

He searches my face for a moment then takes my hand again. "It's just up here." We walk for a few more minutes then come to a clearing with a large rock wall. He pulls a flashlight out of his bag then ducks inside a hole you have to bend double to get through. I follow behind him and inhale a sharp breath as I enter the cave and look around the large open space. The walls are white and look smooth and shiny, like they are wet. A waterfall shoots out of the ceiling into a pool of water that's in the middle of the cave, and along the edge of the water, large stalagmite formations have formed, some so high they look like they reach the ceiling.

"Holy cow." I spin in circles, taking everything in. I cannot believe how magical the space is.

"Surprised?" he asks, and I finish my spin and face him.

"It's amazing! How did you find this place?"

"Me and Everett used to go caving in California. We heard about some of the spots out here and decided to see what we could find. We were on the other side of the hill when we saw an opening, and we came in through there." He points the flashlight off to the side, where it's completely dark, but I can still make out a small hole. "When we got into this section, we saw there was another exit that led to the trail."

"I had no idea places like this even exist."

"They're all over." He smiles, crossing his arms over his chest.

Until Jax

"YOU MAY NOW kiss the bride," the pastor says, and Wes bends July backwards over his arm, kissing her in a way that I'm surprised Uncle Asher doesn't get out of his seat.

"Oh, God," my sister sitting next to me cries, and I look down at her as she wipes her eyes while wrapping her arm around mine. "They are so perfect for each other," she says then looks at me, smiling before standing up when everyone else does.

"Ax," Hope calls from my other side, and I pull my eyes from my sister and hold my breath as Hope Ellie's Daughter smiles up at me. *She looks like her mom...her mom, who has taken up my every thought since meeting her.*

"What's up, sweetheart?" I ask softly, still unsure of what to do with a three-year-old little girl.

"Can you pit me up so I can see Mama?" she asks, and my heart does a tug, the same tug it's done since the moment I met her mom then her.

"Sure," I say, and she holds her hands up to me and I pick her up in her big poufy pink dress then lift her to my shoulders so she can see her mom walk down the aisle behind July, holding onto Harlen's arm, which causes a different kind of tug to pull at my chest.

She looks beautiful today. Her long brown hair is tied up with a white ribbon that is woven through a braid, which is wrapped behind her ear with small pieces framing her face. Her body is incased in a dress that is so formfitting that I know just from looking her breasts would fit perfectly in my hands. Hell, her body fits perfectly against mine. I know this, because every chance I get, I have her close.

She's mine. She may not understand it—hell, I don't even know if I understand it—but she was made for me.

From Me to You

I started this writing journey after I fell in love with reading, like thousands of authors before me.

I wanted to give people a place to escape where the stories were light, funny, sweet and hot.

I wanted my books to leave you feeling good maybe something to clean your pallet after a dark romance or a book that tore out your heart before putting it back together again.

I have loved sharing my stories with you all, loved that readers message me to say that even for a moment they were able to escape into another world.

I started writing for me and will continue writing for you.

Acknowledgments

First I want to give thanks to God without him none of this would be possible.

Second I want to thank my husband. I know I drive you insane and that there is a lot of weight on your shoulders but thank you for being strong enough to bare it all while helping with the laundry, cleaning the house and making sure that we have food. I love you babe always and forever.

Natasha Gentile. You my crazy friend, you brighten my days and force me to push myself even when I want to say screw it and give up. I would be lost without you lady I love you and your crazy biker knowledge.

Kayla, You know I adore you woman. Thank you for always knowing exactly what I'm trying to say even when my words are a mess.

Tina Harris you've become such a good friend and you truly saved my ass with Until July. Thank you so much for not only being such a great friend but for taking the time to help edit Until July. I love you girl.

Thank you to my cover designer and friend Sara Eirew your design and photography skills are unbelievable. I love that you accept my craziness and me and that you know what I'm looking for even when I just have a vague idea.

Thank you to TRSOR you girls are always so hard working, I will forever be thankful for everything you do.

To my Beta's, I think I have said it a million time's but I couldn't ask for better, thank you all so much for always encouraging me.

Aurora's Roses I wish I could hug each and ever one of you. I wish you could all know how much you all brighten my days.

To my Dirty Dozen when I told you guys I may push back this release you didn't stone me or make me feel horrible you all sent me words of encouragement and told me to do what I thought was best. Thank you all for coming along on this journey with me love you girls.

To every Blog and reader thank you for taking the time to read and share my books. There would never be enough ink in the world to acknowledge you all but I will forever be grateful to each of you.

XOXO Aurora

About The Author

NEW YORK TIMES & USA TODAY BESTSELLING AUTHOR Aurora Rose Reynolds started writing so that the over the top alpha men that lived in her head would leave her alone. When she's not writing or reading she spends her days with her very own real life alpha who loves her as much as the men in her books love their women and their Great Dane Blue that always keeps her on her toes.

For more information on books that are in the works or just to say hello, follow me on Facebook:

www.facebook.com/pages/Aurora-Rose-Reynolds/474845965932269

Goodreads

www.goodreads.com/author/show/7215619.Aurora_Rose_Reynolds

Twitter

@Auroraroser

E-mail Aurora she would love to hear from you

Auroraroser@gmail.com

And don't forget to stop by her website to find out about new releases, or to order signed books.

AuroraRoseReynolds.com

Other books by this Author

The Until Series

Until November – NOW AVAILABLE

Until Trevor – NOW AVAILABLE

Until Lilly – NOW AVAILABLE

Until Nico – NOW AVAILABLE

SECOND CHANCE HOLIDAY – NOW AVAILABLE

Underground Kings Series

Assumption – NOW AVAILABLE

Obligation – NOW AVAILABLE

Distraction – Coming Soon

UNTIL HER SERIES

UNTIL JULY – NOW AVAILABLE

UNTIL HIM SERIES

UNTIL JAX – COMING SOON

Alpha Law

Justified – NOW AVAILABLE

Liability – Coming Soon

Verdict – Coming Soon

Made in the USA
Charleston, SC
12 June 2015